T0193486

THE
WORST ATROCITY

THE
WORST ATROCITY
Best That They Fail

A Historical Novel Set in World War II

BY

DAVID EPSTEIN

The Worst Atrocity
Best That They Failed

iUniverse books may be ordered through booksellers or by contacting:

iUniverse
1663 Liberty Drive
Bloomington, IN 47403
www.iuniverse.com
1-800-Authors (1-800-288-4677)

Because of the dynamic nature of the Internet, any web addresses or links contained in this book may have changed since publication and may no longer be valid. The views expressed in this work are solely those of the author and do not necessarily reflect the views of the publisher, and the publisher hereby disclaims any responsibility for them.

Any people depicted in stock imagery provided by Thinkstock are models, and such images are being used for illustrative purposes only.
Certain stock imagery © Thinkstock.

ISBN: 978-1-4759-7599-4 (sc)
ISBN: 978-1-4759-7600-7 (e)

Print information available on the last page.

iUniverse rev. date: 11/05/2013

Map 1. First Battle of the Bulge. Normandy 8/7-14/1944

On 8/7/44, to split the Allied forces, the Germans thrust westerly from Mortain toward Avranches. The offensive was immediately blunted. German army reversed direction, fleeing east toward Falaise. Not much of a 'bulge', but an extraordinary gift for the Allies! End result? Group Eberbach (consisting of the German 7th Army and the 5th Panzer Army; two of OBWest's best) was trapped within the pocket formed by the US1A, the US3A and the British 21AGP, and except for those remnants who managed to escape via the Falaise Gap, was virtually destroyed.

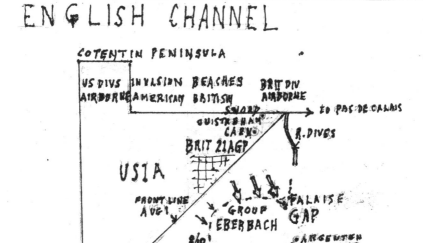

Map 2. Second Battle of the Bulge. Ardennes 12/16 – 26/1944

With Antwerp as ultimate objective, the German Army launched an offensive from the West Wall (a fortified line in Germany , near its boundary with France and Benelux extending roughly from Switzerland to the North Sea) , against the US1A, on a wide front. The assault petered out at Dinant (Belgium), on the Meuse River, after a heroic stand by units of the US3A at Bastogne. End result? The exhausted German Army was unable to defend 'Der Vaterland' leading to an early collapse of the Western Front. By Spring 1945 the Allies 'bounced the Rhine' and the War in Europe was just about over.

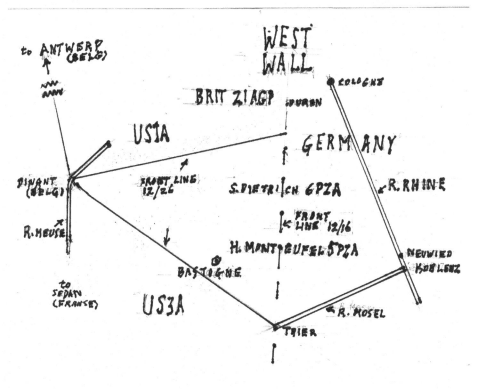

Map3. Operation ZITADELE

This 'bulge' differs from those previously cited. Here the Russians were concentrated inside the bulge.

To trap the Russian Armies within the Kursk salient sandwiched between FM Kluge AGPC and FM Manstein AGPS, Von Hoth's 4th Panzer Army attacked from the South and Model's 9th Army from the North. This double- envelopment maneuver didn't make much progress.
End result? Hitler called off Citadel, but the Soviets had only 'just begun to fight'. In undisputed possession of the initiative, and using the Kursk salient as a spring-board, the Red Army launched a massive counter-offensive, that didn't stop until Hitler's suicide in Berlin, two years later.

F.M. VON KLUGE AGpC

OREL

MODEL 9A

RED ROKOSSOFSKY CENTRAL FRONT

⊙ KURSK

ARMY VATUTIN VORONEZH FRONT

VON HOTH 4 PZA

KHARKOV

F.M. VON MANSTEIN AGpS

Map 4. Kesselschlacht, Road to Moscow
6/22/1941 – 12/5/1941

Although Moscow was not the main objective of BARBAROSSA, von Bock's Army Group Center headed straight for it. Progressing in stages: Minsk (7/16), Smolensk (8/04) fell. After a delay of over two months, the drive resumed; the Bryansk – Vyasma pocket was closed 10/18, but the offensive couldn't quite reach Moscow. Operation Typhoon was called off 12/5/41.

6/22/41   7/16   8/04   VYASMA 12/5/41
RUSSO-GERMAN   MOSCOW
BORDER   M   S   10/18
                                    BRYANSK

Contents

DEDICATION

This book is dedicated to the German Resistance movement and the Allied—mainly British-Secret Intelligence Agents, who, despite Allied Official Policy, as expressed in Absolute Silence' (Jan, 1941) and 'Unconditional Surrender' (Jan, 1943) tried to persuade the Allies to join with the Widerstand in its monumental struggle against 'Hitler and the Nazis'. Unfortunately their valiant efforts were ignored; they were unable to get the 'twin doctrines' rescinded or even modified. The Widerstand had to act alone, with disastrous consequences.

FOREWORD & ACKNOWLEDGEMENTS

Needless to say, I have nothing but the highest praise for the legions of historians and authors, allied and German alike, who strenuously toiled to establish the true historical facts that constitute the back-drop to this book. Many of these works have been cited in the text; some that I have found particularly useful are listed in an appended brief bibliography. I must say that it is not easy to fit a novel into an actual historical framework, while keeping the 'history' intact, but that is what I have tried to do. This work is part 'autobiography', part 'history', and part 'novel', but it may be classified as a 'historical novel'. The novel itself is fiction: a creation of the author's imagination. While some of the characters, locales, and incidents may be real, they are used fictitiously. Any resemblance to persons living or dead is entirely coincidental.

PREFACE

I. A forgotten epic

Twice in the 20th century, epic events occurred on the 20th of July, precisely one-quarter century apart. In 1969, the American Astronauts, 'Buzz' Aldrin, Neil Armstrong, and Michael Collins, accomplished what people have dreamed about, from time immemorial—they walked on the moon!

This amazing feat was greeted by universal acclaim—as it should be. The earlier 'epic event', however, was greeted with universal opprobrium. The 'Revolt of the Generals' was condemned alike by Hitler (understandably) and the Allies (unbelievably). It was probably the only time throughout WWII that they ever agreed on anything. Reading contemporary accounts, one can scarcely distinguish between them; they were equally vitriolic.

As post-war historians started to uncover the facts surrounding this attempt on Hitler's life and the overthrow of the Nazis, what emerged was a totally different picture: It became evident that what actually took place was one of the most extraordinary episodes of the war.

We are all familiar with the names of the 3 Apollo Astronauts, but what of the members of the 'Widerstand', as the anti-Nazi movement came to be called? Its titular head was a Colonel-General L. Beck. "Who was General Beck?" the German military historian W. Goerlitz asks, rhetorically, in his brilliant "History of the German General Staff."

He was the Third Reich's first Chief of the Great German General Staff. Appointed to that post by A. Hitler in 1933. Fearing that Hitler's Rearmament Program and truculent Foreign Policy would put Germany on a collision course with the major European powers, Britain, France, and Russia, leading to a war that Germany could not win, but might possibly result in the complete annihilation of Germany,

General Beck resigned his position on 08/18/1938.

R. Whelan in his book 'Assassinating Hitler' put it neatly: 'Beck's objections to Hitler were first tactical, then strategic, and finally moral.'

Who was Colonel Klaus von Stauffenberg?

He was a much decorated, severely wounded officer, but there were many Colonels in the German Army who fit that description.

What makes him so special?

A man of high ideals, unusual courage, and nerves of steel, he master-minded and carried out the assassination attempt.

As Chief of Staff, to the 'Home (or Replacement) Army'), he attended a meeting at the Fuhrer's Headquarters, the 'Wolf's lair', and planted a bomb meant to kill Hitler.

Hitler survived the blast, the conspiracy collapsed, and those associated with the Widerstand were rounded-up, tortured, tried, and ultimately executed.

It took the Astronauts three days to reach the moon, but the journey of Gen. Beck, from enthusiastic supporter to inveterate foe of Hitler, lasted 11 years, ending on 20 July 1944, a suicide.

Colonell Stauffenberg was executed by a 'firing squad' in the courtyard of Widerstand HQ in the Bendlerstrasse, Berlin.

Words are simply inadequate to describe the incredible heroism of these men.

But the hardest part to take is that they didn't have to do it.

Like many of their inactive fellow generals, all that they had to do was sit-out-the-end-of-the-war (and write their memoirs).

To us, in hindsight, it all seems to have been so unnecessary.

But, their hatred of Hitler and his gang; their desire to put an abrupt end to the 'horrors' of living under a brutal dictatorship; their desire to stop the remorseless battering and destruction of their beloved Germany, and to salvage some vestiges of the honor left of the German Army, was so great that they took the risk, and paid the ultimate price.

It is no exaggeration to say that if the conspiracy had succeeded, millions of lives would have been saved:

'VE Day, Liberation Day, Revolt Day, would all have been celebrated on the same day—20 July 1944.'

As for General Ludwig Beck, he isn't particularly well known today (even in Germany), but he would have been in a class with our own General George Washington.

But, as they say, that's the difference between 'winning and losing'.

II. A WWI observation, updated.to WWII

Winston Churchill, in his book "The World Crisis." tells us that In the First Word War, Admiral Sir John Jellicoe, Commander-in-Chief of the British High Seas Fleet, was the only man who could lose the War in an afternoon.

Well, the "20th of July1944" carried this observation a step further. 'The Revolt of the Generals' was the only action that could end the Second World War (in Europe) in so short a period of Time.

III. Everything Flows

They say that the philosophy of Heraclitus of Ephesus (540-480/ BC,) of the Ionian School (thought to be the birthplace of Greek Science) may be summarized in 100 Epigrams. I don't know about the other 98, but the two of most interest here, may be succinctly written as:

1. War is the father of all things.
2. Everything flows.

What is so profound about this?

In his time, the basic constituents of matter were air, water, solid earth, (and fire).

Air and water flow, but solid earth?

Heraclitus argued that everything was in a state-of-flux and that means solids, as well as fluids.

Heraclitus has been called the patron Greek Philosopher of the Modern Science of Rheology which Treats the Creep or Plastic flow of solids.

Yes, Everything Flows! Why not historical events?

ANECDOTE

A short, entertaining account of some happening usually personal or biographical, and generally of interest to the person involved (and his friends and his relations). So why am I telling it to you?

May 10, 1940: On this day the German people living between the Rhine River and the Belgian-German border were treated to an amazing spectacle. They were astonished by this display of German military might: the First Panzer Army stretched out over 100 miles from Neuwied on the eastern bank of the Rhine westward to the Ardennes.

The order-of-battle is quite interesting: the units and their commanding officers (highest rank achieved) were: Field Marshal G. von Rundstedt, Army Group A; Colonel-General E. von Kleist, First Panzer Army: Lieutenant-General G. Reinhardt, XLI Panzer Corps. (To extend von Kleist's reach through the Ardennes to France, his force was augmented by Colonel-General H. Guderian's XIX Panzer Corps which crossed the Meuse River at Sedan, France, on May 13 1940.) Bringing up the rear on the eastern bank of the Rhine (at Neuwied) was the 6th Panzer division, Major-General W. Kempf commanding with Captain (later Colonel) Klaus von Stauffenberg, Quartermaster. It crossed the Rhine, at Neuwied, reaching the French coast, near Calais, about ten days later.

This is all very interesting, but so what?

May 8, 1945: Move fast forward 5 years.

My outfit, the 1280th Combat Engineer Battalion, was engaged, *inter alia,* in maintaining and rebuilding the infra-structure that had been badly damaged during the last days of the war. The US Army provided the heavy-equipment while the Germans supplied the building-material and the day-laborers drawn from the immense German POW camp at *Andernach* nearby. I was on guard duty that morning when a German let himself into the warehouse with a key. I challenged him and he replied that he was the owner, and was keeping track of the material that the US Army was requisitioning. (Apparently the army was expected to pay for the lumber, gravel, cement etc. that was needed for the day's construction job.) Between his broken English, and my Yiddish, combined with my high-school German, we managed to communicate with each other. The first thing he said to me was "We are not enemies anymore!" He heard on the radio that this day May 8, 1945 Colonel General A. Jodl and Grand Admiral Friedeburg signed the articles of Unconditional Surrender. But this news was anti-climactic—we had been acting as if the war was over for some time now. The 'officer of the guard' arrived and walked over to us. To my astonishment, the German turned to the Lieutenant and said that I was one of the best interpreters that he, personally had dealt with. The Lieutenant laughed, but despite a shortage of competent interpreters he had no intention of recommending me for the position.

We were housed across the river from Neuwied, on the western side of the Rhine, not far from what was left of the original bridge. I never saw, close-up, a bridge—someone called it the Reichsmarshal Herman Goering bridge—so thoroughly destroyed. As an old demolitions man myself, I must admit that the German *pionieren* did a great job. Much of the mangled wreckage protruded from the water. Possibly one could traverse the river by climbing over the exposed rubble. No doubt some of the more intrepid of us did try—but as for me I didn't see much point to it. I'd rather use the replacement for the demolished bridge located nearby.

May 10, 1945:

Colonel Stauffenberg was in Neuwied on the day that Germany invaded France and the Low Countries. This is the same town where I happened to be, five years to the day, later.

Coincidence, perhaps? True, there were hundreds—maybe even thousands—of GIs in the area, so what makes my presence unique? Well, I'll bet that I am the only one in that vast multitude, who sixty-plus years later, has written a book, one of whose principal historical characters is none other than Colonel Klaus Stauffenberg.

In short: On 5/10/1940, the 'day that the War in the West' began in earnest—using the bridge facilities available at that time—the Colonel's unit traversed the Rhine from East to West.

On 5/10/1945, a couple of days after VE-Day—using the US Army erected replacement for the demolished bridge—I had occasion to cross the Rhine from West to East.

In our Anecdote, in a manner of speaking, the 'war in the West' opened and closed, at the same place—Neuwied on the Rhine—but, measured in Time, they were five long years of the most appalling events in the history of the world, apart. Another example of the proverb which, some say, dates back to biblical times:

"What goes around, comes around."

A brief digression on the strange history of the Sixth Panzer Division.

(Remarkable in its own right, I would be remiss if I didn't say a few words about it.)

The tanks 'in the independent, mechanized, strike-force' model of the new German Army were organized in regular armored divisions (1935) and considerably smaller Light Divisions (1938).

Major-General E. Hoepner was given command of the First Light division; a junior officer Captain (later Colonel) K. von Stauffenberg joined it as number 2 staff officer. The 1st Light div made its debut on the international scene during the Munich crisis (1938).

After the Anschluss (The absorption of Austria into the Third Reich (3/38).) Hitler started making noises about the self-determination of Germans living in the Sudetenland region of Czechoslovakia. Fearing that this saber-rattling might lead to a 'collision' with the major European powers, Britain, France, and Russia, the German Army vigorously opposed the threatened invasion. According to the 'Halder plan' (General Halder was General Beck's successor as the chief of the General Staff, who had resigned on August 18, 1938.) If Hitler carried out his threats and issued the order to march, Army units in Berlin, loyal to the General Staff, would arrest him.

General Hoepner's 1st light div played a key role in this operation; it was to position itself to intercept any attempt by strong SS forces near the Czech border from reaching Berlin during the up-rising. This showdown never occurred as per the Munich agreement because Britain and France sold out Czechoslovakia; the Czech's withdrew from the border and the German Army entered the Sudetenland unopposed (September 1938).

The 1st light div participated in the war with Poland (9/39) and in October 1939 was brought up to full strength and renamed the 6th Panzer division. The other light divisions were upgraded as well, bringing to ten the number of Panzer divisions available for the invasion of France and the Low Countries on May 10, 1940.

This is all history; but here we are concerned with the events surrounding Operation Valkyrie, four years later, in July 1944. We have to ask: was the impressionable junior officer unduly influenced by the active role of the commanding general during the Munich crisis? The record seems unclear on this point. It was only after the cumulative effect of years of mindless, monstrous Nazi brutality convinced him that Hitler must be eliminated, that Colonel Stauffenberg joined the Resistance. All that we really know is that Colonel-General Hoepner and Colonel Stauffenberg met again in the ill-starred 'Revolution of the 20th of July, 1944'.

CHAPTER 1

At the Armed Services Club

Section 1.1 Reminiscences

The club was rather crowded. I spied a vacant seat, next to a man who appeared to be unaccompanied.

"Mind if I sit down?"

"No, not at all, what are you drinking?"

"Nothing so far."

I'm not much of a drinker, but at social gatherings I've been known to down a few.

"Come here often?", he asked.

When I come to London, on NATO business,

I usually come a little early so that I can do some sight-seeing.

I was scheduled to give a presentation on what we called Sentinel, a long-range Early-Warning Anti-Submarine Warfare system, utilizing Underwater Explosion signals, that I had been instrumental in developing.[i]

One never tires of London. In the evening, I like to visit the Armed Services Club. If lucky, I find a veteran of 'my war', but the ages of the lads, seems to be getting younger, as the number of WWII vets dwindle.

"Once in a while. "I replied.

He looked to be about my age, maybe a couple of years older, but he obviously kept himself in good physical shape.

I mentioned that I had been stationed in England, with the U.S. Army Combat Engineers, awaiting transport to France. We spent a lot of time practicing 'how to quickly erect a Bailey bridge', under enemy fire. (The 'Bailey bridge'—the low-tech marvel of WWII—contributed as much to winning the war, as many of its more glamorous brethren.)

The Germans as they retreated, had been systematically destroying the bridges, but as fast as they were being blown up, the Army Engineers were throwing up these Bailey bridges across the rivers. The 'big' one of course, was what Monty had facetiously referred to as 'bouncing the Rhine'. I surmised that we would be urgently needed for the final push across the Rhine, into Germany proper, in the Spring of '45. I had gotten into the fray rather late, and we anticipated a fierce fight, but Herr Hitler made it relatively easy for us by obligingly squandering what was left of his 'Army of the West' at the 'Bulge' (December 1944). (See Map 2.)

"You sound disappointed."

He countered with, "My story is a little different. I got into the fray rather early. I was a glider pilot with the British 6th Airborne Division, and in conjunction with American Airborne units (the 82nd and 101st, Div.) we spearheaded the invasion on D-Day (June 6 1944). The 6th's job was to secure the Eastern-most flank of the invasion beaches. To this very day, I still don't know how we managed to fake out the 21st Panzer Div. lurking in the vicinity."

Thinking that the main thrust of OVERLORD would be at Pas de Calais, the German's miscalculated: By nor committing their Armor clustered around Calais immediately, they missed their first, last, and only opportunity to 'roll up the landing', clear the beaches, and hurl the Allies back into the channel before they had time to establish a beachhead and push inland.

"Speaking of squandering, later, during the breakout from Normandy, Hitler ordered an offensive to split the British and the American forces and race for the coast. This salient, directed from Mortain—towards—Avranches was destroyed, and two of his best units, (the 5th Panzer and 7th Armies) were sacrificed in this venture, although some of the encircled Germans did manage to slip through the Falaise Gap and flee back towards Germany, (August 1944) (See Map 1.)"

"I see what you mean. Lunacy is catching!

There were really two Battles-of-the-Bulge. I'd like to think of the earlier one that you mentioned, as the 'first'. Having all but wrecked OB West, at the Falaise Gap (08/'44), he tried the same trick again at the second Battle-of-the-Bulge in the Ardennes (12/'44).

"Ha! You can always depend on Adolf for a 'blunder or two'."

"Oh" I said, "So you were an enlisted man like me."

During the '30's, with the 'clouds of war' overhanging Europe, it was natural for the young chaps to wonder what role they would play in a war, in the event that it materializes.

"The Army? Memories of trench warfare in WWI precluded that. The Navy? Traditionally, the English followed the Sea, but I loved flying with a passion, and besides, 'Aviation' was the wave-of-the-future."

"Why didn't you just join the RAF?"

He laughed. "In those days one 'just didn't join the RAF'. A pilot has a unique social standing and it wasn't easy for the son of a middle-class family to get his wings. We did have those so-called auxiliary flying groups that we joined, grateful for the opportunity to learn how to fly, and hoping for a chance to get a shot at being accepted by the RAF. The RAF left the door slightly ajar by taking on a few of us as trainees. But, there were many guys like me, and I missed the cut.

After being drafted into the Army, my education and prior military training gave me an edge. I quickly got my stripes. Since I couldn't fly with the RAF, I did the next best thing: I volunteered to become a glider pilot."

"We in the U.S., of course, didn't have this built-in class stratification, but it was still rather difficult for a G.I. to get to be an Officer. One could substitute, for the lack of wealth and social status, one year of college (e.g., if one was interested in being an Air Cadet), but who went to college in those Depression years'? Upon graduation from high school one worried about getting a job. Few families could afford the luxury of sending their sons off to college, no matter how talented and academically qualified.

We had to wait for the G.I. Bill, after the war, for the opportunity to continue our education."

"Similar situation here. After the war, with the Labor Government, and the country's new found egalitarianism, opportunities arose. With a few good words, from my former superiors, and a couple of breaks, I enrolled in Sand Hurst, and here I am—a Captain—in Her Majesty's Intelligence Service, Retired, at your service."

The connection between Glider Pilot and Intelligence Officer, escaped me, but who am I to quibble? Finishing his drink, and calling for a refill, he waxed sentimental:

"Yes Sir, those were the WWII days, my friend. British and Americans, comrades-in-arms, fighting side-by-side against the common foe. But, tell me: what do the Americans think of the British today"?

Section 1.2 Anglo-American Relations

"You can't tell by me. I'm the wrong guy to ask. Although the U.K. is our staunchest ally, it seems to me, that the Americans are not particularly fond of the British today. The demographics are working against you. As our English heritage fades, new political trends are fast taking shape. All Western Civilization is under siege. There is little interest in European History and the Europeans, including the English, in general.

"But it wasn't always like that. In the 1930's, we Americans were pretty much in awe of Great Britain. Every schoolchild knew that the 'Sun never sets on the British Empire', and that behind it all stood the 'might' of the Royal Navy.

"I was always a keen student of Naval Affairs. Paraphrasing Gilbert & Sullivan's Major General Stanley I could quote the 'Naval fights historical/ From Salamis to Jutland', in order categorical'.

"Until the Japanese attack on Pearl Harbor (12/07/'41), naval history read pretty much like the 'Story of the English Fleet.' Early in the game, (Centuries before our Admiral Mahan!) England recognized the critical importance of a 'strong Navy' to any nation aspiring to be a 'World Power'. It all started with King Henry VII, (the Shipwright), (1485-1509). A frugal monarch, it was only poetic justice that he left a 'pile' to his profligate son, although to be fair, Henry VIII (1509-1558), didn't skimp, but greatly expanded the scope of English Sea-power.

There may be some question as to who the 'Father of the Royal Navy 'is, but there is no doubt about who the 'Mother was'. It was in 'Good Queen Bess's' glorious days that England emerged as a world-class Naval Power. Successfully taking on all comers, she defeated the Spanish Armada (1588), the Dutch in the 17th century, the French in the 18th and 19th centuries, culminating in Lord Nelson's decisive victory at Trafalgar (1805).

"From the 16th century onwards, Britain had been strengthening its grip over the world's oceans and achieved what appeared to be absolute control of the Seas after the Grand Fleet settled the German High Seas fleet's hash at Jutland."

"For an American you seem to have a rather thorough knowledge of English history."

"I have always thought very highly of the British."

Section 1.3 Anglo-American Culture

Steeped in History, rich in Literature, Arts and Sciences, English Culture has permeated all phases of American Life.

"You may not believe this, but back in college I used to entertain my friends by reciting Rudyard Kipling's epic narrative poem 'East and West' from 'beginning to end.'"

He laughed, "You I can believe. But, he's sort of passé' now. RK was still quite the rage, during, and even after, WWII. Soldiers like to sing, and one of my favorites was 'By the old Moulmein Pagoda/ Looking eastward to the Sea . . .'"

I chimed in with "There's a Burma girl a—setting/ and I know she thinks of me". Some of the fellows gathered round, with a rousing rendition of the refrain:

'On the Road to Mandalay/ where the flying fishes play, And the dawn comes up like thunder/ out of China across the Bay.' "'Mandalay' always brought down the house, but I never realized how dated it was— why, there isn't even a Burma today, and the 'Little Tigers' as they are now called, are fast becoming industrial powerhouses. Can you imagine the youth of today getting excited over that?"

"Yeah, I guess you are right, but RK wrote quite a few other poems, besides the Barrack-Room-Ballads. He was extremely perceptive. Years ago, I remember reading somewhere that after the Bible, he was the second most often quoted author in the English language. But that was a longtime ago; like you, I wonder if anyone quotes him nowadays.

Still, one of my favorite poems is his 'Recessional', written near the close of the 19th century. Britain at that time was at the peak of its power. She had taken on the awesome responsibility of controlling the lives and destiny of hundreds of millions of people. Kipling cautioned Great Britain against arrogance, hubris, over-confidence and exaggerated self-importance that seems to be the traditional 'fate of the superpower'. In his own words,

> Lest we forget-Lest we forget.
>
> Far-called our Navies melt away
>
> On dune and headland sinks the fire.
>
> Lo, all our pomp of yesterday
>
> Is one of Nineveh and Tyre.

No one could have possibly foreseen the disintegration of the British Empire so soon: from Zenith to (not quite) Nadir, in less than a century! A super-colossal empire had been displaced by the U.S., the new reigning champion. One wonders who will compose the 'Recessional' for the 20th century, and what will it say? What warnings will he give to keep the U.S. from falling into the 'trap of the superpower'?"

"Do I detect a tinge of 'fatalism'?"

"I'm not a clairvoyant. All I know is that Superpowers come and go; that's the way it has always been, and as they say, 'Past is Prologue'."

Section 1.4 English-Heritage

"I can only repeat what I said before; you seem to know a lot about the English."

Acknowledging the compliment, I replied. "You might say that I am an Anglo-phile, but that's mainly because Mother was a Londoner." "Grandfather had a Men's' Clothier shop on Tower Bridge Road in Bermondsey. I was there a few years ago, during a visit to the light cruiser 'Belfast' docked in the Thames River nearby.

"When Mother was a child, at the time of the Boer War (1899-1902), the children sang a little ditty, which she recited to us kids:

> When I was young, I used to be
>
> The strongest man in Bermondsey.
>
> The 'Prince of Wales' he ordered me
>
> to join the British Army.'

but her older brother, my 'Uncle Sam', didn't heed his call. He became a 'British tar' instead serving aboard the 'Lion', Admiral David Beattie's Flagship, of the British Battle Cruiser squadron at Jutland, during WWI.

"Jutland?" he laughed, "That's the third time you have mentioned it. You must have a fixation with that name. I doubt if you will find many in England today who even remember that key naval battle, let alone its significance. "I seem to recall from my schooldays, that we took quite a pounding, losing more capital ships, but in the end, the German High Seas Fleet limped home to port, to be heard from no more. Our naval supremacy was never challenged again, as Germany was strangled by our 'Economic Blockade'."

But, after the 'fall of France' (06/22/40) this picture of invincible Britain changed abruptly. Rather than a 'bastion of strength' she was seen to be quite vulnerable as she faced almost certain defeat.

I continued my narrative: "My parents had a candy-store in the Bushwick section of Brooklyn; nearby was Ridgewood, which was pretty much a German-American neighborhood. In general, we got along okay with them. A few doors down from us was the 'Doc', as we used to call him. He had a short-wave radio and listened regularly to General Dittmars reports on DNB, (German Newscasts). "With Britain isolated, and facing the Nazi fury alone, he couldn't understand why the British didn't make Peace. Hitler was offering them such 'generous terms'.

"If they try to hold out, they face certain annihilation".

Mother would look up at him—he towered over her by well over a foot—straight in the eye, and sing the refrain from 'Rule Britannia'—"Britain's never, never, never will be slaves."

"Despite her outward defiance, Mother was very worried, since all her folks were in England . . . GP interrupted my monologue with the observation : "You've told us at some length about your mothers fears and concerns during those perilous times, but what about your father? Didn't he have anything to contribute?"

I regret having to say this, but although I was rather young at the time, the bitter fact was that I didn't have the patience to listen to his boring military experiences. A Polish Jew, he was conscripted into a cavalry unit of the Czarist army, during the 'Revolution of 1905'.

However, he did converse a lot with my older brother, who appreciated his stories—which in retrospect, were astounding—but that, as they say, is another tale.

What did warfare at the turn of the twentieth century have to teach me? For all practical purposes, from the military point of view, his experiences and the first World War itself might just as well have been ancient history.

Ah! But as for the Russo-German conflict, in the Second World War, (June 22 1941-May 8 1945), that was another matter! He summed it up by an old Russian saying

"Russia is easy to get into, but hard to get out of."

The misbegotten adventures, over the centuries of would-be-imperators, dating from the incursions from the west by the Teutonic Knights in the thirteenth century A.D., stopped by Alexander Nevskii, at the 'battle of Lake Peipus, (immortalized by S. Eisenstein's film masterpiece of the same name) attest to the duration and sagacity of this aphorism: To name a few more recent ones, Charles XII of Sweden, not content with the occupation of the Baltic States and large areas in NW Russia, plunged deeper into Russia where his invading forces were checked and completely destroyed by Czar Peter the Great at the battle of Poltava: (1709). Charles himself was extremely lucky, barely eluding capture as he and his army fled the field in disarray; Napoleon I of France was stranded in Moscow (1812); Kaiser Wilhelm II of Germany, despite the stunning triumph at Tannenberg (1914), and the occupation of huge tracts of Russian territory, was lucky to limp home after the Treaty of Brest-Litovsk (February/1918).

Tired of being persecuted in Czarist Russia, my father (like thousands of other Russian nationals) emigrated to England, during the years prior to the first World War, where he had the good fortune of meeting my mother.

I wasn't merely consoling my mother when I insisted that the threatened invasion would never succeed, because at that time I was absolutely sure that the Royal Navy would control the Channel and prevent the German Army from landing on English soil. The German Surface Fleet, which had been decimated in their Scandinavian adventure (04/40) (which turned out to be a blessing in disguise) could offer little protection. Later on, after Pearl Harbor (12/07/41) and the sinking of the new British battleship 'Prince of Wales' and the old battle-cruiser 'Repulse' a few days later, off Singapore, by a few dinky Japanese Torpedo Planes, clearly signaled the start of a new age of aerial domination of Naval operations, I might not have been so sure. But at that time, I was certain that just as the Royal Navy had successfully defied *Der Luftwaffe* at Dunkirk (05/27-06/04/'40) and evacuated the bulk of the British Expeditionary Force, so would it have stopped 'Sealion' cold.(see Section1.6).

Section 1.5 English-American

Droning on-and-on, I feared that I was boring him with my brief autobiographical sketch, but he urged me to continue.

"No, no. Go on. I know how it was over here, but how did it play over there, on the other side of the Atlantic? I'm curious: How did the Americans, in general, and you, an English-American in particular, and one very concerned, but not directly involved, think of our plight?" Concerned? Not involved? Some say that the Germans had a love-hate relationship with the English—but with the Jews in England they dropped the 'love' part. Hard as it might be to live under the heel of a conqueror, in Western Europe, the general population was not severely oppressed, but only the 'Biological and Political enemies' of the Third Reich were rounded-up, while the active collaborators (with the Nazis) thrived.

"English-American? That's a new one. It's customary to refer to those of English-heritage as WASP—a misnomer. As Voltaire might have put it, England is neither White, nor Anglo-Saxon, nor Protestant. You might say that I am more like a WASH, than a WASP."

I'm sorry but it did sound kind of silly: me comfortably ensconced, an ocean removed, telling him how things looked in those days. He who lived through terrible times, under the threat of invasion, destruction from the air, even a submarine economic blockade, should be telling me how it was in 'Blighty', not the other way around. But, with the onset of the 'Battle of Britain' a resurgence of affection for the British people swept America. First with sympathy, and then with admiration. the

Americans were electrified by their showing in the face of adversity and possible obliteration.

Those were the days of Edward R. Morrow's reports on the 'Blitz':

"This is London calling . . ."

Section 1.6 Hitler's Directives

Directive 16, for the invasion of England, codenamed SEELOEWE, or 'SEALION' was belatedly issued on 16 July '40, many weeks after the 'miracle of Dunkirk'.

(Sea-lion! The greatest battle never fought, went down in history as one of a long list of battles that did not take place, and might well have dramatically changed the course of world history, but on which we can only speculate.)

The Wehrmacht was sharply divided on Sea-lion.

What did the Armed Services think about it?

Das Heer (the Army)? Ha! The English Channel is nothing but a wide river.

Der Luftwaffe (the Air-force)? England can be defeated by *Der Luftwaffe* alone—without any help from the Army or Navy.

(If the Luftwaffe couldn't prevent the evacuation from Dunkirk, under conditions most favorable to them, and the worst possible for the Royal Navy and the RAF, how could anyone lend credence to Goering's bombast, and think that it could drive the RAF from the skies, while keeping the RN out of the invasion zone so that it could proceed unmolested?)

Die Kriegsmarine (the Navy)? Couldn't guarantee safe passage nor could it provide logistical support, in the unlikely event that some of the German Army managed to make it safely across the Channel.

BARBAROSSA

The signal event of the 20th Century was the Second World War. The events of the first-half century (such as WWI, the Great Depression, the 'Rise of Militant Dictatorships', etc.) flowed into it, while those of the latter half (such as 'Dissolution of Empires, the United Nations, the abundance of new countries, the 'Cold War', etc.) flowed directly from it.

The main event of WWII, was BARBAROSSA, the codename for the 'invasion of the USSR (June 22 1941). Serious planning commenced with the infamous Directive 21 (December 18, 1940). In it Adolf Hitler laid out his strategic objectives. His plan ran into stiff opposition from the German Army. The main bone of contention with OKH was over Moscow. The more that OKH insisted on the obvious, e.g., that Moscow be the prime objective, the more insistent Hitler became that it wasn't even to be considered until other, more important objectives be achieved. Finally, in exasperation, he declared the capture of Moscow irrelevant, and that it could only be contemplated after Leningrad had fallen, certain economic areas rich in foodstuffs (e.g., *Ukraine*), natural resources (e.g., *Donets Basin*), and petroleum (e.g., *Caucasas*) were taken, and the complete destruction of the Red Army in European Russia accomplished. This fundamental disagreement, which should have been ironed out before the invasion, was to haunt the entire German operation, leading inexorably to the *Disaster at Moscow* (12/41).

What was the connection between Sea-lion and Barbarossa? Ostensibly, they both had the same goal—to drag Great Britain to the 'Peace Table'. Grand Admiral E. Raeder dissuaded Hitler from Sea-lion, declaring that it was the hard-way to go, and substituted an assault on the British Empire's vulnerable, far-flung life-line in its stead. Sea-lion was first postponed, and then abandoned in the Spring of '41. Hitler finally concurred with the grand admiral, but held fast to his obsession that conquering Russia was the easy-way!! Bizarre! (See Section 4.10).

Section 1.7 Pre-Pearl Harbor Recollections

"With such a broad and deep interest in Naval Warfare, how come that you wound up in the Army?"

"To tell you the truth, I really don't know. My older brother signed up with the Navy and it was natural to assume that I would do the same."

But, in the late spring of 1941 rumors began circulating that an 'Invasion of Russia' was imminent.

"Almost 16, I had just graduated from Eastern District High School, and I recall greeting the news with disbelief, but unrepressed joy. If true, Hitler was about to take the 'Free World' off the hook.

"What the Western diplomats had vainly striven for, to get Hitler and Stalin to lock horns was about to become a reality."

"I suppose that my fascination with land warfare was inspired by the monumental battles shaping up in Russia. (True, there were some great naval battles in the Pacific, but after their initial string of sensational victories, the Japanese quickly became out-classed by the industrial and military might of the U.S. and its Allies. Besides, this was later, after Pearl Harbor. Whatever, I was more interested in the European war, where a titanic struggle was taking place, than in the Pacific War, where the outcome seemed inevitable.)

"In our store, we had one of those old-fashioned, waist-high, fire-engine red Coca-Cola coolers where soft drinks were kept cold. When the daily newspapers arrived, I would spread them out on the ice-box and pore over the latest news reports, articles by commentators, and communiqués from the front. Between waiting on customers, I assiduously followed the progress of FM F *von Bock's* Army Group Center as it wended its way towards the capital of the USSR.

"Why von Bock? Simple. It seemed to me that he was following the 'old Napoleonic Road' towards Moscow, which was what I, and most everyone else thought was the primary objective of 'Barbarossa'. I viewed the map with astonishment, as the 'unstoppable German war-machine ate up the miles', and with horror, as it closed the *Minsk* (7/16/41) and *Smolensk* (8/4/41) pockets.

The Red Army suffered staggering losses. Millions of men, thousands of tanks, guns, warplanes and comparable quantities of other equipment and supplies were lost. No army could possibly survive such horrific losses. The way seemed to be wide open for a wild-dash-to Moscow! People, who should have known better, had been talking about a six-week war,—and damn it all—they seemed to be right!"

"Why did von Bock stop?"

"I don't know. Why did he?"

"Why only 200 miles from Moscow, did he waste two whole months of ideal tank-warfare-weather before resuming the offensive?"

Without waiting for an answer, GP interrupted my harangue: "Sea-lion was successfully parried, but the outlook was still grim. We had fought the Germans to a standstill in the 'Battle of Britain', but how do you exit the war? By a negotiated peace? By outright victory? Not much chance of that (strange to say, the Germans faced the same dilemma.) "Hitler's quest for a quick victory had been thwarted: Sea-lion was delayed until 15 Sept '40 and abandoned in Spring, 1941."

Like the powerful tides of the English Channel, the spirits of the English 'rose and fell' with the news from Eastern Europe. The impact of these events covered the entire spectrum of emotions. They were:

Floored by the Russo-German non-aggression pact (8/23/39).

Ecstatic at the prospect of the German invasion of Russia. (6/22/41).

Alarmed by the ease at which the mighty Wehrmacht smashed its way through Russia.

Dismayed as their relentless advance carried them to the 'Gates of Moscow' (12/41).

All that kept their rapidly receding hopes alive was that somehow the sheer vastness of Russia, the legendary toughness of Ivan, and the meager (but rapidly increasing) Allied aid would help sustain her, until her most dependable Ally, 'General Winter' took over.

Resuming, after this brief digression, my personal recollections and reactions, I continued, "Russia is not France. Back in '41, I estimated that it would require 3 consecutive 'French-style' blitzkriegs to reach Moscow. By midsummer, blitzkriegs 1 and 2, had already attained their objectives (See Map 4.) But, it was not until years after the war, that I learned of Directive 21 wherein Hitler ignored Moscow . . .

"True to his original plan, Hitler, denuding Army Group C of its armor, dispatched *von Hoth's* 3rd Panzer Army north to Leningrad, and *Guderian's* 2nd Panzer Army south towards Kiev. Finally, in synchronization with his Generals, he changed his mind on 5 Sept '41. Emulating, the famous Duke of York, 'who, with 20,000 men marched them to the 'top of the hill' and then marched them back down again' he countermanded his earlier orders, recalling the two Panzer Armies, and added *Hoepner's 4*[th].

But, Army Group Center wasn't ready to roll until 3 Oct. There was still plenty of time, but the *Rasputista* came early and was particularly severe in 1941. Largely because of these time delays and the horrendous weather conditions, the 3rd blitzkrieg, after encircling and destroying several Russian Armies in the *Bryansk-Vyazma Kesselschlacht*, fell short of Moscow.(See Map 4)

In all the 'employments of Life', the military, more than any other, demands perspective. It is not my intent to 'lionize' von Bock, but for the final assault on Moscow he did command the largest and most powerful Field Army ever assembled—a mind-boggling 80 Divisions (nearly a million and a half men), including 3 Panzer Armies.

(This is to be compared to the 40 Division thrust—almost the entire Allied combat force in Normandy save for Gen. Patton's 3rd Army— proposed by FM Montgomery to 'end the war in '44'. (A heavily watered down version of this plan, 'Market Garden', ended in the debacle at Arnheim (09/44).) Or, to the much smaller U.S. force of 37 Brigades, (including women and children) in the Iraq-American War.)[ii]

Nothing could withstand such a force. Nothing—that is except the weather! Egged on by orders from 'above' (e.g., Hitler and OKH, in Berlin); restrained by warnings from 'below' (e.g., his generals in the field), FM von Bock was in a quandary. The Autumn rains turned roads and tracks into a quagmire. Men, horses, trucks, even tanks, were unable to make any progress in this 'Sea of Mud'. His generals urged him to call off the attack, withdraw to prepared defensive positions (as far back as Smolensk, if need be) and resume the offensive in the Spring.

But, after so many disappointments, he was not to be dissuaded. Rejecting their admonitions, he exhorted; On to Moscow! For a while he looked good; the temperature fell, the ground froze, permitting the resumption of vehicular traffic. Confidently, he set 7 Nov '41 as the date he intended to invest Moscow. But then the thermometer plummeted (with a vengeance) reaching –45 degrees F. The German Winter Supply system broke down. Without Winter clothing; with 'starvation rations' for the men and animals, with the vehicles frozen immobile, the weary German Army came face-to face with Red Army reinforcements fresh from Asiatic Russia. Under incessant snowfall. and the intense cold, the Nazi offensive, gradually reaching the Moscow-Volga canal, ground to a halt almost in sight of the Kremlin. On 5 Dec 1941, 'Barbarossa' was 'Kaput'.

For the British, Arnheim (September 1944) may have been a 'Bridge too Far', but For the Germans, Moscow (December 1941) proved to be a 'Blitzkrieg too Far'.

Section 1.8 Ironies

Never in the 'History of Warfare' were battles conducted on so grand a scale. The German Army was destroyed in 3 great battles in Russia, codenamed Operations *Typhon* (12/41-1/42), *Blau* (11/42-2/43), and *Zitedele* (7/43), or more commonly known as the Battles of Moscow, Stalingrad, and Kursk, respectively.

But none of these would have taken place if it were not for England's gallant stand, during their 'finest hour' in the 'Battle of Britain'. It was her dogged determination to continue the war, despite all 'odds' that forced Hitler to take the long (long!) land route, via Moscow, rather than the short hop across the English Channel, to drag England to the Peace Table.

"You know, the World owes Great Britain an immense debt of gratitude not only for its unparalleled contributions to the advancement of Modern Western Civilization, but for being the bulwark against the Nazi menace, when single handedly she held them at bay until, with the Soviet Union and the United States at her side, the Grand Alliance crushed Nazi Germany."

I thought that I might have poured it on a bit thick, but what of it? Not noted for effusive praise, the encomium surprised me. However, my panegyric delivered, I felt satisfied. I was feeling a little high, perhaps, but good. I've been told that I have a tendency to wear a 'silly grin' on my face under such circumstances, but with good company, good conversation, and a good story, I can talk about the 'Campaigns of the 'Decisive Battles of the Western World', for hours.

I looked around; the Club seemed more crowded than before. Maybe it was time to leave and give up our table to some other party. He glanced at his watch; 'mingled with the mirth', I detected a slight hardening of his features. Was he giving me a hint? Suddenly, he stood up, and stretched himself; he sat down, twisted his glass between his fingers, took a couple of sips, and matter-of-factly, without pretense, in a clear, firm voice, he commented on my remarks.

"Yes, there are many reasons for an Englishman to be proud, but, our behavior, in the later stages of WWII, was not one of them."

"How's that?"

I wasn't sure that I heard him correctly, but, undeterred, he continued:

"In a war full of atrocities, the English, not the Germans, had committed the worst."

Had he too much to drink? Had he taken leave of his senses?

"Forbear! Sure, there are times, when all Armies, caught up in the 'heat of war' may be guilty of terrible deeds, such as the 'Firebombing of Dresden' (02/45), or even the dropping of an Atomic Bomb (08/45), that might be construed by some as atrocities, but . . ."

Curtly, he brushed aside my protestations,

"In a war replete with ironies, *it was Allied policy, not German, which greatly prolonged the struggle,* and dragged out the pain and suffering that went along with it.

"Please reserve your observations on my degree of intoxication and, more seriously, my mental state, until you have heard my story.

Without waiting for my reply, he went on

"It is not often that one gets the chance to save millions, but, in the summer of 1944, I had mine."

CHAPTER 2

64 Baker Street, SOE HQ. London

Section 2.1 D-Day

In the pre-dawn hours of 6 June 1944, the British 6th Airborne Division boarded their *Horsa* (and some *Hamilcar*) Gliders, and together with the U.S.82nd and 101st Airborne Divisions launched OVERLORD, the codename for the Allied invasion of 'Fortress Europa'. Thousands of Paras—paratroopers and glider troops—rained down on Normandy spearheading D-Day.

The job of the 6th was to take control of the Invasion Beach area, between its eastern-most boundary, the River *Dives*, and the village of *Ouistreham,* and hold it until relieved by elements of the British 1st Corps.

As Gen Gale explained, the 6th had 3 primary tasks: Capture intact the *Orne* River and *Caen* Canal bridges (perhaps, better known as the *Pegasus* bridge), the destruction of the bridges across the River Dives, and the 'silencing of the *Merville Battery'.* Overlooking Sword Beach, its big guns potentially posed a grave danger to the British forces. The importance of these tasks cannot be over-estimated.

Aerial reconnaissance and Intelligence reports put the armament of this heavily fortified battery at four 150 mm (large caliber) guns completely enclosed by casements with walls and roof of reinforced concrete. The MB, a vital outpost of the Atlantic Wall, was expected to be fiercely defended. A multi-pronged operation involving heavy bombers, paratroopers, and assault and supply gliders was envisaged. Operating under tight time constraints this operation had to be successfully completed ½ hour before daybreak.[iii]

"I was a glider pilot of an assault glider. Making a pass over the supposed location of the battery, I couldn't see a thing: no flares, no signal lights, no nothing!"

Encircling a few times, he spotted a heavy concentration of 'tracer fire'.

Assuming that was where the action was, he released the tug and spiraled down, Peppered by MG34 bullets and dual purpose 20mm flak, he was badly wounded, but managed to veer away and crash-land the glider nearby. Scrambling from the wrecked glider, the men joined in the assault, while GP was tended to by the medics. Everything had to go right, but almost everything went wrong. Yet, the MB was demolished in record time so that the British 3rd Division could make its way up from Sword Beach unscathed.

Without thinking, I muttered under my breath, "Sort of a Marshal *Grouchy* in reverse."

"Who?"

"One of Napoleon's generals."

"Thanks for the promotion, but I fail to see the connection."

"The Marshal marched his Army (45,000 strong) *away* from the firing, and missed the Battle of *Waterloo*. You flew *towards* the firing but missed the 'Battle for the Merville Battery' Although reacting in precisely the opposite manner, the end result was the same: You both *missed* the Battle."

"That's a good one. I'll have to remember it."

Section 2.2 Hospital stay

Because of a perceived shortage, it was policy to evacuate wounded Glider Pilots to Hospital in England as quickly as possible. A healthy, strong young man, his recovery was quite swift.

Battalion Major made a point of trying to get back to England to visit with the wounded men from the 6th.

As he (not so eloquently) put it, "I've more of my boys here in hospital than at the front."

The men looked forward to his visits and got a boost-in-morale from his news-from-Normandy.

"The 6th performed brilliantly, but Jerry is putting up a tough fight, and casualties have been higher than expected. The lads are interspersed with the 3rd Infantry, while waiting to be assembled for shipment back to England to get ready for their next assignment."

The Major asked GP. "Well my boy, what would you like to do while recuperating? I've been informed by the Doctor that your wounds preclude an early return to action as a glider pilot. "You could do nothing, I suppose, but just hang around here fooling around with the Nurses, but I don't think that you will find that very satisfying." They both laughed at how that came out.!

Smiling, GP thought for a while, "You know, Sir, I've always had a yen for flying. I've been hanging around airplanes since I was a kid. I was a pretty good seat-of-the-pants flyer, but whatever the RAF was looking for, it wasn't me. Under the circumstances, I would like to make use of my skills, by flying non-combat missions."

"Nothing is too good for a boy from the 6th. With the acceleration in flow of cross-channel traffic you might be of some use. How does the ferrying of SIS agents between England and the Continent strike you? I know some people in the Intelligence service. I might be able to get you assigned, on temporary leave, to their flight pool."

I wasn't too thrilled; I never thought of myself as a trans-English Channel ferryboat captain, but I get the chance to 'hone my flying skills' and besides I would be lending a helping hand to the 'war effort'.

Section 2.3 An urgent call

"Good morning B, good of you to come. We should get together more often. You know how much I appreciate our conversations, Pull up a chair."

B wondered: *What's this all about*? He and the Director hadn't had much to say to each other since D-Day. SOE had been a relative bee-hive, but he hadn't been involved. He had expected a surge in activity, but it didn't materialize.

Ostensibly, as Head of the German Resistance (German anti-Nazi) Desk, it should have been his job to maintain contact with the *Widerstand*, as the German Resistance movement came to be called (referred to here—simply as W). (Although there was a large civilian component, in practice, only the German Army had the strength and organization to effectively oppose Hitler, Consequently, W became synonymous with the German Generals.)

But the catch-22 is that the Allied twin doctrines of' Absolute Silence' (January 1941) and 'Unconditional Surrender' (January 1943) prohibit all intercourse with the enemy, and that includes W. Of necessity, our dialogues were limited to informal, off-the-record exchanges.

Suddenly, Dir arose from his chair, walked to the window, and stared outside. B hadn't seen him so agitated: What was up? Dir returned to his desk, and sat down,

"I have something to tell you, but I don't know where to begin."

"Its customary to start at the beginning, Sir."

Dir frowned, then smiled, "Good show. See, I can always rely on you for good advice." Tension evaporated, he said that "SOE has known for some time about a contact between the OSS agent A. Dulles and a certain *Gisevious*, of doubtful reliability, an emissary of W, about a month ago. Meetings like that are expressly forbidden by the twin doctrines, but it apparently didn't bother the Americans. "Without going into details, the W plan was ignored in Washington and London."

However, Dir was intrigued by the 'OSS-W' contact. Were the Americans on to something? "I get the impression that OSS would like to play *'Let's make a deal'*. I don't think that they would be shy about beating us 'to the punch'. They are even talking to the Nazis. Negotiations with the notorious SS General K. Wolff, to 'end the war in Italy' have been going on for a long time now".

"Strange, Un Su was their idea, but they don't seem to be taking it seriously."

All of this would have remained academic, but for an urgent call from an SOE agent in the Netherlands. Dutch Resistance has arranged a tete-a-tete, with a German General, a leading member of W to discuss their latest plan for the 'overthrow of Hitler and the Nazis'. The new-plan is a variation of the 'old one' with most of Allies objections removed, and adapted to the current situation on the Western Front.

B listened to Dir remarks with apprehension. He knew where all this was leading. He didn't want to go on another wild-goose chase. Besides, he just about had his fill of the GGs. "I know that those in W are different, but they all have one thing in common: Their arrogance can sometimes be insufferable. Ha! Despite being supplicants, they still think they can call the shots,"

B heard of these plans to eliminate Hitler before, but they always turned up empty. Besides, the twin doctrines pre-ordain their failure. But he was now being asked to meet with W once again. The urgent 'call' apparently induced SOE to consider the new-plan.

Why do they bother?

"I needn't tell you, Sir, how many false alarms these blokes have triggered."

"Maybe we shouldn't be so rough on them. Maybe it isn't so easy to keep a plot going in a brutal totalitarian state. It's not cricket, what the Nazis play!"

Despite the rapid deterioration of the German position, W remained true to its convictions and reaffirmed its plans to overthrow the Nazis. They knew full-well that the war cannot last much longer, but they hold getting rid of Hitler quickly to be of paramount importance and have no intention of sitting idly by waiting for the inevitable Allied victory. However, now more than ever, they desperately seek British support for the 'enterprise'.

B took it all in. After a pause he said, "I'm sorry, Sir, but I am not the man for this job."

"On the contrary, you are tailor-made for it. You know how much I value your judgment in these matters." Sternly, he continued, "I, of course, would prefer that you display a little enthusiasm, but, "he added acidly," in any case, you must go." I'm not asking you to make any spot decisions. In fact that is precisely what you shouldn't do. Just take what the General tells you under advisement, and immediately report back to me."

Silence. On the one hand B cannot stomach their posturing, but on the other, the mere fact that he will be meeting with them, cannot, but be, misinterpreted as 'encouragement'. B had the contorted expression, of a man, who knows that what he is about to do is not for him, but he's going to do it anyway. He thought for a moment,

"Can you supply me with some information about GG?"

Fiddling around in his briefcase, he replied, "Here is a fact-sheet summarizing the extent of our knowledge. Aside from the leadership of W, we know little about the others."

"If this is all you have, you can't be very serious about the meeting."

"Nonsense. While we don't want you to get too friendly with them, we are counting on you to bring an 'open mind' to the proceedings I want you to report on their commitment, their new-plans, their ability to deliver, what they want from us, and, of course, what's in it for us. Listen carefully to what they have to say, but you must never—I repeat, never promise them anything. I rely on your discretion. By the way, anything that you can pick-up, unobtrusively of course, about the Americans will be greatly appreciated. Good luck. Relax, don't look so worried. It won't be as bad as all that,"

"Whew. That's a tall order," B said to himself, as he exited Dir's office.

He muses: *If that's what he wants, that's what he's going to get. He may not like what he hears, but I have no intention of being a sounding-board—a mere fact-finder.*

Section 2.4 German Resistance Desk

I arrived at 64 Baker St.

"So this is the HQ of SOE. Not a very impressive site."

I entered and identified myself.

"What's your business here, soldier?"

"I was ordered to report to SOE German Resistance Desk.'

Directed towards a small dingy room, I knocked on the door.

"Come in. Take a seat, I'll be right with you."

I placed my dossier on the desk, and looked around. Amazing! GR Desk? Ha! They weren't kidding. That's precisely what it was: A desk, a chair, a telephone, a filing cabinet, an over-flowing bookcase and for effect, no doubt, a large wall-map of Northwest Europe, showing Northern France, Southern England, the Low Countries, and NW Germany, Superimposed on the map, was the latest position of the front line. Not much progress, since D-Day. The British were bogged down at Caen; the Americans were inching their way south towards *St. Lo* and slowly working their way up the *Cotentin* Peninsula towards *Cherbourg.*

"So you're to be my pilot." Thumbing through my papers, mumbling to himself, he said, "I see where you were shot down on D-Day. Too bad I missed that show, but we all have our little part to play, eh, what?. Right now, mine is to run the GR Desk, not a very busy place, as you can see."

GP smiled, and concurred (aside), "*Leicester Square it isn't.*"

"Sometimes I get the urge to chuck it all in and volunteer for overseas duty."

GP thought: *"Yeah, I can just see this 'old fart' giving up his cushy job here in London to be up-front with the 'boys in Normandy.'"*

Rhetorically, B notes," No Hurricanes or Spitfires here."

"Ever fly a Lysander? It may be one of the slowest birds around, but it's terrific for cross-channel covert operations with the Continental Resistance Groups. It can fly under the Radar undetected, and almost any patch of open country suffices as a landing field,"

Although more than a bit irritated, GP smiled "I don't mean to be rude, Sir, but if you had taken the time to read my dossier, you would have discovered that I wasn't a fighter pilot with the RAF, but a Glider Pilot with the 6th Air-landing Division. A hybrid: Trained as a pilot by the RAF and as a soldier by the Royal Infantry.

"I didn't fly a Spitfire—nor even a Hurricane—for that matter, but a *Horsa* Glider—the 'slowest and most silent' ride in town. Furthermore, I was not shot out of the sky in a dog-fight with an Me 109, but was wounded, and severely injured, crash-landing my glider on D-Day."

B listened in amazement, while GP couldn't believe that he that he had the nerve to talk like that to a Brigadier. (By nature reserved, he felt uneasy in the presence of Senior Brass, but he didn't seem to have that problem with B Perhaps in GP's eyes, he was 'just a windbag' and not a genuine high-ranking Army Officer.)

"Right. Whatever, let's get on with it, shall we? He spread a detailed map of the landing area on his desk. The plane is to land on a field adjacent to a secure farmhouse, arranged by courtesy of the

Dutch Resistance. "There we will meet a representative from the GR movement. We leave tonight."

Naively, GP asks," German Resistance, Sir. I didn't know that there was any."

B found it amusing., but replied cryptically: "Neither did I."

Chapter 3

Flight out

Section 3.1 Sketches

We drove out to Tempford Airport in Bedfordshire. The Lysander was waiting for us; GP filed the flight plan.

A ground-crewman assisted GP into the cockpit. B boarded the plane with trepidation.

"Are you sure that you are up to this?"

"Never felt better, Sir. Come on in, I can't wait to get started."

A smooth take-off allayed B's fears, but only after they crossed the English coast did he relax and loosen-up a bit.

"Tight-lipped, he didn't tell me anything, and I didn't ask. It was evident that he was reluctant to discuss the 'mission' with a layman not schooled in the 'Methods of Military Intelligence'. But, his 'days at the University' got the better of him. He couldn't keep quiet for long. A veritable storehouse of knowledge he was always ready to impart information to anyone who would listen. To pass the time and make for a more pleasant trip, he entertained me with an autobiographical sketch and the elements of SIS.

Aside, GP noted, "*I had heard of MI6, but who the devil was SOE?*"

An offshoot of MI6, External Intelligence, it was a brainchild of PM, who, obsessed with the idea of 'setting occupied Europe ablaze', thought that 'Subversion and Sabotage' should be a separate entity. MI6 was not thrilled by this proposal. There was no love lost between the two agencies.

Broadly speaking, SOE was organized to cooperate with anti-Nazi Resistance elements in occupied Europe but, strange to say, it virtually ignored German Resistance movements. Some trace this limitation to the ill-starred *Venlo* incident (11/39) which led to PM's famous dictum Absolute Silence (1/41) and with FDR, to, 'Unconditional Surrender' two-years later at *Casablanca* (1/43).

These twin-doctrines shaped Allied-W policy; despite vigorous efforts to get them retracted, or even modified. They persisted to the end of the war. What was worse, SOE was ordered to ignore any approaches from W or to pass them on to FO and SIS.

Section 3.2 B's story

Feeling more comfortable as the flight progressed, B began his lecture:

"Twice my studies were interrupted by war: As a newly graduated college student in the First World War and in this war, as a University Professor. In my opinion, WWI was much worse; the casualties amongst junior officers were so great, that by the time it ended, I was discharged as a Captain.

I resumed my studies at Oxford specializing in 17th century Continental History. The signal event of that century was the conflict which started with the' Defenestration of Prague' in 1618, and ended in 1648, with the 'Peace of Westphalia'.

Under his breath, GP muttered, "I guess that's why they call it the Thirty—Years war'."

B got a kick out of that, but added sarcastically," I'm glad to see that you are paying attention. Step to the head of the class, young man. Even my better students would have had trouble with that one."

We both laughed. First impressions went out-the-window.

"My hasty judgment quickly changed to admiration, upon learning that he had seen action in the Great War'.

The fact is that I began to think more and more highly of him as time progressed. But frankly, I wasn't in the mood for a history lesson. Still he continued, "Now that was a War! "In its own way, it was more devastating than either of the two World Wars. According to some historians, it was the precursor to the 'Modern Age'. It started, more or less, as a religious and dynastic struggle, and ended, more or less, as a 'nationalistic war'. Religious wars are notorious for their inhumanity, since they worked on the premise that there was only one 'True Religion', and it was theirs. Thus, Catholics and Protestants had no particular qualms in 'savaging each other'. During the later phases of the war, however, the protagonists became preoccupied with national ascendency and the acquisition of territory, as they battled for the hegemony of Europe."

B lapsed into silence, but it was only to get-his-second-wind'. "Before the war, I was a rather well-respected, if undistinguished, Professor. After the war began, the government began recruiting academics for the Secret Intelligence Service. For some ridiculous reason (for which, in the words of the 'Pirate King', I have no desire to be disloyal) known only to the bureaucrats, they thought that we would make fine secret service agents. They raided the faculties, and it was just my luck to wind up in the 'Special Operations Executive'.'

"They must have been disappointed with my performance, when the Director called me in and proudly announced:

"Congratulations, You have just been promoted to head the German Resistance Desk."

"But, Sir", B protested, "There is no GR Desk to speak of."

"That's true", he said, "but, nevertheless, we always get communications from people in Germany, who claim to be anti-Nazi, or are acting on behalf of the Widerstand, but they never amount to anything, They promise, but never deliver."

I had written extensively on the strategy and tactics of the '30 years war' but I never could understand how my meticulous investigations in depth, of the Battles of *Rocroi* (1643) and *Luetzen* (1632) had any bearing on WWII. From the disposition of Allied forces Dir had deduced that Northwest Germany would most likely be the British 'zone of influence'. B had spent several years in the Duchy of *Cleves-Julich* region in particular, and NW Germany in general, researching the archives of that war.

B recalled the meeting with Dir accompanying his appointment. "Your knowledge and experience are of great interest to us."

Baloney. He knew full well that the 'twin doctrines' had made a shambles out of our intelligence activities in Germany, and left the Widerstand all but dead.

"I had about as much chance as a dreaded-Stuka, (JU87 dive-bomber) with a Spitfire on his tail, of making any meaningful contacts with German anti-Nazis. That's why I was so surprised, when he called me in and informed me about the 'mission'. He told me that if 'upstairs' thinks that the Americans are getting too chumy with W, then a chink in the wall separating us from W may be developing."

"But Sir", B interjected, "I thought that you were dead-set against any formal meetings with W. Although we weren't supposed to make any contact with them, as a practical matter, they are a persistent bunch, and, unavoidably, on occasion, we do 'bump' into them."

Immediately, he replied, "Like the rest of us, all I can do is follow orders."

"Yes, I know. England's most distinguished poet laureate, Alfred, Lord Tennyson, put it magnificently, 'Ours not to reason why/ Ours but to do or die'"

"Right! They tell me; 'Absolute Silence and Unconditional Surrender'—so I tell you 'No Deals!—regardless of my personal opinion. Now if an opening in the barrier is really developing, then maybe it can be exploited to our advantage. But remember, this is only speculation; it is up to you to find out what W has in mind. I repeat, as far as I know, the old orders still stand: Listen, like the well-bred English Gentleman that you are, to what they have to say, but no promises, no negotiations! Understand?"

Bravo! B thought, "*Another wild-goose chase!*"

B was not happy with this assignment, but this time he chose to read between the lines. Maybe Dir is right; maybe something can come out of this. *Maybe, as the American's say, the GG will make us an offer that we cannot refuse.*

Chapter 4

Rendezvous

"The Fuhrer, Adolph Hitler gives us the example. We will follow him gladly into the German future—come what will."

Gen. Frederici (30 Mar 1939).

("The German Army and the Nazi Party, 1933-39", R.J. O'Neill.)

Section 4.1 The meeting

The GG, attired in his casual, undress, summer uniform, with all insignia and other references to his rank removed, accompanied by a boy, his interpreter, was seated in the kitchen of the farmhouse, anxiously awaiting the arrival of the British Agent. (Although Holland was occupied, he had to be given safe-conduct by the Dutch Resistance, to protect him from the Dutch partisans who were all over the place, and would like nothing better than to capture (or knock off) a German General.)

Their Dutch guide introduced them. He held the meeting in high regard; a clandestine rendezvous between an agent from London with a GG must be very important.

Upon closer examination. GP could see that the interpreter was really a young woman, disguised as a boy; with a short haircut, a bulky,

loose-fitting light jacket, German Army regulation trousers and boots—
the impersonation was quite effective.

GP had never been so close to a British, let alone a German, general
before. He tried to imagine how the GG would have looked in full
uniform, stern-visaged, with the familiar thin-red stripe, of the General
Staff, running down his pantleg.

The meeting got off to an inauspicious start. Neither of them
wanted to come. It was early summer, but the icy, formal greeting
between the two men left them all cold.

GP *thinks: "No need for Air-conditioning here."*

B *thinks: "What's the point of this charade?"*

GG *thinks: "What's the use." But, he had to control* his feelings.

He repeats (to himself) the words of Colonel General *Beck*, when
first asked to undertake this mission. *"A great deal hinges on the outcome of
this meeting. This may be the last opportunity that we will ever get to influence the
British. Their active engagement could very well spell the difference between success
and failure. of our great 'enterprise'."*

GG resolves to take whatever measures are needed to persuade the
British to come along with W.

B, smiling, breaks the ice. "Well General, after a 5 year hiatus, we
finally get to finish our conversation."

GG, perplexed says, "I beg your pardon. You've got the advantage."

"Venlo is a town nearby. Shortly after the German Army over-ran
Poland in Sept. 1939, British Intelligence was tricked into thinking that
they would be talking to a disaffected German general, representing the
'peace party', but our agents were kidnapped instead (11/39).

As far as I know they are still imprisoned in *Sachsenhaussen.*"

"Oh, I vaguely recall that British agents were implicated in an abortive plot to kill Hitler, It was plastered all over the newspapers at that time. I'm sorry for those men; it wasn't us, but the *Sicherheitdienst* who were responsible."

GG stood up, and after a brief pause, continued:

"You don't have to tell me about Venlo. I come from this region. In Germany. of course, between the Dutch border and the Rhine".

B's face lit up, "You do? I have fond memories of time spent in the, Palatinate researching the origins of the 'Thirty Year's War'.

"Es ist ein kleines Welt, nicht wahr?"

GG smiled, and replied, "Smaller than you think. I learned a little English while serving on the staff of the German Military attaché in London. I became deeply interested in the early history of England, from the time of the Anglo-Saxon migration, and was struck by the same Teutonic heritage of the Germans and the English". GG lightly observes, that with each of them having a working-knowledge of the others language, they will have to be careful of what they say.

"Enough of these pleasantries. Let's get down to business."

B and GG adjourn to a makeshift 'conference room' adjacent to the kitchen. The girl notices his limp "Oh, that?

It was a present from your countrymen on D-Day."

"D-Day? What's that?"

"That my dear girl, *is the Allied name for the 'Invasion of Fortress Europe."*

Section 4.2 The Old-Plan

B calls the meeting to order. GP wasn't sure if it was okay for him to listen in. Since B raised no objection, that's what he did. Whatever, after eavesdropping for a while, he slipped out to check up on the airplane.

"Why did you request this meeting? I understand that one of your emissaries, a certain *Gisevious*, contacted the American Allen Dulles, the OSS agent, and submitted a plan which called for, *inter alia*, the elimination of Hitler and a' quick end to the war'"

This plan foundered on an ill-advised attempt to '*split* the Grand Alliance' and to '*scrap* Unconditional Surrender' It was ignored in Washington and London.

"It's bad enough to agitate for the 'repeal of UnSu—but to 'break-up the Grand Alliance—Never!"

B, berates GG for the waste of valuable time.

"Frankly, you may have procrastinated too long already. In May, before D-Day, you had something to peddle. In May, there was a sense of urgency.".

Rumors of the impending cross-channel invasion were rife. Obviously maximum impact of the Revolt would be achieved before D-Day. Time was rapidly running out for the conspiracy. The Gestapo was breathing down their necks. Civilian leadership in W were in particular jeopardy. (The Socialist J. *Leber* was slated to be picked up, while the ex-Mayor of *Leipzig*, and the Chancellor-designate of the Provisional Government, K. *Goedeler*, went into hiding.)

W had to make its move!

Despite absolute control of the Sea and Air, the outlook for OVERLORD was uncertain. How strong was the Atlantic Wall? No one knew for sure. Amphibious operations are notoriously treacherous.

Would it be successful, as it was in Italy (at *Salerno* and *Anzio*, in 1943) and in the Pacific Islands, or would it be more like a rerun of the 'Disaster at *Gallipoli*' in the first World War?

No operation anywhere near the size and scope of Overlord had ever been contemplated. Will the casualty lists be so long as to cause the Allies to 'lose heart' and abort the invasion?

"But, now that we have absorbed the losses, and the invasion is a success, what incentive is there to deal with W?"

"I protest. We have been trying without success to get support for our efforts to oust Hitler, at least since 1938, but these attempts were all sabotaged by the Allies."

"To insinuate that we stopped you from getting rid of Hitler is absurd."

Exasperated, the GG replied, "No that is not what I am saying. You must understand that it takes a long time for a conspiracy to develop. Especially in a brutal dictatorship like Nazi Germany. Now, while the core conspirators never wavered, it took time to bring other generals around. Very few of them were openly supportive; some were sympathetic, but most were non-committal. It's a tribute to the generals, that even if some of them thought our plan treasonous, they never informed on us.

For the most part, however, their attitude was: "Make your Revolution, overthrow the Nazis, then we'll come along for the ride."

(Come to think of it, this wasn't very much different from the British government's official position.)

W needed some action from the Allies to get the generals to jump on the bandwagon. A sizable opposition stretches back well into pre-war days. Early W plans were based on the premise that the Allies hated and feared Hitler as much as we did. We knew that if the Allies had taken a firm stand, Hitler would have backed down; or, in the event of war, the German Army was so weak that it could easily be overwhelmed."

B replied simply, "What you say may be true. but all I can say is that if you hadn't cluttered-up your plan with that *split and scrap* nonsense, it might have gotten a better reception."

GG defends W position: He still thinks that a 'crusade against Communism', isn't such a bad idea.

Wasn't this Allied policy in the 1930s?

"Russia, not Germany, will be your main post-war worry."

B retorts sarcastically, "Thanks for the warning, but if I was you, I would be worrying more about the Russians, right now!"[iv]

Angrily, B continues, raising his voice: "Don't you people ever learn? Can't you get it through your thick skulls that there is no way that you can split the Grand Alliance? It is even weirder to suppose that you can get the Allies to join with OB West, and the German forces on the Eastern Front, to shield Western Civilization from the Red menace."

B has no illusions about the durability of the Grand Alliance, but after all that the Western Allies and the Soviets have gone through together, he had high hopes that the wartime partners can at least co-exist in 'peace and harmony'.

"Be that as it may, this is neither the time nor the place to engage in geopolitical speculation."

"You are so right. I'm not here to preach for a 'Crusade against Bolshevism'; but despite your protestations to the contrary, you will need our help to deter Russia. She is already laying the groundwork for the Communization of Eastern Europe, and perhaps, Central Europe as well. You should be listening closely to what I am saying: A word to the wise is sufficient."

What infuriates B, is that he may damnably well be right. There are already rumblings about having it out with Russia, and as a practical matter, having Germany on our side.

Section 4.3 The New Plan

Annoyed by the effrontery of the GG in presuming to lecture him on post-war European Affairs, B threatens to leave. Hastily GG unveils the new-plan—a variant of the old-plan—with the anti-Soviet elements deleted, but it still insists on the retraction of Un Su. He seeks to impress upon B the quickened pace of W activity.

B, likes what he hears. Mollified somewhat by W's apparent return to sanity, B shifts gears; GG listens impassively, as he continues in a more conciliatory tone:

"Look, I know that you want to keep the Russians out of Germany, but it cannot be done except by an unconditional cease-fire on both the Eastern and Western Fronts. You must capitulate before the Red Army crosses the Russo-German border, if you want to shield Germany from the full fury of Russian vengeance. Otherwise, if they have to fight their way in, they will 'Kill and Destroy' everything in sight.

If it wasn't for what the Nazi *Einsatzgruppen* (mobile killing units) did to the Russians, I could almost feel sorry for the German people. But, this is how it stands—Un Su now—or brace yourselves for the onslaught."

"I appreciate your concern, but the situation on the Western Front is deteriorating rapidly. The Allies arrived, uninvited, but the invitation for an Allied Airlanding on Berlin still stands. For politico-military reasons, the need for a British contingent is more urgent than ever"

Even at this late date, W still thinks that collapsing the Western Front is a good idea. Supposedly, the Field Marshals in the West and Adm. *Canaris* are intrigued by it.

"I cannot speak for the FMs or the Admiral, but rumor has it that FM *Rommel* is prepared to act on his own, independent of W, but his plans seem rather vague.

"I, for one, am not impressed—after all he is one of Adolph's fair-haired boys. Rommel has been sharing command of OB West for quite a while. Unlike W he is in control of a large Field Army and in an excellent position to carry out his plans—if serious. The fact that he hasn't acted, brings into question his sincerity. Here we are well into the invasion, and he has yet to make a move towards seeking an Armistice. FM von *Rundstedt* is non-committal, but is due to be replaced by FM von *Kluge*. This sounds like a major plus for us, but he has been in-and-out of the conspiracy for years, and where he actually stands is anybody's guess. Adm. Canaris, the ex-Head of the *Abwehr* (roughly the German equivalent of MI6) is an enigma, but with his power base taken over by the SD, there really isn't much that he can do.

"At any rate, we hope that the FMs will come to their senses, and cast their lot with W so that German Resistance can present a united front against Hitler.

"But, even without them, we have a strong organization in the West. Many of the other Senior Officers are poised to join. It all hinges on the revocation of Un Su. How can we expect others to come along with us, if they are to be treated no differently than the Nazis? Why should they?"

GG's logic is irrefutable. He pulls no punches. Adherence to that bankrupt policy turns everyone off. Coming as it did on the heels of Stalingrad (12/42-2/43). it was the worst disaster to strike the German Resistance movement.

"It was a body-blow from which W has yet to recover. It is only a slogan—scrap it and everything falls into place. It isn't worth the expenditure of any further American, British, Russian, and 'occupied European' blood. What the Germans really desire is an end to this infernal war, but they don't know how to go about getting it. In the final analysis, success of our enterprise depends on convincing the German Army and the *Deutsche Volk* that W can do business with the Allies." ("You can't do business with Hitler", But what *S. Lewis* forgot to tell us was that, with Un Su in place, you couldn't do business with the anti-Nazi GR movement, either.)

GG has made his move. Right now, B was listening. He has to be careful not to turn him off'.

Pouring himself a glass of water, he resumes, in a conversational manner, "It isn't as if Germany has no legitimate demands. Unless these issues are openly discussed and resolved, to our mutual satisfaction, grounds for potential conflict will continue to exist. There will always be demagogues around who will try to exploit an imposed '*Carthaginian* Peace'.

"Everyone agrees that the Versailles Treaty was an abomination. This terrible war is a direct consequence of its repressive measures, Germany wants the iniquities of Versailles redressed."

GG claims that Germany wants to replace enmity with friendship; that Germany does not covet any conquered territory, but does seek restoration of lands ceded after WWI, that are inherently German. Germany wants to resume its traditional role as a leading member of the European Community. These are all pre-requisite to an enduring Peace.

.

"With the 'seeds of discontent' eliminated. the 'Cycle of 20th Century European Wars' will be broken."

B dryly remarks, "That's quite a list.

"The last people in the world that the Allies would entrust with the maintenance of the 'peace and security' of Europe, are the GGs.

B laughs: 'I know that you are serious, but I can't help finding it rather amusing. The absurdity of your claims must be obvious even to a German General. For unleashing, the most 'sadistic attack on humanity since the *Assyrians*, you expect to be rewarded? Do you think that we are fighting this war so that you will benefit territorially?"

B's visage solidifies, "Let's get a few things straight. I am not interested in your fantasies about Allied injustices, although from the point-of-view of a professional historian, I am willing to concede that you may have some valid gripes—however, with the seizure of the *'Rump of Czechoslovakia'*, in 1939, and the wholesale occupation and annexation of non-German regions, all claims on erstwhile German lands are forfeit."

B is just warming up; unable to contain his scorn, he explodes: "Legitimate demands, indeed! I wasn't aware that you were in any position to make demands, legitimate or otherwise. Pre-1914 boundaries? Greater Germany? Leading Continental Power? What's this nonsense all about? There is a 'school of thought' in Allied circles' that advocates wiping Germany off the map. Consider yourselves lucky if *there is a Germany still around after the war.*"

GG bitterly accuses B of agreeing with Dr. Goebbels that the extinction of the German State is the real Allied goal. He uses that argument as justification for his call for 'Total War' behind Der Fuhrer. 'This war must be made as costly as possible. We should murder and plunder without remorse leaving nothing but scorched earth behind.

"Even Goebbels didn't go quite that far, but there are others, amongst those who wield the power in Nazi Germany today, who will."

Taken aback by the vehemence of his reply, B quickly reassures GG: "Preposterous! You can't believe that. While eliminating Hitler and a 'quick end' to the war, are laudable goals, this war cannot end until all Allied war aims are achieved. Un Su simply means that we intend to impose terms that are in the best interests of Europe and Germany alike, without any argument and interference from you. You'll just have to trust us to be 'fair and just'."

GG perplexed, asks, *"Gott in Himmel!* Why this hesitancy, you seem to be taking this matter rather lightly. It is to everyone's interest, combatant and civilian alike, to end the war in a hurry. Allied forces alone cannot bring about an immediate cessation of hostilities. Only an internal military coup can do that."

"But, my dear General, there is another sure-fire way-' just give up'.
You know, *"Heben Sie die Hande hohe."* B demonstrates by raising his
hands over his head. A sick joke. B wanted to recant, but GG seized the
gambit.

"That's a specious argument. True, if Germany surrenders, the war
is over. But who is going to do it? Us? Hitler? We can't and he won't.
Why should he? 'UnSu' is his insurance policy. It guarantees that he will
be around to the final days of the war, although millions won't. The
Allies will have to occupy every square-meter of Germany and even
then he won't give up—but will probably commit suicide."

"I know that it is difficult for you to grasp, but German Resistance
plays no role in Allied thinking.

What Germany does, or doesn't do, is of no consequence. But,
we will do what we must—insist upon Un Su. This is Germany's only
choice, and the sooner she recognizes it, the better for all concerned. It
certainly does not mean 'obliteration' nor does it mean that her rights
will be disregarded. What it does mean is that Germany will be governed
by an Allied Control Council. We tell you what to do, and you do it. It's
as simple as all that."

Temporarily deflated, it took a while for B's remarks to penetrate.
Carefully choosing his words, GG replies, "You're dreaming. No matter
how and when this war ends, nothing short of obliteration, to borrow
your terminology, can prevent Germany from resuming her historic role
as the 'leading continental power'. "Such a policy is bound to fail. You
will not be able to control our destiny for long. In a few short years,
you will be desperately seeking German help to maintain the 'peace and
security' of post-war Europe. Your ACC will have to enlist the aid of

Germans to govern Germany. The only question is: Do you want to deal with dedicated anti-Nazis, like W or a bunch of de-Nazified ex-SS gangsters?"

The GG pulls himself up to his full height, standing at rigid attention as if on the 'parade ground' proudly admiring his troops as they' pass in review.' Defiantly he resumes his fiery oration with renewed vigor, 'No matter how powerful the Allied forces, there is no way that external pressure alone, can shorten the war by a single day, but it will play itself out to the bitter end, with all the pain, suffering, torment, and even death, that entails.

"I repeat; only an internal coup can do that, W offers what no one else can—a feasible plan!

But, we need your help."

B interrupts, "But, we don't need yours."

GG responds, "I beg to differ. If you want the war over quickly, so that it will do the most good, you certainly do.

"You British live by the slogan'; here is another one to ponder:

Externally? No way,

Internally? The only way!'"

Not to be outdone, and wishing to make absolutely certain that the GG understands W's precarious position, B replies, with barely concealed annoyance, "At the risk of sounding repetitious, you just don't seem to get it. Overthrow of Hitler is not enough. Germany must be crushed. She must never again be able to threaten the 'peace and security' of Europe—and that, my dear general, means Un Su."

"It's now my turn to exclaim nonsense'. Can't you see Un Su talks to Hitler—not W? You are confusing us with the Nazis."

GG thunders, "Threaten the Peace? Ha! With Hitler gone, Germany won't be in that business anymore."

Despite his cogent arguments, GG did not seem to be making much headway. If anything, B's position seemed to be hardening. GG had to take this badgering, but F didn't. Unable to restrain herself any longer she bolts from the room, into the kitchen.

GP pauses briefly before continuing his story. For refreshment he pours himself a drink. He raises the glass, rubbing it gently between his fingers and 'quaffs out the wine'. (Unlike Sir Lochinvar, he didn't 'throw down the cup'.)

Smiling, he picks up his account from there.(in the first person).

"I wasn't sure if it was okay for me to 'listen in'. Since B raised no objection, that's what I did. (I assumed that he had already made up his mind, that we were just 'going through the motions', so that it really didn't matter.) Whatever, while B and GG (and the girl), were having their discussion, I slipped out to check up on my airplane and discuss return flight procedures with our Dutch guide. To keep the airplane out-of-sight, I help push it into the barn and cover it with camouflage netting."

On the walk back, DG reminds GP that this is enemy territory and there may be a German Patrol lurking in the area,

"We don't usually do things this way. It is rare for a *Lysander* to hang around so long. It lands, drops off and/or picks up an agent and immediately flies back to England. But, to stick around for a few hours may be downright dangerous. I advise you to inform the Brigadier to quickly wrap up his business and vacate the area as-soon-as-possible."

Upon returning to the kitchen, GP pours himself a glass of wine, and is about to sit down and savor his drink, when suddenly the door swings open.

F storms into the kitchen, accidently colliding with GP

GP turns to me, and takes up the story from there.

"I went outside to check up on the plane.

Thirsty, I returned to the kitchen for a drink. Suddenly, the door from the 'conference' room, flung open, the girl bolted out, and ran right into me—almost bowling me over.

"Blimey, can't a bloke get a drink around here?"

Without warning, she disparages B

"Listening to him tell it, you'd think that it was us (e.g. W), not Hitler, who, was the enemy."

I take umbrage at this outburst. "Forbear! How dare you attack a British Officer in such a fashion?"

Realizing her error, she apologizes contritely. "I'm sorry. It is not my place to criticize, but he is insufferable, all the same." Why isn't he listening to what GG is trying to tell him? He is such a *dummkopf.*

He fails to understand that W offers what no one else can.
It is W, not the Allies that holds the key to a 'quick end to the war'."

I laugh, "We and the Russians are doing okay without W. What do we "need them for?"

Boy. was that a mistake. Like a fury she vented her wrath on me. "So, you think that you are doing great. Do you know that while we are talking, those in the Concentration Camps are facing misery, torment, and even death? By the time you fly back to London, thousands will have been murdered in Extermination Camps, constructed solely for that purpose? What good is your D-Day to them?"

Knocked off balance, I ask. "What are you talking about? How come you know so much about what's going on inside the CCs? How come that I have never heard of this?"

Sarcastically, she replies, "You British are great at keeping secrets. You see only what you want to see."

"Were you ever inside? Did you actually witness these murders?"

"No, but I know someone who was."

I press on, "An inmate?"

"No, a guard."

"A guard? How come that a staunch anti-Nazi like you, pals around with a Concentration Camp guard?"

"He's no Nazi. Never mind, it's enough for you to know the truth about what's really going on in 'hostage Europe today."

Section 4.4 War Crimes

'Atrocities attributed to the Hun (in WWI) were unsubstantiated.'

Lord Ponsby's Report (1924)

'Distortions of WWI, obscured the Realities of WWII'

P. Taylor, 'Munitions of the Mind'.

B and GG. emerge from the 'conference room'. They stand in the doorway listening. She turns, sees the General, and abruptly stops.

B enquires, "what is all the commotion about?'

GG gruffly waves the girl aside, turning to us, he says, "Ach, she's always worrying about the Jews."

B asks sharply, "Aren't you?"

Caught off guard, GG hesitates, "*Bestimmt*; it's in the manifesto, but we must get rid of Hitler first. before we can take care of the victims of the Nazis."

B mutters, "Yeah, then you can solve the Jewish question your way."

GG bristles, "I resent your innuendo. The German Army does not wage war against unarmed civilians. In all of its modern history, you will see that the German Army has never engaged in wanton slaughter. *Friedrich der Grosse* (in the 7 years war) didn't; Marshal *Bluecher* in the Napoleonic wars didn't; *Bismarck and von Molkte*, in the Franco-Prussian war, didn't. On the contrary, it ran counter to Bismarck's policy of reconciliation with our defeated foes. We didn't do it in the last War, and we certainly wouldn't have done it in this one either, if the German Army had its way. Most of the atrocities attributed to the 'Hun' in the First World War have proved to be unfounded.

"The German Army has no quarrel with the Jews. In WWI, they fought side-by-side, with the general population, roughly in proportion to their numbers. On many occasions, the old Field Marshal, *Reich-President von Hindenburg* publicly praised the patriotism of the Jewish War Veterans. Their Scientific and Technological contributions were outstanding. Without the *Haber* process, for example, Germany would not have been able to continue the war, due to a lack of gunpowder. Don't think that the Wehrmacht, for its own selfish reasons, hasn't regretted the exclusion of non-Aryans. It's a shame that we couldn't make use of their talents. What a waste!"[v]

"That may be, "B replied sardonically, "but what about another German invention, "unconditional submarine warfare in WWI?"

"The old-rules favored the Allies. The British blockade squeezed us unmercifully, and this was the only means to get back at them: Use the U-Boat to strangle Britain! Even so, many of our leaders, members of the old-school were vigorously opposed, but circumstances silenced them, especially after the U.S. entry into the war."

Not to be outdone, GG continued unabated: "I could level a similar accusation at you. What about the indiscriminate aerial bombing of civilians in this war?"

"Huh?", flabbergasted, B retorted, "You are a fine one to talk. You started it with a deliberate, systematic attempt to destroy London, and other cities, such as Coventry, during the Blitz."

"That's a laugh. The Luftwaffe had no strategic bombing capability. How can you compare the few hundred He 111 medium bomber raids with the 'thousand Lancaster heavy bomber, firebombing of Hamburg?.

(A favorite trick, developed by 'bomber command' was first to firebomb, and then, with the streets flooded with torrents of fire, follow it up with high-explosives, to prevent the firefighters from controlling the blaze.)

"If that's the case, you are crazier than I thought. Why did you start it? You must have known that the Allies were great believers in 'strategic bombing'. You knew full well, that with the under-manned, under—equipped, under-trained British Army, no match for the Wehrmacht, this was the only way that she could strike back."

GG was about to retort, but B, held up his hand, "I didn't come here to play 'Can you top this'. These mutual recriminations could go on all day, without getting us anywhere."

To get in the last word, GG quickly adds, "What I am trying to show, is that these unfortunate incidents occur in every war, on both sides. All armies engaged in a long, fierce, desperate struggle, tend to commit so-called 'war crimes', but not as a matter of policy."

B nods disinterestedly, "Yes, yes, let's move on."

Section 4.5 Legacy of General Blaskowitz

GG shakes his head. "It is really of no use, me telling you this because you probably won't believe it. Like all the others, you classify all German generals as militarists (whatever that means) cut from the same cloth, and not to be trusted, but I'll tell you anyway. "You may not be aware of this, but there was a powerful struggle between the Army and the SS over jurisdiction and administration of the occupied territories. "Have you ever heard of General *Blaskowitz*?

"No. I'm afraid not. Should I have?" I don't really know very much about the personal, or professional, lives for that matter, of you generals."

"General Blaskowitz was one of the most successful generals in the Polish campaign. After the defeat of Poland he was appointed Military governor. Appalled by the SS treatment of the populace he had the temerity to complain directly to Hitler. In payment for his clash with Himmler, the German Army was denied the use of this gifted general throughout the war. He recently resurfaced as Commander of Army Gp.G in Southern France. The grim lesson, which he learned the hard way, was that active opposition to Hitler's racial policies was a losing proposition.

If you want to keep your job, you follow orders, and keep quiet, if not, you are sent packing, or worse. Proficiency in the field, was subordinate to 'toeing the National Socialist line'. Most of us suppressed our anti-Nazi sentiments. Realistically, what else could we do? Defy the legal government in wartime? In every country in the world, that's treason. One can be cashiered, or even executed, as an enemy of the state, for that."

Section 4.6 Dilemma

Accusingly, GG continues," Dual allegiance is a phenomenon unknown to the Allied commanders, but we had to face it daily. Our problem has always been that we were fighting 'under two flags'. Simply put, for W to win, Germany must lose. That is a dilemma that no German general can view with equanimity. I would be lying if I told you that I wasn't intensely proud of the performance of the invincible German Army, but the dark side is that if the German Army continues to win, we will never be able to get rid of Hitler. War takes on a 'life of its own'. Before you know it, you get so involved that you cannot think of anything else. So here we were in the midst of this terrible war, making use of our expertise and professional training to defend the Third Reich to the best of our abilities.

Can anything be more ironic?"

B responds laconically," I wouldn't worry about that. You've lost the war already."

Section 4.7 Double-crosses

GG went on the offensive. In the pre-war years the GR Movement looked to the British for leadership. Reasoning that Britain and France, and W, were all playing-the-same-game, and that like themselves, they understood that to avoid a catastrophic European War, Hitler must be ousted.

GG points out that on at least three separate occasions, W counted on Allied support, but each time they were double-crossed, citing Munich (1938), the 'Phony War' (1939/1940), and Casablanca (January1943) where the doctrine of Un Su was first proclaimed. These were the most propitious times to act against Hitler and his gang. But, the Allies had erected an un-scalable barrier, so that from then on, W was strictly on its own. The other generals asked ingenuously, "Why should we join with W? Even your new comrades, the British, don't want to know from you." You must take the responsibility for that!"

The 3-double-crosses alluded to were the following:

1. Britain and France, before the war, at Munich (1938).

Neville Chamberlain, the British PM didn't come to Munich during the Sudeten crisis, to see Colonel General. L. Beck, he came to make a deal with Hitler.[vi]

"Now the British have the audacity to ask." Where were the 'good Germans' when we needed them? Ha!"

2. Britain and France during the 'Phony War'(1939/1940).

The German Army was terrified. Its main force, with all of its armor and aircraft, was hotly engaged with Poland in the East, leaving the Franco-German border, in the West, virtually defenseless. There

Army Group C, Colonel General—(later FM) von Leeb commanding—consisting of a small body of under-manned, ill-equipped, poorly-trained, second tier troops, faced the full might of the French Army. It should have been a 'walk-through', but the French did not budge.

3. The Anglo-Americans at Casablanca, (January1943). Coming as it did, at the time of the monumental GA defeat at Stalingrad, it was probably the best opportunity, during the war, to overthrow Hitler. But, what did W get? Un Su! It all but wrecked the German Resistance movement.

Section 4.8 Recriminations

B angrily rejects GG's assertions.

"Hold-on there. Back off! Don't try to shove the blame on us. I won't have it. If you deluded yourselves into thinking that the Allies would take action, you did so at your own peril. It is idle to suppose that the Allies could, or would solve the problems that German Resistance had with Hitler. We had enough problems of our own.

"Munich? We were completely unprepared; We had been sleeping in the post-WWI years. Plans for rearmament were on the drawing boards, but we didn't have anything comparable to the Germans in production. We desperately needed that year's breathing space' to modernize.

"Phony War? France dawdled. What the French High Command was thinking about in those days is still a mystery. It is not that their planes and tanks were inferior—far from it—their heavy 'Somua' tank outclassed any PzKw in the field. But, their production rates were low, and besides, they didn't know what to do with the equipment anyway. They fumbled that decisive opportunity. If the French Army, couldn't overwhelm the 'border guards' what could they do against the full might of the Wehrmacht?"

It is ironic, that the two pioneers, General J.F.C. Fuller and General Charles DeGaulle, were English and French, respectively, but only the German, Colonel General H. *Guderian* (who read their works) fully understood the lessons of 'Mechanized War'. You should know this better than I do."

Still bristling, B blasts GG, "Talk about double-crosses! "The one time that we tried to work with the so-called 'Peace-Party' at *Venlo*

(November 1939), after the German Army over-ran Poland (September 1939), what did we get for our pains? Two of our agents kidnapped and a Dutch police officer slain. I'll bet that back in Germany, the *Huns* had a good laugh over that one.

"Where were your good-Germans, when we had our back to the wall? Now with the Americans and Soviets at our side, where do you fit in?"

"Why do you persist in blaming us? We had nothing what-so-ever to do with that. It was the SD *Sturmbannfuhrer W. Schellenberg* who abducted your agents."

B calms down, saying, "I'm sorry, I didn't mean to be so harsh, but in Britain the hatred of Hitler is so deep, that by inference, justified or not, it extends to the GGs as well. Hitler without the magnificent German Army is just another petty despot. But with it, he is a menace to the entire world."

Section 4.9 Mindset

After this outburst, GG realizes that he still has his work cut out for him. He tries to shake the British mindset about the GGs. Anxiously, he moves to set the record straight. GG complains that even B has succumbed to this animosity directed towards them, but the fact was that they acted as a 'brake' on Hitler's ambition. Their failed attempt to curb his adventurism; was a tremendous source of friction between Hitler and his generals.[vii]

Cryptically, GG adds. "Neither you nor I, nor anyone else, knows how many GGs (and in what way, and to what extent) may have tried, in secret, to thwart his grandiose schemes. "Please permit me a few words to clarify our position and give you English cause to rethink yours. Perhaps a brief review of the GA's actions, which must be viewed in the context of the 'events of the times' will give you a better appreciation of what we had to contend with in Hitler's Germany".

B replies," That's not quite the way we saw it in Britain. Maybe the GGs did try to restrain Hitler, but like him you thought the USSR an easy mark—ripe for the picking, It's only now, when the 'pipe-dream' has faded away—and in the face of certain defeat—that you have seen fit to come up with a real plot to get rid of Hitler."

"Just a minute! Nothing could be further from the truth. That's not the way it was at-all.

GP wondered:

"Why is B listening to this 'bull-shit'? I was all ears, because, well, it was all news to me."

It may have been B's innate sense of fair—play that made him listen, but it was the historian in him, that kept him interested. As GG began his 'Apologia for the Defense of the German Army', B seemed transfixed. It was sheer luck that proffered him this unique opportunity to get an Adler's-eyed view, while the war was still raging.[viii]

Section 4.10 An Adler's Eye View

"What was evident to Colonel General Beck years ago was becoming apparent to us now: Adolf Hitler was insatiable. There was no end in sight to the war. But, with his amazing string of victories many of the doubters' thought: *Maybe he knows a lot more than we gave him credit for. Maybe he has the 'right stuff' for the job; maybe the German Army is 'invincible'.* Whatever, General Beck's crystal—ball was murky. Murky? It was more like opaque. He was looking bad. The younger officers scoffed at his 'powers of clairvoyance'; he was dismissed as an old-fogie, who hadn't learned a thing since the last war."

"We had an old score to settle with Poland, so there really was no conflict there. Our swift victory was supposed to be followed up by a negotiated peace with Britain and France. With Poland out of the war, there was no point for the Allies to stay in it any longer."

"Frankly, we were deathly afraid of taking on the Allies. Memories of the First World War were not easily forgotten. But, with the smashing defeat of France, we were sure that this was really the end of the war.

"We had unified the German nation: Austria, the *Sudetenland*, the provinces ceded after WW1, were all back where they belonged—in Greater Germany. *Versailles* was avenged, and Germany was restored to its historic position as the dominant continental power. This was as far as most of us were willing to go. We had proved our point: it was now time to enjoy the fruits of victory. A Bismarck would have had a field day negotiating reasonable peace terms with our erstwhile foes. We wanted peace, but the British demurred. So much the worse for them.

"After a delay of 7 weeks from the evacuation of the BEF and remnants of the French Army at Dunkirk, orders for Sea-lion were issued. The 'invasion of England' seemed like a trivial exercise to the army, but the navy and the Luftwaffe were not up to it. The Grand Admiral told us flat out that there was no way that his ships could guarantee safe passage for the invasion barges, nor the transport of reinforcements and supplies, in the unlikely event that some of them managed to make it to the English shore unscathed. And when that pompous ass Goering, couldn't blow away the RAF, Sea-lion was postponed. Never the less, the army, supremely confident in its ability to make short-shrift of the British defenders and overrun the island, still thought it was worth a try. Of course, the longer we waited the more difficult this would be. Hitler, however, had lost interest.

But, to the Grand Admiral the course was clear: Sea-lion was a dead issue, but the 'War against England' had only just begun. Admiral *Raeder* pushed an alternate plan, codenamed FELIX. England, an island, fighting on alone, is exposed everywhere. The easy, risk-free, way to get at England is to hit her where she is most vulnerable—along her far-flung shipping and communication lanes—with everything they've got: U-Boats, Commerce Raiders, Aircraft, and where necessary, the mighty Army. The army is essential to close the Mediterranean Sea, by taking *Gibraltar* in the West, *Suez* in the East, and the islands of *Malta* and *Crete*, in between.

"Hitler concurred. But he had convinced himself that the shortest way to get at England was not by taking the 'jump across the English Channel' but via Moscow! "The Grand Admiral, whom Hitler never listened to anyway, put it this way:

Felix is the no-lose approach. To attack England (e.g., Sea-lion) is hazardous, but to invade Russia (e.g., Barbarossa) is disastrous."

"When Hitler started muttering about Russia, we thought he was a lunatic. On 12/18/40, Directive 21, codenamed BARBAROSSA for the invasion of the USSR was issued. This directive was greeted with dismay. Though thoroughly disconcerted by the proposed venture only the Field Marshal F. von Bock had the temerity to question its wisdom.

It wasn't a military question. He had no doubt that we can destroy the Red Army, if we can make it stand and fight, but can we force Russia to make peace? Ironically, though we didn't realize it at that time, the FM gave a succinct one-sentence summary of the coming Russo-German war. How can we even think of going to war with Russia, without first polishing off England? Clearly he was in danger of resurrecting that 'old German Army nemesis'—the two-front war. For a brief three-month campaign, it could, perhaps, be ignored but what if the war drags out into the winter (a remote possibility, of course!)? What about the pitfall of a multi-year war of attrition' as in WWI—the kind of war that Germany cannot possibly win, considering the overwhelming resources of our potential adversaries?

These fears unnerved us. Colonel General L. Beck was right after all: enough will never be enough. If we generals felt so uneasy about a Russo-German War, what must the troops, who are going to do the actual fighting, think? Adolf Hitler took care of that by trumpeting it as an 'ideological war'; not an 'ordinary war', but as a 'war of annihilation' against the Jew-Bolsheviks, the enemies of 'Western civilization', and the subjugation of the 'Untermenschen', the Slavs (March31 1941). We took this message back to the soldiers."

The GG's pallor abruptly changed. All color vanished from his face. With a cadaverous look, he intoned, "Now is the time for complete honesty. The days of dissembling are over. Immediately prior to the invasion of the Soviet Union, I like other GGs in the orders-of-the-day spread this Nazi racial propaganda to the units under our respective commands."

With his fingers interlaced behind his back, GG turned his back on us. Stiffening visibly, he continued: "I never think back on those days without shame. I would like to say that the words got stuck-in-my-throat, but they didn't.

"Psychologically, to inspire, and bolster the morale of men facing an especially grueling war it did seem to make some sense—but, militarily, it made none at all !

"Why anger the populace unnecessarily? Especially in Russia, where the supply-lines are so long, the paved roads, so few, the railroad equipment incompatible, and the transport of men and material depends critically on the goodwill and cooperation of the occupied areas. The people in the disaffected Soviet States, were appalled converting potentially willing Allies into inveterate foes.

"The infamous 'Commissar Order' caused severe logistical problems to the front-line commanders. The Field Marshals vigorously protested. The 'Commissar Order' was rescinded in spring of '42, after the damage had been done."[ix]

GP was electrified by the GG's presentation. He said to me. "I didn't know what to make of this presentation. I didn't know what to make of GG. All my instincts said—'A German general? Hate him!' But, I rationalized my opinion by thinking: 'Oh well. He's the exception that proves the rule.' But to hear him admit that he passed on Hitler's infamous order to his troops, and to maintain that, at that time, it didn't sound so bad, left me thoroughly confused. His apologies and regrets, notwithstanding, sounded self-serving.

Although some might argue that these admissions went to the heart-of-the-matter and showed conclusively that the German Army was a willing accomplice of the SS in committing 'War Crimes', I decided to let it pass."

Section 4.11 Jews, Bolsheviks & *Untermenschen*

B hears him out. After a few moments reflection, he replies. "Its a good story. We enjoyed your little lecture. It gave us insight into the workings of the GG's mind, as well as a view of the war from the German side. After the war we will have to invite you to repeat it at the 'War College'. But, for now, let's get down to business.

"Are we talking about the same war? What gives with you Germans, that the mere juxtaposition of the two words Jew-Bolshevik drives you into an uncontrollable frenzy. What made you think that you could bring your 'brand of hate' to Eastern Europe and get away with it?

"Even when it was clearly in your best interests, to enlist the aid of those anti-Soviet elements, writhing in Stalin's grip, you still continued this pernicious racial policy unabated."

Amazing!! It was more important to kill Jews and Bolsheviks and to subjugate the Slavs (e.g., the Untermenschen) than 'win the war'!

It's not that you didn't know. You cannot plead ignorance. You just got through telling us about the 'legacy of General Blaskowitz'. How could you generals be so ingenuous as to think that things would be any different in Russia? If you, an avowed anti-Nazi, could subscribe to this policy, what could be expected from the others?

No. These tactics back-fired. Was it not the partisans behind the lines, astride the long supply routes, stretching from the old Russo-German border to Moscow, making life miserable for the

German Army that soured you on this policy? It was certainly not for humanitarian reasons!

No, my dear general, there is something missing from your tale. You and the other generals reneged on your solemn duty to the soldiers under your command and the best interests of your own country. It's one thing to exhort troops—all commanders do that before battle. One only has to recall the English King Henry V before *Harfleur* and *Agincourt* (in France, during the 'Hundred Years War'). But, to allow—nay encourage—your troops to repeatedly violate the 'Rules of Civilized War'—concerning non-combatants and POWs, spelled out in conventions, stretching at least as far back as the 'Peace of *Westphalia* (1648)—is indefensible. By doing so, and descending into the abyss of Nazi brutality, the good name and reputation of the German Army is forever forfeit."

B wasn't through castigating GG just yet: "In other words, you GGs saw nothing particularly evil with Hitler's premises for waging war 'Nazi style'."

"Realistically, what else could we do? But, we had no intention of carrying out those orders that we found particularly repugnant. Hitler couldn't rely on the collaboration of the army, so he turned the task over to the SS."

"So you just washed your hands of it? You just tuned out those 'horrible crimes' perpetrated in the name of the army and left it like that?"

Exasperated, GG ignored B's remarks and continued, "No. That's not the way it was. Although many did react that way, some of the more intrepid GGs barred the SS from 'local military zones' under their control. The partisans were wreaking havoc with their supply lines.

Einsatzgruppen bred the Partisans. They committed the atrocities, but the German Army paid for them in full."

"I don't mean to minimize the difficulties of living in a brutal dictatorship, but you people did disseminate Nazi racial propaganda. The infamous 'order' was issued months before Barbarossa (06/22/'41). If the GGs were so concerned about the army's good name they had plenty of time to solidify their opposition before disillusionment set in. Perhaps, pressure from the GGs may have gotten it rescinded, but it didn't put a stop to the inhumane treatment of the populace and POWs. You must take the responsibility for that!"

GG argues that in the pre-war years Germany was weak. "Had you collaborated with us, together we could have made short-shrift of Hitler."

Annoyed, B replies, "There you go again. What are you saying ? W didn't even exist at that time. Ever since the Venlo incident, British Intelligence has mistrusted the GGs."

"Why do you persist in perpetuating that fiction? It was the *Sicherheitsdienst*, not us, who was responsible. Is it the purpose of impugning W's motives, to transfer the British hatred of Hitler to the entire German nation? Ha! I thought that Great Britain was above such chicanery, but it appears that in the interest of political expediency, they don't draw-the-line at tampering with the facts".[x]

Contemptuously, GG adds, "Had BIS. the fortitude to admit (to itself) that they were careless, and were out-foxed by German double-agents, much misunderstanding and grief could have been avoided."

This unexpected riposte stopped B cold. It took guts for GG to challenge British official policy, at the highest leve.l GP thought: "*Uh, oh, it's all over now.*", but B adroitly fielded GG's biting but perspicacious' observations,

"Right! There may be an element of truth in what you say, but British foreign policy has not been stagnant. GR no longer plays any role in Allied thinking". It had been taking on a harder line as the war progressed. It had shifted from Cadogan-ism (A readiness of the British to work with the so-called 'good Germans' to restrain Hitler.) to Vanstittart-ism (All Germans are our enemies. Overthrow of Hitler, will not suffice. Germany must be crushed.) This was the genesis of the twin doctrines Abs Sil (01/41), and Un Su, two years later at Casablanca (01/43).(Sir A. Cadogan was the permanent under-secretary to the FO and Sir R. Vanstittart was the chief advisor on German affairs serving under PM Neville Chamberlain and his successor PM Winston Churchill.)

Section 4.12 Responsibility

GG lamely responds, "There is no way that we can absolve ourselves from the consequences of our actions, but it is of prime importance to us, that you recognize that the atrocities were committed by the SS."

Impatiently, B continues his diatribe, "When we talk about 'war crimes', you keep on insisting that it was the SS. When we talk about responsibility, you keep on repeating, realistically, what can we do? The GGs must have realized that without the victorious German Army, there are no *Einsatzgruppen*. Ha! You can be proud of your handiwork. You GGs built the most magnificent fighting machine ever assembled, and to what use did you put it? You gave to a megalomaniac Hitler the wherewithal to act out his wildest fantasies, and commit the most monstrous crimes since the Assyrians. The German Army must shoulder its share of the blame!

I am not here to assign guilt. You will have plenty of time to tell your side of the story to the 'War Crimes Commission' after the war."

GG was stunned; F bewildered, and GP aghast. The tension was rising rapidly. GP thought, *"That's nasty". B's accusations may be correct, but he is being much too hard on W. Why doesn't he save his venom for the Nazis."*

Recovering quickly from his blunt outburst, B says, "I'm sorry I didn't mean to lump all of the GGs together. But the fact is that even if a few of you are decent and honorable chaps it doesn't change a thing."

The room fell silent. B didn't want to get swallowed up in a wave of sympathy for the conspirators.

He continues on his fact-finding mission. "Let's put this matter into proper perspective. How many German generals are firmly committed to W?"

"About two dozen."

"Out of how many?"

"Over two thousand."

"Hmm. So you only make up about 1percent of the 'corps of generals'. What about the other 99 percent? They don't seem to in any hurry to dump Adolf."

Again GG takes up the gambit. "All the more reason to scrap Un Su. Adherence to that pernicious doctrine turns everybody off. Of course, I can't speak for the others, but the numbers belie the true extent of the opposition to Hitler." Disturbed, GG knots his brow, and continues,

"It seems to me that we are going around in circles: First you proclaim Un Su—this discourages the GGs from joining the German Resistance. Then you complain about the paucity of GGs committed to W."

GG still insists that there are many more poised to join, but de facto recognition, a willingness to negotiate, and a pledge of military support, are pre-requisite, if W is to be taken seriously, as a viable alternative to Nazism by the German Army and the Deutsche Volk. He concludes with an impassioned plea: Un Su must be scrapped!"

Section 4.13 Anglo-W Enterprise

Just when it looked as if they had reached an impasse, B suddenly shifts gears: 'Up until now, we have been talking in generalities—probing each other's positions and discussing background material. Important I suppose, but we are not getting anywhere fast. What exactly is it that you want from us?"

GG replies," Un Su must go.",

"I know. I know. Besides that, tell us more about your plans."

GG elucidates upon some of the points made before. He notes that events have overtaken the old—plan, drafted before the invasion. "The Allies arrived uninvited, but for politico-military reasons the need for air-landings on Berlin, are more urgent than ever."

"How large a force was requested?"

"Three divisions."

Taken aback, B replies "Wow! That's a tall order. I don't think that we could muster remotely that many. They were extensively employed on D-Day, you know."

"And to great effect, I am told. We know from firsthand experience that your airborne troops are a tough bunch, probably the toughest we have ever come up against."

Aware that the size of the British contingent might be a problem, W sharply scaled down its requirements to a brigade, or even a few battalions, if that's all that can be spared.

Smiling, B calls over GP, "Well, my boy, compliments from a German General, no less. What do you have to say about that?"

To GG, he says, "My pilot here, was with the gliders on D-Day, you know."

GP turns crimson, "Really, you flatter us, Sir. We are good, but not that good. What can a few battalions do against the German Army?"

GP took a giant leap in GG's estimation. Addressing his remarks to him, he continues: "The regular Army is not expected to be there. What is in Berlin is the 'Replacement', or 'Home Army', which is under our control."

B asks, "Is the Commandant in the conspiracy?"

"Colonel General Fromm? No, he is one of the most prominent 'fence straddlers', but, Colonel Stauffenberg, his deputy, is. Your troops will not be needed for actual combat; if, for any reason, such a situation develops, the 'Home Army' will take care of it. The British detachment will form a compact, superbly trained, hard-fighting, reliable core, well suited for special tasks. It isn't that we don't trust the 'Home Army', but you cannot be too careful."

B dryly remarks, "You yourself just told us that Fromm isn't in the conspiracy, but will look the other way. You certainly need people more enthusiastic than that."

GG declares: We are all talking straight now. You may as well know that at first, I was not happy about this arrangement. I felt that British troops running around Berlin, even though in league with the 'Home Army' might precipitate a Civil War, and even in the event that the 'Revolt' succeeds, they could compromise our position at the Peace table."

"But, Col Gen Beck didn't really care what the size of the British contingent was. Its mere presence will show unequivocally, to the

German Army and the Deutsche Volk, that we can do business with the Allies."

Reflectively, GG continues, "It will replace despair by hope. The German people haven't thought for themselves for so many years that they simply respond to whomever shouts the loudest. All they hear, all day long, and every day, is Dr. Goebbels and company shrieking 'Total War'. But self-preservation is more powerful than the loudest exhortations, and once they get the idea that there is a better way out of this mess, they'll seize it. The commitment of British soldiers to the struggle will help convince them beyond all doubt that the Allies do distinguish between the German people and the Nazis, and further, that W is a viable anti-dote to Hitler-ism."

B plays the 'devil's advocate'. "Frankly, I don't know if you can deliver. Your plan is fraught with uncertainty. Let's see, you plan to 'collapse the Western Front'; though none of the Field Marshals are in the conspiracy. You claim control of the 'Home Army', but the commandant is non-committal. Doesn't sound too promising."

B notes, "It seems to me that you need people more zealous than that. You expect the Generals, in command of field armies, to transfer their allegiance, and turn their forces over to the Provisional Government. The obvious question is: Why should they?"

GG admits that this is a serious problem, but with Hitler out of the way, there will be no more oaths for the GGs to worry about. With the Home Army in control of Berlin, and the Provisional. Government firmly ensconced, it's a good bet that the Field Armies will join up with W. All the while, B's mind is working rapidly. *It isn't easy to simultaneously listen to the GG and keep one's thoughts in order. With the possible involvement of*

British troops, this was no longer 'just W's party'. He couldn't just wish them 'good luck, as he waved them good-bye' (Despite what Gracie Fields used to say.) They need something more substantial than that.

As it turned out, luck was a commodity that W sorely lacked.

B was in a quandary. He didn't want to encourage them but he did need to know more. "What if an attempt is made, and it fails?"

"But, it won't fail."

"That is easy enough for you to say, but there have been many prior attempts, all to no avail. What makes you so sure that it will succeed this time?"

GG replies, "We have the man, the means, the access and the opportunity. Our assassin is a man of high ideals, unusual courage, and nerves of steel. The Home Army is under our direction. All that he is waiting for is the most propitious moment to strike."

"You seem to be relying an awful lot on his judgment. But, with British soldiers possibly engaged, I must consider all possibilities. Is W prepared to vigorously proceed with Op Valkyrie, even if Hitler survives the assassination attempt?"

GG hesitates, GP thought that he could detect from GG's reaction. that he didn't want to even contemplate such a possibility, but B continues,

"Think of it in terms of traffic lights'. Red Light flashes: Attempt postponed. No problem. Green light flashes: Hooray! Hitler eliminated. British gliders arrive; Op Valkyrie is triggered, activating Home Army. Revolt is in full swing. Yellow? Detonation cancels yellow. It must be clearly understood that if the bomb is exploded there is no yellow light, but W must go directly to green. The revolt must proceed as if he was assassinated.

"I have to ask you: Is W committed to continue knowing full well what the consequences will be?" No answer.

"I would presume that you really have no choice. No matter what, once started there is no turning back. If the 'enterprise' fails, then British troops will most likely wind up in a POW's cage, but all of W is doomed."

GG thinks awhile before replying with what passes for a smile on a GG's face: "The Col Gen was right. The token British contingent might just be the catalyst needed to make the whole thing work!"

Section 4.14 Tell it like it is

Despite B's ghoulish scenario, and the seemingly endless recriminations, GG felt good. All things considered, the meeting, hectic as it was, didn't turn out too badly.

"I appreciate your concern, but be assured, we will adhere to our part of the bargain." For the first time, in this rotten war, GG feels confident. Finally events seem to be going W's way. Their man is patiently waiting in the wings, ready to strike.

"Here we are, having this productive meeting with British Intelligence.

Something that W had sought for a long time, without success, and more importantly, with you giving serious consideration to W's plan."

B didn't like the direction that the conversation was taking. He had to temper GG's enthusiasm. He endeavors to curtail the meeting. B cautions the GG not to misconstrue his curiosity as a pledge of Allied support. He didn't want to raise false hopes.

"I am ambivalent about your plan to include British troops. Dragging Gliders from England to Berlin is a long haul. But such an operation was an integral part of the old-plan, so there must have been some feasibility studies made. "My pilot here can't wait. But, it's not that simple. As you correctly perceived, Un Su is the big hurdle. The problem is that it was proclaimed to the world by the 'big chiefs'. Unless the President and the Prime Minister themselves relent, it is hard for me to see anyone else having the temerity to moderate it on his own."

B continued, "Look, it not my intention to disparage your plan, but I have misgivings. The plan seems to be leaving too much to chance.

I can't in good conscience extend hope for a change-in-policy, which is unlikely to be forthcoming. As it stands, Un Su is still very much in effect."

"I understand. I know that you are not fully convinced, but at least you've listened. I know that Allied cooperation is a long-shot, but I am sure that you will see to it, that W gets a fair hearing. Perhaps a joint-operation is too much to wish for, but I fervently hope that the British will see themselves clear to join with us in the 'enterprise'.

"Please do not tarry. You have at most a few days to come to a decision and a few weeks to prepare. We desperately want you to come along with us, but with-or without—your help the 'plot' moves forward as planned. If you are to play a decisive role in this unique 'enterprise' you must move with alacrity. There is 'so little time'."

B listens impassively to his appeal. But right now there is a 'war to be won'.

"You've told us, at some length, how we fit into your plans. However, the real question is precisely how does W fit into ours?

"That is the main purpose of this meeting."

B softens his position somewhat. Maybe he went too far. "I realize that I must sound harsh, but I am only trying to impress upon you the realities of your situation. Unless the PM throws his weight behind it, the mere thought of an Anglo-W collaboration will be greeted with derision."

B worries that he may have talked too much already. "My advice to you? Pack it all in. Disband, and sit out the remainder of the war. How much longer can it last, with Germany being pounded incessantly from the West, by the Anglo-Americans, from the East, by the Soviets, and the 'thousand plane heavy bomber raids' from above? But, my guess is that you will do what you have to. As you say, regardless of what the Allies ultimately decide. I sincerely, hope that you know what you are doing: That you fully understand the risks involved, and that the consequences of failure are too gruesome to contemplate."

As the meeting progressed, B had developed a genuine liking for GG, and a healthy respect for W, but, all the same, there was something gnawing inside, that he couldn't shake. The Allies neither needed nor wanted the revolt. W didn't have to go through with it. At this stage of the game, it seemed superfluous.

"It's all so unnecessary."

"Unnecessary? You British do not understand, do you. If that's what you think, then you have missed the point and this meeting has been for naught.

"For the future of Germany, and the German Army, it is our solemn duty to carry out the W plan, come what may. Posterity must know that there were Germans who had the conviction and courage to stand up, even at this late date, against Hitler and the Nazis.".

B, applauded the succinct, simple, stirring, and inspirational statement rendered calmly, and free from mawkish sentimentality. (GP was grateful that GG spared them a 'Ciceronian' oration on the matter.)

"I am very glad to have met you. Otherwise I might have gone through the whole war thinking only 'evil' about the GGs. It is enlightening to learn that at least a few of them are honorable chaps, much like most of the Allied Generals. It was their misfortune to be caught in the jaws of a vise—albeit, not entirely of their own making."

B wondered how he would have reacted under similar circumstances. *Fortunately, as GG noted earlier, Allied officers were never put to the test.*

On a more cheerful note, B adds, "If you succeed in 'lifting the curse of Hitler from the brows of mankind', you will have fulfilled one of the PM's most ardent wishes. Bravo!"

"Did he really say that?"

"Years ago, right after the 'miracle of Dunkirk' in a speech before the 'House of Commons'".

GG winces, "Don't remind me of that fiasco."

"Were you there?"

GG replies with a glint in his eye, "Not exactly. That was the responsibility of FM von Rundstedt's Army Group A. I was with FM von Bock's Army Group B driving towards the French coast via the Low Countries. Not to take anything away from Col Gen E. Kleist's 1st Panzer Army, but I don't think that we would have let you off the hook so easily."

"Why do you say that?"

"To answer that question, you have to understand the temperament of the Field Marshals.

. von Leeb, Army Group C, an anti-Nazi from way back, despised Hitler. A world-renowned expert on Defensive Warfare, he lacked 'Battlefield experience from the War in Poland', and couldn't be expected to lead the assault.

von Bock would argue with Hitler, if he disagreed with him. Hitler didn't take kindly to subordinates who questioned his military decisions. But, von Bock would have found a way to circumvent them, and complete the annihilation of the British Expeditionary Force before it could be evacuated. von Rundstedt obeyed orders. The order from Hitler at Dunkirk was 'Stop!'—so he stopped, It is no coincidence that of the 'big three', he is the only one left on the active list at this late stage of the war"

B mused, *"Ha! Once a GG always a GG."*

GP, bracing for another lecture on the 'Art of Mechanized War', was relieved when GG continued, "We GGs are not numbered amongst Mr. Churchill's greatest admirers, but I must admit that he has a remarkable way with words. Too bad, he couldn't see his way clear to work with us, as you say, years ago. Talk about squandering valuable time! You English take the prize."

To this B responded, "Maybe, someday after this war is over, when the killing has stopped, and our sole concern will be the rebuilding of a new, peaceful, tranquil Europe, we could meet in a London pub, or a Berlin Brauhaus, and over a few beers, you can tell us how von Bock, would have done-the-British-in at Dunkirk."[xi]

The meeting was drawing to a close. Impulsively, B offers to fly them back with him.

But, with the Director's admonitions ringing in his ears, suddenly, it occurs to B that this might lead to all sorts of complications. "I would like to invite you to return to London with me, but that's premature. It exceeds my authority. Quite a bit of spadework is needed before that can be done."

"That's all right; I have to report back to my comrades anyway. But can you take the girl?" (The Lysander, the workhorse of BI, and one of the unsung heroes of the war, could carry 4 men in a pinch.)

B smiling, replies, "It will be tight, but I think that we can squeeze her in,"

"Go with him. It will be a great service for W. You are familiar with the plot, and could be of invaluable assistance to the Brigadier in the presentation of our case to his superiors."

F replies directly to B "No. I can't go, but I thank you for your kind offer."

Annoyed, GG tells her, "Go to England. Things are apt to be very chaotic and dangerous around here very soon. Germany will not be a good place to be."

"I'm sorry, but I must insist on staying here with you."

GG threw up his hands, "See, it isn't only the Englishwomen who talk back. Even die Madchens are doing it now. "With a shrug of his shoulders, he adds, "Ach, she has a mind of her own."

GP and B watched this display of filial affection, with a tinge of amusement. F looked plaintively at GG, as if she sought his permission to say something. He smiled thinly, and nodded imperceptibly. F turned to B

"Believe me, I would love to go to England, but before you leave. with your permission, I would like to say a few words, if I may."

B, raised his eyebrows, "This is a bit irregular, but if your comments are pertinent to this meeting, why not?"

Struck by the lop-sided distribution of risks, she notes that the Allies have everything to gain and nothing to lose, while W has personally precious little to gain, but everything to lose—their lives! Allied reluctance to participate is incomprehensible. Bizarre! Briefly she repeats some of GG's arguments, but with a bias towards the plight of 'occupied Europe', the POWs, and particularly those in the Concentration Camps, living in mortal fear

"Of all the atrocities perpetrated against them, the worst would be for the Allies to make no attempt at rescue, but to cut them adrift and leave them to the tender mercies of their Nazi captors."

But, nobody except GP was really listening. B and GG were skeptical. They both thought that she was being melodramatic and that the actual dangers facing these people was somewhat exaggerated. GP on the other hand, listened intently, because what she said made sense. Whether she realized it or not, by design or accident, she hit upon the transcendent reason for all this urgency.

"I'll have to talk to B about this."

Chapter 5

Return Flight

Section 5.1 Learning experience

Save for the drone of the Lysander's propeller, all is quiet. B was buckled in beside him, deep in thought. I was grateful for the opportunity to digest what I had heard during the meeting, while it was still fresh in my mind. So much of it was news-to-me. I was sure that this war was the greatest adventure of all time. I was glad, and proud, to be part of it. True I was knocked out of it on D-Day, but 'those are the fortunes of war'. To me and the other chaps, it was all so simple and uncomplicated: 'kill Germans and win the war'. This attitude served us very well. It's not that we were unaware of the 'big issues', but we had more important things, like survival, to worry about. I wasn't sure that I appreciated my new-found-knowledge, and it was all her fault. Her tale transformed me from a happy-go-lucky guy to a thinker. (Nothing worse than that! Wasn't it Frederic the Great who said, "If my officers ever started to think not one of them would remain with the colors."). A man cannot really think and fight at the same time. War is hell—as the American Civil War General Sherman, so aptly put it—if you stop to think of it, it will drive you crazy.

I had successfully thrust the 'horrors of war' from my mind. I wasn't at all happy that she shoved them back—in spades. It had been a profound learning experience.

Of course, I like most everyone else, knew that there were many so-called good-Germans—dedicated anti-Nazis, who wanted to get rid of Hitler, but not to the extent that they were well organized and had hatched a 'plot to kill Hitler'.

Of course, I knew that there were some German generals who opposed Hitler's adventurism, but not to the extent that, although the German Resistance movement had a large civilian component, they were the engine that drove W. True, there weren't many, but that there were any at all was refreshing. We all thought of the GGs as a 'gang of militarists', so it was enlightening to learn that there was this nucleus of anti-Nazi Generals, and also that there were many others poised to join W, with proper encouragement.

Of course, I knew about the pain and sufferings of the Jews herded into CCs, but not to the extent that they were being systematically murdered, by the thousands, in extermination camps, set-up specifically for that purpose.

Of course, I had vaguely heard about Un Su, but what did that have to do with me? I never dreamt that this 'slogan' had such far-reaching, devastating consequences. That it was the worst disaster to strike W—a body-blow from which it has yet to recover. That it was an 'insurance policy' for Hitler, assuring that he will be around at the 'end of the war'—while millions of others wouldn't. Since the Allies wouldn't talk with W they ceded the initiative to Hitler. Every square-meter of

German territory will have to be occupied—and even then, he won't give-up but will probably commit suicide.

GP wonders: "*All of this was going on, and I barely knew of it. Which Allied soldier ever heard about W and the Plot? Or even thought about Un Su and its impact on the war? We couldn't even imagine what life was like in the CCs, let alone the existence of 'death camps'.*"

Having learned of the full extent of the atrocities inflicted on 'hostage Europe', particularly on those in the CCs, he realizes that their rescue cannot wait for the inevitable Allied victory, but that action must be taken without delay. Since the only feasible way that this can be done was, as the GG explained, via an internal coup, he positioned himself four-square behind the W plan.

Maybe I was being super-naive, but I bought the GG's argument. I made a mental note, "I'll have to talk to B about this."

Section 5.2 Sold

GP is sold on the W plan. It's tailor-made for glider troops. He is excited by the prospects of a 'joint-operation'. The long haul from England to Berlin made the 'adrenaline run faster'. It would be a real *tour-de-force*; the longest glider operation over strongly defended enemy territory in history! GP extols the virtues of airlanding forces; their unique capability allows them to perform missions that others can only dream of. In his mind's eye, he could visualize gliders landing on the *Tiergarten*, or other suitable park like areas. Joining up with units of the 'Home Army'; they disperse, to carry out vital tasks where-ever our special expertise would do the most good. He whistled an 'air' from the 'Gondoliers', smiled and sang (to himself):

'Now that's a sight, you could not beat,
'Krauts and Brits on a Berlin Street.
Battling with no little heat,
Uncle Adolf's minions.'

Suddenly, all becomes clear. He is finally able to put the girl's remarks into words. Forget about the Americans, the British, the Russians, and the Germans, but remember 'hostage Europe'! The Allies have everything to gain and nothing to lose. All that they have to do is walk in, if the 'revolt' succeeds, or walk away if it fails. W takes the risks, and the Allies reap the benefits.

Section 5.3 The Old-Plan

B interrupts GP ruminations. He doesn't share GP's sanguine outlook. B is unconvinced. He shakes his head, wondering aloud,

"Why did they have to clutter up the old-plan with all that nonsense? Split the Grand Alliance? Indeed!"

Any Allied leader making such a suggestion (at that time) would be lynched. Although unalterably opposed to Communism, the Anglo-American peoples have a genuine affection for Ivan, admiration for the exploits of the Red Army, and amazement at the heroic stand, and resiliency of the Russian people. GG may be correct in his assessment of post-war Europe, but this is neither the time nor the place for geo-political debate.

"According to GG, the revolt is imminent. Time-wise, this puts us in a bind. This delay puts the entire enterprise in jeopardy. Even under the best of circumstances, joint operations can be quite tricky. Its hard enough to get Anglo-Americans—who are old friends and Allies—to cooperate, but Anglo-Germans—actually Anglo-W, is another matter. Ostensibly, the GGs in W seek our friendship. The last time that English and German (i.e., Prussian) Armies fought alongside each other, was at *Waterloo* where the forces of the Duke of Wellington and Marshal *Bluecher* united to defeat Napoleon."

B briefly rehashes the chronology of the old-plan. The Dulles-Gisevious meeting was in early May, roughly a month before D-Day. W was quite slow to realize that the time for action was before the invasion, while the Soviets were still far from the old German-Russian border. But, really who needs them now?

GP muses, "*Right! But as the GG pointed out, W may not be needed to 'win the war', but it is essential, if you want to rescue 'hostage Europe' immediately, when it counts the most. We have at most a few weeks to coordinate our operations. What an inexcusable waste of valuable time!*"

Section 5.4 The Third Party

B wonders aloud. Oblivious of GP, B frames his thoughts in a flurry of rhetorical questions (answering some of them himself). What do they really want from us? What motivates them?

Save Germany from obliteration? Salvage honor and reputation of the German Army?

Who cares?

Resume her historic role as the leading continental power? Address the wrongs of Versailles? They are hallucinating.

Save Allied lives?

We'd love to, but sad to say, that is the 'price of victory'!

"Why this sense of urgency?"

GP blurts out, "If that's the whole story—there isn't any." He quickly covers his mouth with his hand.

"I'm sorry for that outburst, Sir."

"No, it's quite all right. I always encourage my students back at the university, to speak their minds. If you've got something to say, then by all means, say it!"

GP, truculently mumbles to himself, "*I'm not one of your students.*"

B enquires, "What are your observations on the meeting?"

"Not being a bona fide intelligence agent, is it proper for me to voice my opinion?"

"Sometimes the amateur sees more than the professional. Go right ahead."

"Well sir, in answer to your question, there isn't any great hurry, unless she's telling the truth."

B is surprised. "She? You mean the interpreter? What does she have to do with it?"

GP briefly recapitulates the essence of his conversation with her in the kitchen where she stressed, in graphic detail, that as they spoke thousands were being confined, gassed, and cremated in so-called 'death camps' constructed specifically for that purpose.

"I had never heard of this before. Surely, she exaggerates?"

B who had been pretty uptight, relaxed a bit. "She's right, you know. We in British Intelligence have been aware of these horrors for some time. Our sources of information may not be the most reliable, since most of our information comes from escapees, who may be prone to make conditions worse than they really are. Remember she is associated with W so it is clearly to their advantage to magnify the severity of 'life in the CCs'.

So you can see that it is hard to say with certainty, but our information does seem to point to the conclusion that no rational person can conceive of the brutality of the SS in the CCs."

B continued. "Perhaps her source is better than mine. She didn't happen to tell you, did she?"

"As a matter of fact she did. He is a former tank commander, seriously wounded in Russia, who was recruited to be a CC guard, but he's not a Nazi."

B smiles, "An anti-Nazi CC guard? What will they think of next? Sounds like an oxy-moron, but I suppose anything is possible."

GP thinks—"*Be that as it may, but there does seem to be an overwhelming reason to move forward without delay.*

"In reply to your question, it seems to me, that you have left out the ones most deeply concerned. This isn't just an Allied-German affair; there is a third-party involved whose situation must be considered. There is a transcendent reason for immediate action, after all!"

B dismisses GP observation. "While I share your concern for their fate, that is not what we are fighting for. It is not of the highest priority. When final victory is achieved, hostage-Europe will be freed."

Sarcastically, GP remarks, "Is that all that the Allies have to offer? Allied victories do nothing for those penned up in the CCs. They cannot wait for the ultimate Allied triumph.

"You and the GG think alike: you both say freedom awaits the final Allied victory.

GG says, "It's in the manifesto, but the profound distinction between the two of you is that only W has come up with a feasible plan—an internal coup, supported by the British."

GP steels himself. (Careful, you are arguing with a Brigadier.).

"I'm sorry, sir, but I must disagree with you.

Liberation day must coincide with the 'day of the revolt', which according to the GG—is imminent.".

Section 5.5 A Sense of Urgency

"Why should it bother you so? Countless millions have been lost in this wretched war. Should we sacrifice any of our war aims, now that it is grinding down to an end, in the not too distant future? Would a few more make such a difference?"

B shuddered. He immediately regretted what he had said. It sounded heartless, not at all what he intended.

GP thought, "*I can't believe that he said that, but I'll let it pass.*"

GP replied, "We can't do anything about them, but now we have a plan to save the rest. W has shown the way. Why hesitate?"

"Don't get me wrong. I am not unsympathetic, but I can foresee serious difficulties. Their plan is flawed. Can they deliver?

There are too many loose ends, too many hurdles, too many risks—and so little time to be prepared. For all their bravado they seem to be unsure of themselves, or why so desperate for a few battalions? The GG gave us some perfectly logical reasons, but I can't help feeling that there is more to it."

Groping for the right words, B continues, "My guess is that they need a *stiffener'*. They are looking for us to be the *catalyst* that would make it all work".

"Personally, I would feel a lot better if they cancelled out. I have a genuine regard for W and I 'd hate to see them go-at-it-alone. While Allied support doesn't guarantee success, without it, its '*Bleak House*' (as my old friend, Mr. Charles Dickens, might have said)."

With conviction, GP replies; "I cannot emphasize this too strongly. You are the only one standing between 'Disaster for W' and for the continued victimization of those in the CCs."

B with a nervous laugh, responds, "You and the GG both seriously overestimate my importance in the scheme of things. I am just the messenger. All I can do is submit my report, perhaps make a few suggestions, but it's up to Dir to carry-the-ball from there."

"I understand. But, can't you see, sir, you are our only hope. Without your vigorous support, it's all an exercise in futility."

B muses, *GG sold plan to GP. GP tries to sell it to me. I am supposed to peddle it to Dir. I sure don't envy him, having to unload it on the Foreign Office. And all the while, I cannot give it my unqualified support.*

Section 5.6 Trump Card

Although in passing, GG indirectly linked the fate of hostage-Europe to the 'revolt', only the girl seemed to grasp its significance. Her strategy of concentrating on GP was paying off.

Why couldn't W see that the plight of the third-party was the Allies 'Achilles heel'?

That it was not only W's trump-card—it was also their only card (as things turned out).

W hadn't played it in the old-plan; W didn't play it in the new-plan;

So GP decided to play it for them.

They were leaving the continent. The Lysander which had been flying under-the-radar, gradually rose to its normal flight level. Approaching the English coast, B glanced out of the window, noticing a few lights here-and-there. Evidently, with German air raids virtually extinct, blackout regulations were no longer being strictly enforced.

B relaxed, closing his eyes, mentally reviewing GP's remarks. In a way he was delighted that he had taken such a lively interest in the proceedings. Most pilots were content to merely fly-the-plane and let it go at that.

Smiling to himself, B got a perverse pleasure at leveling a few potshots at Allied inaction. "This ought to jar them out of their complacency. Imagine having to go on-the-record, admitting that although W showed them the way, they were still dragging-their-feet.

The irony is inescapable: it is the German Generals—you know, the ones that we all love-to-hate who committed themselves to the immediate liberation of 'hostage Europe'—and that it was (the hostages so-called friends), the Allies who balked!'"

Chapter 6

A Call for Volunteers

Section 6.1 Mission

"It's a suicide mission, you know. "This is not like D-Day, where the regular army was quick to come to your relief. There is no way that you can be rescued if W's plan goes awry. Normally, I suppose that complete units would be preferred, but under these circumstances we might have to call for volunteers. This is your bailiwick. Think that we will get them?"

"You worry too much, sir. When it comes to Intelligence, you are the expert, but when the discussion turns to gliders, I'm your man. Have no qualms on that score. This is their *raison d'etre*. That's what they have been trained to do. That's what they want to do. You will have to hold them back."

"Before you let this romanticizing get the better of you, let me tell you a little story about an incident that took place in late 1942. SIS got word that a large heavy-water (deuterium oxide) plant in *Vermork*, Northern Norway, had a sudden increase in output.

Along with the fissionable isotope U235, it is believed to play a key role in their atomic bomb research program. The threat was so real that Operation Freshman, a glider attack to destroy the plant was organized. Most of the men in that ill-fated raid were lost due to flying errors and equipment failures, but ten did manage to survive. The Wehrmacht wanted to treat them as POWs, but the Gestapo executed them as *saboteurs*.

"Even if taken prisoner, a man has to be lucky. If captured by regular German Army units, he may wind up in a POW camp, but those who have the misfortune of being picked up by the SS, most likely will be tortured and killed."

GP is visibly shaken by B's tale, but he still held his ground, "That was a terrible story, but I still think that we will have no shortage of volunteers. If it's okay with you, sir, I'd like to pay a quick visit to my old outfit and sound them out."

B thought a while: "I have no objections to your proposed visit. I can see where you might be excited to 'sound out' your comrades, as you say, on a possible operation. But, you must be discreet. You can talk in generalities, but under no circumstances, are you to divulge anything about the mission or even that the meeting with the GG ever took place. Remember—this mission is covered by the Official Secrets Act."

"I understand sir, but you implied that the men might savor their comfort and may be quite content to sit-out-the-war, in England. Maybe you're right; maybe I'm being overly 'romantic' about this, but I have to find out for myself. Don't worry, I can get the information that I want, without a breech in security'".

B replies with scorn, "Don't think that just because the 'cause is just', they will volunteer to get themselves shot at. Maybe, they are quite content the way things are. This is no reflection on your comrades, of course, but that's just human nature. To many of us, survival means 'don't volunteer'. We'll only know for sure. when, and if, there is a call for volunteers."

Section 6.2 Home Base

GP arrives at his former 'home base' at Bulford. He is stopped by a sentry at the gate. He identifies himself. Unlike the days before D-Day, the place was eerily quiet.

"Where is everybody?"

"Where have you been? Haven't you heard? The Sixth is still in France. It has been commandeered by the Army to alleviate a shortage of infantry."

(Stupid! I should have called first.)

GP couldn't explain it. Suddenly he felt a 'sinking feeling', but it vanished as quickly as it came. Given the tight schedule, it was doubtful if the 6th could be withdrawn to England, refitted and regrouped, in time for W's enterprise.

"I'm sorry that you came all this way for nothing."

"Not quite. What about the First.?"

"As far as I know they are still unemployed. Their base isn't far from here, if you want to pay them a visit."

Dismayed by the thought of the 6th still languishing in Normandy, he decides to 'drop in' and visit with a good friend from Glider Pilot School, who is with the 1st. While he would have preferred conferring with his mates, the fact is that the British contingent to W's enterprise will be culled from the 1st. He hitches a ride.

GP thinks: *"Maybe it is better this way. They are well-rested, in peak condition, and much better prepared to fight than the 6th, which had suffered severe casualties in Normandy."*

Section 6.3 NCO Club, First Air-landing Division

He hitches a ride over to the 1st. He seeks his friend out; locating him in the NCO's club His friend is overjoyed.

"What are you doing here? I thought that you would still be in France."

"I've been temporarily assigned to Military Intelligence, ferrying agents over to the Continent."

"With Intelligence? Well, well. This war gets more interesting all the time. But tell me, what brings you up from London?"

"Homesick, I guess. I had a yen to visit my old outfit, but there was nobody home. So that the trip wouldn't be a total loss, I decided to see how my erstwhile buddies from GP school were making out at the 1st."

"Gee, it's great to see you again, but what happened to you over there?" He couldn't contain his exuberance.

Before I could reply, he burst out with, "Hey, fellas, I want you chaps to meet a pal of mine, a genuine hero from the 6th."

"Throw the bum out, as the Yanks would say", a voice hollered out.

"Before we give him the old—heave-ho, remember England is still a Democracy. Let him tell us his side of the story." Hear, hear!

Of course, they all knew that the 6th (together with the American 82nd and 101st) performed spectacularly in spear-heading the invasion, but even those actually participating up-front, had only a vague idea of what was actually taking place.

I really didn't want to talk about my experiences, but, reluctantly, I gave them a brief run-through of what transpired on D-Day. General Gale impressed upon us the importance of our role. The plan was to seize the *Orne* bridges, destroy the bridges across the *Dives* River, and secure the eastern flank of the invasion area. Specifically, I was attached to the 9th Paras battalion engaged in taking out the guns of the *Merville* Battery, a part of the Atlantic Wall, which allowed the British infantry to move up from Sword Beach unimpeded. I was badly injured in crash-landing my glider, evacuated to a hospital in England, and am now temporarily assigned to ferrying British agents over to the continent, until I get fit to rejoin my outfit on its next mission."

The men listened in hushed silence. One of them suddenly jumped on the table, and yelled, "Let's give a rousing cheer for the 'boys of the 6th'. "Laughing they gathered round to greet the 'wounded hero'. After a round of introductions, his friend said: "You guys have all the luck."

"I wouldn't exactly call it that, being stuck in France as infantry. What a waste! Don't get me wrong. I have the utmost respect for the British Infantry, but we are special-purpose troops, and are neither trained, nor equipped, to do their job"

"That's a tough break, but think of us poor lads sitting on our butts, watching the war-go-bye."

GP presses on, "I wouldn't complain. I'll bet there are plenty of guys in the 6th, running around the 'Normandy hedgerows' getting their asses shot at, who would be delighted to exchange places with you."

"Awwe, don't be so serious; you know what I mean, We've been training ad nauseam to do a job, and we aren't doing it. We want action!"

Section 6.4 Battalion HQ. Fieldhouse

In general, the men of the 1st take a dim view of future airborne operations. They just could not understand why they were being 'kept on the shelf'. All missions, suggested by them, were respectfully declined.

"To be fair, it seems to me, that the Army High Command does not want to fritter you away on local tactical missions. But, if that is the case, and Monty wants to conserve his Airborne troops, why is he keeping the 6th in France to fight as infantry? Why not just send them home to regroup?"

"Because he doesn't have to, *dummkopf*—who says that I can't speak German?

He's got us, remember? When you want to make the big push you call for the big boys—you don't fool around with the second best."

Before GP could get off an angry retort, smiling he continued, "I'm only kidding. Don't get so excited. Of course, I have to admit—grudgingly—that you men did one terrific job, in starting the 'Battle for Europe' on D-Day, but we will be the ones to finish it on VE-Day. Yes, Monty talks about 'winning the war in '44', but I'll tell you one-thing he isn't going to do it without us."

"Look, I have a meeting with the Major over at Battalion Headquarters. Why don't you come along. I'm sure that he'll want to chat with you."

"That's what I'm afraid of." Instinctively, he didn't feel at ease talking to a Battalion Commander, but he quickly overcame his qualms and agreed. Actually he had no reason to worry. The Major was a friendly, talkative type, and GP took an immediate liking to him.

As they walked across the field, on the way to BN HQ, they passed a number of gliders strewn about.

"Hold up just a minute." GP walked up to one of the *Horsas*,

Affectionately, he ran his hand over it, as one might an old horse that one has grown to love. He marveled how a platoon from the old 'Ox & Bucks' loaded down with equipment, piled into it, and were carried away on a journey from which many of them failed to return. Despite surprise, casualties were high.

His reverie was interrupted, "Take a look at that Hamilcar over there. Isn't it a beauty? It can carry a jeep, or a small piece of artillery."

"I guess we're not as vulnerable as we used to be. I'll bet that if the war lasts much longer, the Airborne will be carrying its own tanks."

"Ha! That will be the day. Then we won't be constrained by the ground forces that we need to support us if we get in a jam. But, we'll probably have to wait for the next war for that." They had a good laugh. Suddenly, they quieted down and walked together in silence. Strange, almost simultaneously, as GP thought about his fallen comrades, his friend had the same thought and commiserated with him. Even though they were from different divisions, there was a very strong bond between the men of the Airborne units. GP wondered if these feelings extended to the *'Fallschirmjaeger'* as well.

"I took the liberty of bringing my friend, a visitor from the sixth. I thought that you might like to have a few words with him. I hope you don't mind, Sir."

"So you're from the 6th. Let me shake your hand,"

The Major called for silence. "Before I begin, I would like to introduce a distinguished visitor. As you know, they did a splendid job on D-Day. I hope that when we get into the fray, we'll do as well,"

Embarrassed, GP nevertheless rose to the occasion. and blurted out, "I'm sure that the First will, sir."

"Well said, my boy. Stick around after my talk and we'll chat." Let's give a nice round of applause, to the 'lad from the 6th'."

After this short digression, the Major got on with the briefing. He was clearly annoyed. Despite the fact that the Allied Armies seemed to be having great difficulty in breaking-out at *Caen*, on the eastern, and, Carentin on the western, edges of the invasion perimeter, respectively, the 1st Div was being held in reserve. A glance at the map, shows that there are many ways in which a well-placed 'drop' could play a key role in breaking this log-jam. Although quite firm now, in reality the German front may well be on the verge of collapse. Should the line break, there will be a mad dash for the Seine River, and maybe even as far as the border, turning the breakout into a rout.

"Yet, apparently, we are not going to be part of this operation". The men groaned, as he continued, "Why?" We finally got an answer. Our divisional General recently attended a planning session with the top-brass'. They recommended that we proceed vigorously with our training, and instead of 'toying around' with limited, tactical exercises, we should focus our minds on the big picture.

Apparently Monty. is obsessed with 'winning the war' in '44. Waxing poetic, General Urquart went on to say—you all know that twinkle that comes into his eyes when he is planning something daring and exciting—well, he said "I've got some great plans—tell your lads to sit tight—I want to keep the Airborne Army intact to help us deliver the coup-de-grace—when the time comes. He had the same glitter flashing in his eyes before *El Alemain*—and you all know what happed then!" Hear, hear!

The Major interpreted this to mean that the 1st Division will only be used after the situation in Normandy clears up, but not by itself. "I am confident that the First Army will be restored to its full fighting strength; the 82nd, 101st, and the 6th will all be withdrawn, refitted, and regrouped, for the major strategic operation that the Army High Command has currently in the planning stage.

I'm guessing, but I can only conclude that somewhere down the line, in the not too distant future, Monty. is going to launch an all-out, no-holds-barred, attempt to wrap the war up this year. If that is indeed his goal, then he must, in his immortal words 'bounce the Rhine' before he can thrust into Germany. That's the most likely place where the First Allied Air-landing Army will be deployed."

After the briefing, we adjourned to battalion HQ office. The Major's orderly brought us a round-of-drinks. We settled back, into our respective chairs, making our-selves comfortable, when I opened the conversation with what may have sounded like the obligatory compliments, but I meant every word of them.

"I found your lecture informative and stimulating, particularly the part about 'bouncing-the Rhine', prior to the thrust into Germany proper.

"I surmise that the intent is to use a variation of the conventional ground support-Airborne strike force strategy used so successfully on D-Day. Let me tell you, sir, we were jubilant at the sight of the British 3rd Infantry scampering up from Sword Beach, coming to our relief, just as Jerry was recovering from the initial jolt and was getting ready to counter-attack."

Inadvertently, the major had presented GP with an entry point. GP played dumb. Ingenuously, he observed that the deeper the drop (i.e., into Germany) the more dangerous the operation. The attraction, however, is that it can perhaps take advantage of the chaotic conditions known to exist behind the front lines, and a home front rife with discontent (as in 1918). With the German Army in disarray, one can easily visualize entire units capitulating, causing a rapid, general collapse of the fighting-front.

("You know, the *Huns* are desperately seeking a way out of this mess, and when you get right down to it, surrender to the Western Allies is really, the easiest, cleanest, and the only way to go. The German soldier doesn't have too many options. Of course, he can always 'fight on', but that's a losing proposition. Those on the Eastern Front are in a particularly bad way. All they can do is follow the American Horace Greeley's advice—"Go West, young man, go West."—or they could flee back home, but the SS doesn't take too kindly to deserters. And as for the Western Front—who's afraid of the Anglo-Americans? Surrender to them, you will be well taken care of, and your private war is finished".)

But the fly-in-the-ointment is that the Airborne forces will be strictly-on-their-own. Should the mission succeed, it would dramatically shorten the duration of the war—but if it failed, the best that can be hoped for is that they will spend the remainder of the war in a German POW camp.

GP wasn't aware that he was so articulate. (As the Greek philosopher Heraclitus might have noted: everything flowed.) Both his friend and the major stared at him. His friend got a kick out of watching GP discussing military strategy with the Major. He didn't know that he had it in him, but the major was sharp enough to observe that the GP's remarks were not simply 'off the top of his head'. Did he have some ulterior motive?

The Major's eyes narrowed. "Got something on your mind, son?" You're down in Intelligence, maybe you picked up some choice tidbits? You wouldn't be holding out on us, now, would you, laddie?"

"No, No." He answers quickly—too quickly.

GP laughs, nervously, "You know that I couldn't tell you even if I wanted to, its just that your commentary set me thinking. My scenario is merely a logical extension of the Army High Command's view, and I wondered what the Airborne troop's reaction would be to such a plan."

Mollified, the Major replied, "It's all very interesting, but it would take a far greater-force than the 1st Airlanding Army to even consider the proposed mission. I don't think that this is the type of operation that Whitehall has in mind, but if they do, we're ready."

GP smiles (to himself) at the Majors acute observation, but what would he think *if he knew that the 'German Home Army' would supply the greater-force?*

"We are the Airborne troops, or have you forgotten so soon? In every mission, we face disaster. Every time a para jumps or a glider crash-lands the odds are stacked against him. The only thing that he has going for him is surprise, and conditioning, and the knowledge that he is the best. Look, we aren't in the business of looking for 'missions impossible'—because that's what they are—impossible—but, if the stakes are high enough, we'll take the risk."

"But, sir, considering the dire consequences of failure, I imagine that a call for volunteers may be in order."

"Volunteers? Yeah—you, you and you. Fall out! Seriously, though we expect every man to fight as a member of the unit to which he belongs, alongside the men with whom he lived and trained. In any airlanding operation, we always try to make sure that there is a way-out. In the mission hypothesized that does not appear to be the case. Although it is conceivable that volunteers are a possibility, it really doesn't make any difference—they'd all want to come along anyway."

The Major reflected, "Your example bears a startling resemblance to the problems faced by the *Fallschirmjaeger* at Crete. There, completely cut-off from the mainland (Greece) by the Royal Navy, they faced utter destruction, but it didn't matter, because they had achieved their objective, captured Crete and compelled us to evacuate the island. A classic example of a pyrrhic victory; their losses were so high, that it spelled the end of independent German Airborne operations—clearly a fate that we want to avoid."

With the interview over, the Major offered to have them driven back to the barracks, but GP preferred to walk—"I need the practice.".

Heartily, the Major patted him on the back. "Good lad. Take care. Get well and come back to us soon. We need all the men like you that we can get." And with a broad smile, he excused himself,

As we sauntered back, my friend openly expressed his admiration. "Boy, that was quite a session. I hope the major is right, This sitting around doing nothing, while the Army lads are running off with all the glory, is driving me nuts."

"Glory? I wouldn't exactly call what they are getting at Caen, glory."

"You know what I mean we-can-make-things-happen! We can accomplish missions that others can only dream about."

GP cautions his friend, "Still. I wouldn't be too anxious to tangle with regular German Army units."

"Okay, maybe it's not that simple, but we are always being held back by the Army. If you ask me the Army High Command is too tradition bound. Even at this late date, they are too timid for Airborne operations. Give them a straightforward, textbook, military exercise and they are unsurpassed, but suggest something new, audacious, and risky, and you might just as well be talking-to-the-wall."

"Well, it looks like you will be getting your wish sooner than you think.

"Lightheartedly, his friend responds,

"Right! Things are not all grim. You heard the major: He doesn't know precisely what Monty has in mind, but one thing is for sure—whatever it is, he can't do it without us," (*Poor chaps.: They had never even heard of Arnheim.*)

My friend insisted that I stay over and spend the evening carousing with the guys and fooling around with the girls at the local tavern.

"Boy, I sure could use a break—I really hadn't had one since before D-Day."

His first impulse was to decline the offer; he couldn't wait to get back to London, but to pass up such an occasion might look suspicious. However, it did flash through his mind that he would have to be careful, to imbibe in moderation—Under-the-influence he might talk too much, and well, you know—'loose lips sink ships'—and all that.

"I promise—no more talk about the war. Tonight is reserved for fun! fun! fun! Don't worry—you can take a day off—the war is not going anywhere, it will still be around tomorrow."

Reluctantly, he allowed himself to be talked into staying.

Section 6.5 SOE HQ, London

GP caught the train to London. He had been under quite a strain.

"Ha! Facing the major was more grueling than combat." But, he flattered himself that he had managed to find out what he wanted to know without tipping-his-hand.

"I was glad to learn that I hadn't been exaggerating the zeal of the airborne troops. While the Major didn't say so, in so many words, I was sure that the 'call for volunteers' would be oversubscribed."

The paras from the 1st, a well-rested, superbly-trained, high spirited lot of dedicated men, thirsting for action, would be a far-cry from the uncertain, untrustworthy, unreliable, war-weary 'Home Army' upon which W relies.

GP yawned, "They would give the boost to their morale essential for the success of the proposed Anglo-W enterprise."

The conductor shook him. "Wake up soldier, we're at Victoria Station—last stop." I must have been exhausted—I had dozed off without knowing it."

On this trip, GP grew up fast. He exuded confidence. No longer was he just a flying-chauffer, but he thought of himself as one of those intelligence chaps—See? I'm beginning to talk like them already."

Upon his return to SOE HQ, he headed straight for the GR Desk. He couldn't wait to recount the events of his visit—from his dismay at learning that the 6th was still in France, to his invitation to the 'briefing' where the Major discussed the situation on the Western Front and the current AHC thinking on how to proceed after Normandy.

B Interrupts, "You must be famished. Why don't we have some lunch, and you can tell me all about it? How did you make out with your friend and the Major?"

"As I figured, I got the expected response from the NCO's but the conversation with the major was an unexpected bonus."

"Did he try to pump you?"

"Not really. On the contrary he made it easy for me. He may have been a trifle suspicious, but he didn't show it. He is a congenial Scotsman, a candid sort, who likes to talk. The more he talked, the 'surer' I was that the W plan was the way-to-go."

GP continued with his rendition, "The Major revealed, in broad outline, an ambitious, audacious plan that involved 'bouncing the Rhine', and turning the Siegfried Line at its northern terminus, in preparation for a decisive thrust into Germany proper."

"Hmm. I haven't heard that expression before, but it is no secret that Monty has repeatedly stressed (for his own reasons, no doubt) that his goal was to 'end the war in '44."

The thought that AHC and W might be thinking along similar lines gave GP a scare. But his fears proved groundless: their time-frames are very different. The Commander-in-Chiefs plan is months away, while Operation *Valkyrie* is in a matter of weeks, and it will probably be launched before the breakout from Normandy. B remarks that he wouldn't be overly concerned with these matters but if Monty is convinced that the 1st Division is vital to his future plans, he may not be willing to risk a Brigade, or whatever the minimum contribution W requires.

GP confides to B the initial misgivings that he had when with a start it suddenly dawned on him that the British contingent will be drawn from the inexperienced 1st. Inexplicably, he was struck by a strange hesitancy. "Now, I have no reservations concerning their ability to perform, but all the same, their minds may be focused elsewhere and I would feel a lot more comfortable with my comrades from the 6th." Then he asked B point-blank, Why this tinge of doubt? Why should it bother me?"

Matter-of-factly B replies, "Intellectually, you are satisfied with this arrangement, but your gut-feeling says otherwise. Maybe it is just 'reality' settling in. Maybe things aren't going as smoothly as anticipated. Maybe it is a harbinger of things to come. Never mind, don't take these things personally. Rather, gird yourself for disappointments—there are plenty more where that came from.

"Whatever, I don't perceive this as more than a minor obstacle; the possible competition for Air-landing troops that may develop is potentially far more troublesome. But, who knows? Maybe this situation can be turned to our advantage. It is precisely because the time-scales do not overlap that it might create a window-of-opportunity. As you pointed out, Valkyrie is imminent and will most likely begin before the 'breakout from Normandy'. Of course, we are not in possession of all the facts, but considering the FM's goals, it does seem that, from the Allied point of view, he would be crazy not to try the W scheme, a limited risk venture, first. If it fails, nothing has really changed. Monty will still have the time and the forces to follow-up with his meticulously planned 'grand war-winning' offensive."

As for the reason that prompted GP's trip in the first place, he could say with conviction that a 'call for volunteers', if necessary, is the least of their concerns. Enthusiasm is catching, but, at times, it can be cloying as well.

Irritably, B retorted, "That's what they tell you. "What did you expect the Major to say? That they will drive the paras into the gliders with whips? But, when it penetrates that it is indeed a 'suicide mission', and if it fails, the best that can be hoped for is a POW's cage, they may not be so anxious to go.

"But, we are getting ahead of ourselves. All of this may come to naught."

Upon reflection, he had to admit—grudgingly—that this discussion with GP brought him a step closer to embracing the W plan. But, alas, he was still unconvinced.

B muses: *So W is being given a second chance. Although before the invasion was the time to strike, they didn't. The Normandy campaign is rapidly building up to a costly time-consuming affair. Again to be of real use to the Allies, now is the time to 'Revolt'—with the British detachment, of course—post-haste.*

Chapter 7

The Report

Section 7.1 Dir Unhappy

Dir was seated, staring at B's report, laid open on the desk before him. Furiously, Dir roars his disapproval. B hadn't seen him in such a state of high dudgeon before.

"You call this an intelligence report? It reads more like a blueprint for a military campaign."

A negative report would have been ample justification for dropping the project. Dir, half-expected to slap B on the back and commend him—"Good show!"—as he stamped "case closed". A team player, Dir felt duty-bound to uphold, not clash with Official Policy.

"I'm surprised that a clever man like you would come up with something like this. Ha! They are a canny bunch. They send their most affable, astute, and knowledgeable general, to the meeting and he feeds you a cock-and-bull story that you are only too eager to pass along to us. I thought that you were more hard-headed than that."

"You were specifically enjoined from giving them any encouragement. Your job was to discourage, not to lend credence to W's schemes."

But B was not so easily dismissed.

Taken aback by this out-burst, he replies, "You sent me to the meeting, over my strong objections—remember? What was I supposed to do? Sit there like a dummy?

"I listened conscientiously to what GG had to say. We had a frank exchange of opinions. Valiantly I tried to dissuade him: My advice to W was to disband and sit-out-the-remainder of the war, it cannot last much longer. My report recounts the meeting as it was. It details the GG's case, and it contains my unbiased commentary. As per your instructions, I tried to banish all pre-conceived notions, and drew my own conclusions based solely on the merits of W's arguments."

Section 7.2 Questions and Answers

"Fair enough."

Dir's testiness subsides. "Don't mind me. I'm sorry. It is not my intention to take my frustrations out on you. As long as you didn't promise them anything, I'll listen to your tale, but it better be a good one."

Before he could get set, Dir surprises B. "By the way is W still dealing with the Americans.?"

"While they would certainly like to talk to them, the feeling is that it is a dead end. As fellow Europeans, they seem to have convinced themselves that we British understood them better. They have the habit of looking to Britain for leadership, that's hard to break.

"There have been many times in the past when the English and the Germans, fellow Teutons, were good friends, and there is no reason why, after they get rid of Hitler and the Nazis, and write finis to this wretched war, they can't be again."

Satisfied that there had been no further contacts of consequence, between OSS and W, he proceeds further with his interrogation of B on his impressions of the soundness of the new W plan: their motives, intentions, commitment, and above all, their ability to deliver.

"What do they want from us? What do they offer? I know that's a tall order, but I think highly of your judgment in these matters. Speak freely. I'm listening."

B reviews the meeting, filling in some of the details of the new-plan. Although more palatable, it remains seriously flawed. The politico-military significance of even a token British Airlanding force on

Berlin, cannot be overestimated. There is a vast storehouse of anti-Nazi sentiment in the German army and German people, just aching to be released. While de-facto recognition of W, as a viable alternative to Hitlerism, doesn't guarantee success, it's bleak-house without it. But, they intend to carry-out their plot, with-or-without-us."

Section 7.3 Control of the Wehrmacht

"They're bluffing. It's just a trick to drag us in with them. You just don't understand the GGs. To regain control of the Wehrmacht, they'll promise anything. They know that they have to get rid of Hitler, if they are to have any hope of talking to the Allies. Ha! They will even empty the Concentration Camps.

I don't doubt their sincerity. I'm sure that they hate Hitler and the Nazis, and seek to end the war in a hurry, if only to stave off obliteration. I don't doubt that they will seek a cease-fire—they know better than anyone else of the sorry state of OBWest. They do want to talk if only to press their so-called legitimate demands, they so ingenuously mentioned to you."

Sarcastically, Dir complains that B is being intentionally obtuse, so that he was having trouble making himself understood. Britain doesn't want Germany to be the 'leading continental power', nor does she want to resuscitate a 'Greater Germany'

"If they thought Versailles was bad, wait until they see what we have in store for them this time around."

Struck by a touch-of levity in an otherwise very serious conversation, with a short, nervous laugh, Dir loudly continues: My dear boy, didn't you know that Adolf Hitler is now the best general that the Allies have, and you want to turn the German Army over to the Professional Soldiers? Have you gone mad? The Wehrmacht may be hanging-on-the-ropes, but it still is a formidable force to contend with, and in the hands of the competent leadership of the crack German generals we may get more than we bargained for—a costly prolongation of the war with all that entails. Wouldn't it be ironic, if we wound up warring against the anti-Nazis?."[xii]

B fails to see the humor. "These men are not like that at all. They are highly principled, dedicated men, committed not only to the 'elimination of Hitler', but for a 'quick end to the war' as well."

"That may be, but once in control of the GA they may not be so tractable. Remember, *once a GG always a GG*. Gloomy as the GA's position is now, I'll bet, that as we speak, they are carefully studying the lessons of this war, as they plan for the next."

Mitigating these scathing remarks somewhat Dir quickly adds, "True, if they were only looking to save-their-skins they wouldn't be active in the conspiracy. They would take your advice and defect, or if that is too distasteful, simply sit-out-the-war as most of the other inactive GGs are doing. This plot of theirs is a high-risk, dangerous game, and I'm not sure that I want to play. Throughout the entire war, we have managed to keep them at arm's length. With victory in our grasp, with fulfillment of our war aims in sight, why get involved with them now?"

Section 7.4 Third Party

"Maybe we should have responded sooner. Maybe we should have tried harder. GG insists that immediately following the debacle at Stalingrad was the most propitious time to overthrow Hitler, but what did W get? Unconditional Surrender! A body-blow from which W has yet to recover."

"That's nonsense. W as a visible, viable, organization didn't even exist at that time. Even at this late date, aside from Colonel General L. Beck and K. *Goedeler*, who are to head-up the Provisional Government, we still barely know who the others are."

B hadn't had much to smile about in this interrogation, but he did now. "That's easily rectified; just invite GG over and he will be glad to give you the whole table of organization."

"Okay, demand Un Su from the Nazis, but for heaven's sake, talk to the dedicated anti-Nazis in W".

You mentioned Col Gen Beck. He has been outspoken, at great personal risk, in his opposition to Hitler, but nobody in Germany was listening. The situation has changed dramatically. There is a torrent of pent-up anti-Nazi sentiment just aching to be released in support of the provisional government."

"While I have no doubt that your German generals in W are honorable and decent men, who mean what they say, but they constitute only a tiny fraction of the total. With Hitler out of the way there may well be a free-for-all, maybe even a civil war, as others strive to take control of the government. What guarantees do we have that these generals in command of field armies, will willingly turn their troops over to the provisional government?

"I personally prefer the Rommel plan (if one really exists), for collapsing the Western Front, and initiating a general withdrawal. It has the aura of simplicity, sadly lacking in the W scheme."

"I would tend to agree with you, sir, but unfortunately, while Rommel has had plenty of time—even before D-Day—to seek an armistice, he hasn't budged.

"It is principally because no Senior General has stepped forward, that W is desperately trying to get us to scrap Un Su and join them in their great-enterprise. But, at the risk of sounding repetitious, if need be, they'll go-at-it-alone."

Section 7.5 Externally? No Way. Internally? The Only Way!

Dir slaps the side of his head. "There he goes again, pushing the GG agenda. Can't you get it straight? We won't relax Un Su. We won't participate in their 'enterprise'—as they call it. But, we cannot stop them. For their sakes, I hope that they don't even try. If they disregard our warnings; if they are stubborn, and go at-it-alone, they do so at their own peril.

"You gave them the best advice; pack it all in. Retire to your homes, 'sit out the remainder of the war', and write your war-memoirs as I am sure, most of the other German generals on the inactive list, are doing.

"I can understand your sympathy for W: but why they—or you, for that matter—worry about the other Germans is a mystery."

"Sir, now it is you who has missed the point. This is not merely an Anglo-German affair, but there is a third-party anxiously awaiting the outcome of this meeting. Subjected to every conceivable humiliation and atrocity, the worst would be for us to abandon them now that there is a feasible plan to 'end the war, in a hurry' on the table."

"We are not insensitive to the pain and suffering of hostage-Europe, but that's not what the fighting is all about. We are not holding back. What more could the Allies have done than what they did?"

"The fact that millions have perished testifies that it wasn't enough. What you are saying only reinforces GG's arguments. Allied forces, no matter how powerful, cannot do the job alone. A successful coup frees all at once, from the Nazi yoke. As GG succinctly put it: Externally? No way. Internally? The only way! The situation has changed drastically. Now there is a feasible plan on the table. For the first time in this rotten war, the scales are tipping in their favor. We can no longer hide behind Un Su! Are we to stifle all initiative? How much longer will these absurd doctrines prevent us from acting?"

"If it will make you feel any better. most of the senior Allied military and civilian advisors, have no use for Un Su in its extreme form. But, the ones who count the most, the President and the PM are adamant: who has the temerity to modify it on his own?"

Pompously, Dir. continues, "Every undertaking must be based on 'sound military principles' and conform to Allied post-war aspirations. Besides most of the CCs inmates, Jews, Bolsheviks, and Slavs, are penned-up in camps in German-occupied Eastern Europe, well beyond the reach and influence of the Western Allies."

B bit his lip. He resented his contemptuous referral to those unfortunates in the CCs, but he let it pass.

Section 7.6 B Takes Sides

Despite misgivings, B feels inexorably drawn into the 'plot'. It seemed as though the more strenuous Dir's opposition, the more vigorous his support. Scornfully, Dir notes B's rapid about—face, from skeptic-to-firebrand.

"For someone reluctant to take on this assignment in the first place, and one who thinks that the W plan is seriously flawed, how come the sudden transformation?"

"You have the persistence of my pilot to thank for that."

"Your pilot? What does he have to do with anything? I'd think that you'd be more circumspect, and not discuss our business with non-intelligence personnel around."

Annoyed B replies defiantly, "Look, sir, I'm just a professor, and he is a Lysander pilot. We're not your ordinary dyed-in-the-wool British agents. He is not an ordinary pilot either. After being severely-wounded as a glider pilot, spear-heading the invasion on D-Day, he volunteered to help us ferry agents to the continent.

"He is particularly excited by the proposed employment of Airlanding troops. He is 'sold' on the joint Anglo-W operation. He has absolute faith in the unique capability of the airborne units—to coin a phrase—to make a 'mission impossible'—well, possible. An outspoken fellow, he hangs in there like a true English bulldog. Yes sir, sometimes the amateur sees more than the professional. If not for his quick, open mind, we might have overlooked the transcendent need for urgency for the survival of those cooped up in the CCs."

GP's enthusiasm is infectious, although a bit cloying at times. He has a tendency, typical of the young, to over-simplify, but B adopts a more sober approach.

"Recall, the old-plan called for three airlanding Divisions, but W will make do with a token British contingent of a brigade or a few battalions, if necessary."

Dir interjects incredulously: "What's this? A joke? Ha! A battalion of glider troops, holds off the German Army, while the GGs carry out their 'Revolution'."

Ignoring Dir's fatuous observation, B repeats the GG's argument verbatim: "The British detachment will serve as a reliable core of superbly trained men of unexcelled fighting prowess to be used primarily for 'special tasks'. The 'Home Army', plus German Army units loyal to the conspiracy, will take care of any fire-fight should one develop."

B however, thinks that there is more to it than that. He sees things differently. It isn't the size, per se, but their mere presence that is paramount. They convey the message of Allied de-facto recognition, making W an effective rallying point for all anti-Nazi dissidents.

"Despite their bravado, they are unsure of themselves. They expect the British troops to act as a *'stiffener'* for the Home-Army, and be the *catalyst* that will make the 'enterprise' a success."

"Dir is impressed by B's choice of words.

"That may be, but we are laying ourselves wide open. This can easily turn into an open-ended proposition. How do we respond to a 'hurry-up distress call' for more battalions? They know full well that if we decide to cast our lot with them, we will make certain that there are sufficient British soldiers to do the job. It would be criminal to do otherwise."

"I thought about that, but as GG bluntly put it,—if more British troops are needed, the 'Revolt' has failed."

Section 7.7 No Turning Back

"That's easy for him to say. If things go wrong, he will be singing-a-different-tune. The presence of British soldiers adds a new element of concern. With our lads possibly involved, there is no room for misunderstanding. My worst nightmare is that we fly in ready for action and W doesn't show up."

"Rest easy. You may fault them for many things, but lack of commitment isn't one of them. With the Western Front disintegrating they could have opted out, but they chose to stay with the 'plot'."

"Yes, but do they fully understand that once started there is no turning back?"

"I impressed upon GG that it is imperative to keep the pot-boiling. The German Army and Die Deutsche Volk will need some time to absorb the rush-of-events. But, even if Hitler survives the assassination attempt, they must act as if it succeeded. They must fight on until the expected surge of popular support materializes, or—perversely—the 'Revolt 'is crushed."

"*Ha! They might as well for if it fails-for any reason—they are all dead men any way.*"

Section 7.8 On the Verge of Greatness

"How did you leave it?'

"GG is ready to come at a moment's notice. You should invite him over to London at once. for further consultation."

Dir demurs. "It's premature. We must first ascertain that Sir Anthony and Monty will see him. Besides, as things stand, W might interpret this invitation, erroneously, as a sign of Allied support. Remember, we must refrain from saying—or doing—anything that might even vaguely be misconstrued as relaxation of Official Policy."

Dir and B, both agree on one thing: If no British assistance is to be forthcoming, they don't want W to even think of trying it on-their-own. The consequences of failure are too gruesome to contemplate.

Finally, Dir and B were in synch. Dir had calmed down and the discussion continued on a more rational level. Still unconvinced, Dir is reluctant to press further (*Why doesn't W just 'go away'?).* B quietly watches as, visibly disturbed, he paces back and forth, like a caged tiger, and equally ferocious. He stops and glares at B *(Accusingly?* B, wonders.)

"It's your party. Where do we go from here? Any new ideas? Anything else to add?"

"I've told my story I've voiced my opinions. It's all up to you now, sir."

Dir sits down, leans back in his chair, interlacing his fingers behind his head. "You know, W is fortunate to have such a powerful advocate on its side."

"I did nothing more than fulfill my promise to GG, to tell-it-like-it-is, and that I would relate their side of the argument without prejudice." And, boy, did he tell it!

Philosophizing, Dir continues unfazed:

"Everyone sees the situation from his own vantage point.

Your ex-Glider Pilot foresees no difficulties.

You worry, but think that with British help the W plan, though seriously flawed, is feasible.

Getting approval for a venture of this type is extremely difficult.

The only prior prospect of seriously working with the German Resistance movement was in the so-called Venlo Affair, and you may recall what a disaster that was.

Getting tricked by the Germans once, is pardonable but twice in the same war is inexcusable."

Dir hesitates before continuing, "How much should I tell you? In the intelligence service it is dangerous to know too much about matters with which one is not directly concerned. Ha! We are not even supposed to be talking to them let alone considering a joint-operation. It's hard enough, to work out the logistics for an Anglo-American venture, but an Anglo-German (more exactly, an Anglo-W) one? Whew!"

Dir ponders awhile. It pained him greatly to think of the daunting task ahead. He stares at the floor, slowly raising his glance towards the ceiling. "We have to go through channels. up the ladder rung-by-rung, where each rung is a veritable minefield."

A holder of two medals of Valor from the First World War, he is not one to shrink from a fight, but frankly, he wasn't looking forward to 'skirmishing 'with the higher echelons of the Foreign Office and the Military. One false step, and his long career of diligent service to King and country goes up in smoke.

"But, these are my problems."

"I don't envy you, Sir. It is not my intention to exacerbate an already difficult situation."

B has no desire to put Dir's career in jeopardy. B does not expect him to take on the project, unless he believes in it. However, he does find his pessimism a bit hard to fathom. SOE dealt so effectively with the Continental Resistance Groups, but pointedly avoided contact with German Resistance movements. B may have been naive, but he never could really understand the rational of not working with them all along. B senses that despite his fulminations, there is a part of Dir that finds the 'plot' irresistible (As A. Dulles had before, in May '44.) But is he really ready for the showdown with C?

Rhetorically, he asks himself: *What is the purpose of SOE if not to take on the 'big gambles'? Of course it performed brilliantly in its mundane business of 'Subversion and Sabotage' but events have catapulted it beyond that: It is now on the verge of greatness."*

The wily old WWI gunnery officer rolled out his heavy artillery,

"The proposed joint-venture dwarfs all prior SOE operations combined. Without exaggeration, it could be the most dramatic single operation of the entire war.

Caught off balance by the vehemence of B's remarks, Dir concedes that he has a point, but quickly interjects, "Alas, unfortunately, on the peace process afterwards, as well.

In this game, what looks straight-forward is often, in reality, quite convoluted. Every move we make has politico-military ramifications, that must be considered."

"I understand, but, at this stage, that's all pure speculation. I am not a soothsayer, and neither are you. But one thing Sir, that we can be sure of is that the actual post-war world will be very different from what any one of us can imagine now."

Dir did not reply, and B continued, "Our exposure is limited to a token British detachment. W risks all; if it fails, we walk away. There may be a disturbing number of casualties, but they will have little deterrent effect on the Allied prosecution of the war. Everyone associated with W, however, faces dire consequences. W will be blown away—to be heard from no more."

They had reached a crucial point in their discussion. Feigning disgust, B was busy collecting his papers. "You know, far from setting Europe ablaze—as the PM put it—SOE is really one-big-bust. Sure it did magnificently in its routine business, but if it shies away from the 'big risks', then C was right: Who needs a separated secret Service in the first place ?"

"By the way, sir, what has C been doing all this time?"

"C does not share its information with us. I cannot speak for them. All I know is that whatever they have, or have not, been doing there is nothing to show for it."

"Nothing?"

"My guess, is that he was scared-off by Official Policy—you know, the 'twin doctrines'."

"This may be the opportunity that we have been waiting for; they left the door ajar, for us. The ball is in our court now. Are we up to the challenge?"

"You asked—facetiously, I hope—what's in it for us?"

B notes that this can be tersely summarized in a single paragraph: *Elimination of Hitler; a quick end to the war; liberation of occupied Europe; release of POWs, and emptying of the Concentration Camps; and last, but not least, the saving of Allied lives. It is evident that not one single item on this list conflicts with our 'War aims'.*"

Dir dryly remarks that while praiseworthy, there is little new in B's presentation. Angrily B retorts, "Yes, but it is where the emphasis is placed that is new: the imminence of the assassination attempt, the feasibility of the Anglo-W operation, the sense of urgency, all have taken on a new-meaning"

"Unfortunately, my dear friend, they are insufficient to modify the Official Position. There is no need for us to stick out our necks. Ultimate Allied victory solves all problems. The CC will be emptied as they are over-run. So you see Victory-in-Europe Day will also be Liberation Day, obviating the need for W's 'Revolt of the Generals'".

Exasperated, B says," VE-Day is simply too long to wait. To liberate the camps piecemeal is absurd. They should all be freed at the same time. Monty has been repeatedly quoted as saying' to shorten the war by a single day is worth everyone's utmost effort'. Paraphrasing, I say that ideally, our utmost effort should be directed towards making VE-Day,

Liberation Day, and 'Revolt' Day, the same day. With his voice rising, he continues,

"That's what W offers us. That's the goal that we should strive for. That should be SOE's motto".

"Steady. Extremely well put, my dear friend, but for the last time I'm telling you that this war is not being fought in a vacuum. The destiny of Germany will be controlled indefinitely by an Allied Control Counsel."

B is not so easily deflected. He interrupts, interjecting, "Control Germany? That's a laugh. Britain will be hard pressed to control its own destiny in the post-war world."

Dir goes on, unfazed, 'We neither need, nor want, Germany as a partner, at the peace table." . . .

B quickly responds, "I can only repeat GG's admonition. That is an illusion. We will not be able to govern that way for long. Their cooperation will be absolutely necessary to be successful. If I read you correctly, what you are implying is that the Allies will just as soon work with a bunch of de-Nazified SS gangsters as with the dedicated, proven anti-Nazis in W."

This conversation was veering into dangerous territory. Clearly Dir didn't like the way things were progressing. He wasn't going to let himself get stampeded. Used to being in control, he resented being dragged, reluctantly, by the 'flow of circumstance'. (*As Heraclitus, told us long ago—, everything—even circumstance—flows.*)

Frankly, he was getting worried. It is one thing to flaunt the 'Rule of Absolute Silence' and quite another to be held in violation of the

Official Secrets Act. He decides to cut the meeting short. With a forced grin, he addresses B:

"I should have kicked you out of my office, when I had the chance. As you know, I have a high regard for your judgment, but I am still unconvinced. I am unsure as to how to proceed further with this matter." Abruptly, he dismisses B.

"Please excuse me. I have some heavy thinking to do. I'll keep you posted."

B takes his leave, returns to his desk, and cogitates on the session. He never expected so much controversy over his report. He thought that it was pretty good: level-headed and fair. Yet it precipitated such a violent reaction from Dir.

B muses: *Where do I fit into all this 'cloak and dagger' stuff? The old faker. Trying to make out that it was all my idea. A negative report? Ha! His conscience is assuaged; like the good trooper that he is, he makes-no-waves. A contentious, fighting report? If 'upstairs' likes it, and it works, he becomes the man-of-the-hour. But if things go awry, then it's all due to my faulty intelligence report!*

I resent being used this way, but, oh well, you can't get mad at your boss. No, I can't be too harsh with him, like he says, these are his problems—and he is being overwhelmed. Caught in the 'jaws of a vise'; (of his own making) he is being forced to choose between maintaining the status quo or embracing the new W plan.

B is confident that Dir will do the right-thing.

He regrets having exerted so much pressure, but he cannot tarry: there is 'so little time'—a decision must be made 'right away'.

CHAPTER 8

The Lights Burn Late at the Foreign Office, Monty's HQ and the Bendlerblock

Section 8.1 Daydreams

B gave Dir a headache.

To relax, he leans back in his chair—interlacing his fingers behind his head. A bland smile suffuses his visage as he lapses into a 'daydream'. In his mind's eye, he rapidly runs through the joint Anglo-W operation, to its glorious conclusion. It all sounds so easy.

The Foreign Office and Monty's HQ. pledge full cooperation. FO gets PM to suspend Un Su. Monty supplies the battalions from the presently unemployed 1st Airlanding Div. Allied 'Blockbusting' will be done with leaflets, not explosives. Airlanding drop on Berlin activates Operation Valkyrie. British contingent joins up with Home Army; units are assigned special tasks. They are immediately dispatched to seize the Communication Center, and to protect W HQ in the Bendlerstrasse.

Col Gen L. Beck addresses the German nation. He solicits the support of the German Army and the Deutsche *Volk* for the W manifesto and the provisional government. A cease-fire is proclaimed on the Western and Eastern fronts. Occupied Europe is freed; POWs are released; CCs emptied. B's ideal conclusion prevails: officially, *VE-Day, Liberation-Day, and the 'Day of the Revolt' are all the same day!*

With a start, he snaps out of his reverie. "I wish it were as simple as all that, but there are powerful elements in the British leadership who are dead-set against ending the war according to this scenario."

Section 8.2 Reflections

Yanked back to reality, he reflects: "How did I get into this predicament?" Was he getting cold-feet? Without any qualms, he could have ignored the frantic call from W reiterating their grim determination, despite rapidly deteriorating conditions on the Western Front, to go through with the 'Plot', but curiosity got the better of him. Intrigued by the Dulles-Gisevious (i.e., the OSS-W) contact, he wonders if the Americans are on to something. Perhaps they are softening their position.

He admires Dulles's boldness, but why no follow through? "He must be having a 'tough sell' with the State Department, as I expect that I would have from the Foreign Office. The State Department and the FO think alike. They both frown on initiatives from subordinates, while the 'twin doctrines' forbid discussion with the enemy.

"If Dulles got away with it, why can't I? Sometimes I think that we British are too much in awe of authority.[xiii]

C was aware of the Dulles-Gisevious contact. Dir had his sources, but what he didn't know for sure, was that C, accompanied by OSS Chief W. Donovan, had talked with none other than Admiral *Canaris*, the head of *Abwehr/Ausland* (roughly the German counterpart of MI6), but had rejected his proposals for Allied-W cooperation, in late 1943.[xiv]

Dir vividly recalls when he first got the bright idea to dispatch a reluctant B as his representative to a fact—finding mission, with a GG, representing W. W had contacted a trusted member of the DR, who brought their urgent-appeal to the attention of an SOE agent in Holland, who in turn forwarded its message to Baker Street.

B had begged off. "I'm not your man."

"On the contrary, none better." Speaking freely, Dir continued,

"Your years between the wars, in the *Cleves-Julich* area, makes you the logical choice. Your familiarity with the German language and the culture of this region, will come in handy, some day." *He thought that B would be pliable and easily manipulated—what a surprise, for the Dir!*

Dir was still smarting from his report, but he grudgingly admitted that B marshaled some pretty powerful arguments in support of his position. He may have been unsophisticated in the ways of SIS, but he learned fast.

"However the trouble with these academic types, is that they turn every discussion into a 'dissertation'."

How do you like that episode with his pilot? Who could have factored him into the equation? He sure gave us old fogies a jolt. *"I'll have to tell B, to bring this 'ex-glider pilot who perceives no problems' along to one of our meetings soon."*

Section 8.3 Quandaries

Dir was in a quandary. Unable to postpone his decision any longer, he has to come to grips with his dilemma. He assumes a Shakespearian pose and cries out (to himself). *"To squelch, or not to squelch? That is the question."*

For his own edification, Dir mulls over his tumultuous session with B Despite B's persuasive presentation he was still of the opinion that these arguments, taken on their own merit, were probably insufficient to warrant a fundamental shift in OP, but when cloaked as a 'challenge to SOE', B struck a raw nerve. He has to ask himself point-blank: *"Did he want to be remembered by posterity as the man who torpedoed the last-ditch-effort to bring the war to a swift conclusion?*

"Sure, I can walk away from all this, but never will I, nor anyone else, for that matter, ever get the stars to line-up like this again". Though no student of Astrology, he had seen too many events occur in war, which can be explained in no way other than by the stars, or fate, or destiny, or whatever name one chooses to call it.

All roads seem to lead to an Anglo-German (strictly speaking an Anglo-W) operation. Ha! The last time that happened was when the combined forces of the Duke of Wellington and FM Bluecher defeated Napoleon at Waterloo.

When will the time be more opportune? He felt like FM F. von Bock must have felt before Moscow in November of 1941. The prudent course was to withdraw, and resume his offensive in the spring of '42. All his senior officers urged him to do so. But, he couldn't imagine the stars lining up for him like this ever again. The chance to become one of the greatest generals in the 'history of war' was not going to slip from his grasp.

"When they speak of Hannibal before Rome, they will also mention von Bock before Moscow!"

But, it unnerved him to think that he might be the only one pushing the enterprise. He notes that they are working under a tight schedule. "The time for a decision is measured in days; if the decision is favorable, then the time for preparation, is, at most, a matter of weeks, if the British are to be of any use to the conspirators.

B's powerful arguments, the 'challenge to SOE', his professional pride, the growing realization that this is what SOE should have been doing all along, all combined to push him over the edge. The course is clear. But, he has to be careful. One false step. and his career is in ruins.

Suddenly, he feels rejuvenated. Miraculously, all doubts and trepidations vanish. Suddenly, he is the man-of-action, with the simple-minded purpose of making the new plan a reality. The adrenaline is flowing. Like in an old-fashioned melodrama, he shakes his clenched fist in the general direction of Bletchley Park, crying out,

"You've had your day in the Sun, now it's our turn. Your triumph's in 'intelligence circles' are legendary. You broke the Enigma code, and Ultra has proved indispensible on the battle-field. Yes, Ultra is great—but this is the greatest!"

Dir muses:" It's awesome. Never in the 'history of war', will so few have stopped so many. A few strategically placed battalions, will bring this titanic struggle, between huge armies, involving millions of men, to a screeching halt! My word!"

Section 8.4 Decisions

Finally, Dir was able to catch his breath. An inordinate amount of nervous energy had been expended in overcoming his self-doubts, but he was absolutely certain, that this was the way to go.

"Here I am, all worn out, and I haven't even started yet." But, that was all in the past. Dir was not a second-guesser. Once a decision was made, he never looked back(or so he says).

"With these preliminaries out of the way, let's get down to business."

This is just the opening gambit. For the moment, SOE's work is done. Now comes the tough part. He has no illusions. There is no getting around it. The decisions needed to advance the matter further have to be made at the highest level. Not only must it be based on sound military principles but it must also conform to our post-war policy as well. There is no doubt that the proposed 'enterprise' will have a profound effect on post-war thinking. But, he needs support of FO or WO, to gain access to the PM. With Sir Anthony or Monty in his corner, pressure could be brought on the PM to modify his stance on Un Su.

. It was common knowledge that meetings were being held to discuss in the light of post D-Day events, what alterations, if any, should be made on the official British response to German Resistance movements. Dir wanted the PM to modify Un Su rules immediately so that SOE could invite GG over to London for consultation.

It has been bruited about (his sources have informed him) that the PM is fed up with the restrictions of Un Su—that it has outlived its usefulness. "If true, now is the time for him to step-up-to-the-plate (as the Yanks might have put it)."

He ships B's report, together with his commentaries, upstairs; requesting a meeting with the foreign secretary; On the pretext of discussing coordination of the army, with SOE and the Maquis, he seeks to arrange a meeting at Monty's Normandy headquarters.

Section 8.5 Anglo-Widerstand Relations

Section 8.5.1 Cross-Channel Excursion

Dir was actually very busy. This was a period of intense cross-channel activity. SOE agents, working with the Maquis—in France and the Low Countries—behind enemy lines, wreaking havoc on the German supply-lines, and gathering information on the disposition of German Army units, were of great assistance to the Allied advance in Normandy.

Dir called in B "I've got another mission for you. Get your favorite pilot and fly over to Monty's Field HQ in Normandy."

"Not again! Me go see Monty? Me talk to the Commander-In-Chief of the Allied Armies in Northern France (Soon to be appointed to FM)? You must be balmy, sir."

Dir laughed, "You're working your way up in the world, You've already met with a general, a step or two below a FM and more than held your own with him."

"Yes, but he is a German General, and he wanted something from me.

Here we want something from Monty."

Grumbling a bit, B continues," If you don't mind my saying so. Sir, I think that Monty may not take too kindly at the prospect of talking to me. He's rather touchy that way; he doesn't like to deal with subordinates."

"Hmm, you may have a point there, but I want you to come along."

B smiled (aside). *"I really think that he got a kick out of all three of us taking this excursion together."*

They arrive at Monty's field HQ. Dir starts to enter the tent, but an aide blocks GP's entry:

"Where do you think you're going, soldier?" GP halted; he didn't say a word, but B exploded: "He's with me." The aide, with a smirk, replied, "I'm sorry, sir, but only officers are allowed at the CIC's official conferences."

Unused to any turmoil at his HQ, Monty rose from his desk, and walked to the door, to see what the ruckus was all about. Observing that he was annoyed B quickly introduced GP to him.

"Sir, please allow me to present my pilot. He was a glider pilot with the 6th on D-Day." Monty's disdain quickly turned to praise, when informed that GP was severely wounded during the pre-dawn raid by the sixth. The CIC. beamed," My boy, let me shake your hand, (GP smiles to himself." *The 6th must have done something memorable. Everyone wants to shake my hand.*)" "You chaps did a marvelous job. It's hard to imagine the Allies having done nearly as well as they did on D-Day, without the airlanding troops. Your actions thwarted a possible German reaction from the east that might have caused us some serious problems. "Flustered, GP did manage to squeak out a "Thank you, sir. You are much too kind."

He surprised himself, by blurting out, "but, we were only doing our job" They all laughed, but Monty said gently, but firmly, that his aide was right, and that GP, like RK's Tommy Atkins, would have to 'wait outside'. He turned to his aide, "See that the lad is well taken care of." he instructed as he, Dir, and B went inside.

Ever the charmer, Monty was lavish in his praise of the performance of the intelligence service, "The Ultra-reports, and the SOE/Maquis operations have been extremely useful. But, you haven't come all this way to hear me tell you that. What's on your mind?"

"You're a hard man to fool. You're so right, sir. I've come to discuss a matter that is of a far more serious nature, It has to do with the future conduct and course of the war."

Monty's ears perked up, "Is this going to take long? I don't mean to rush you, but I have an important meeting scheduled with General. Eisenhower. Why don't we adjourn for lunch, then you can tell me all about it?"

"I understand. I'll be as brief as I can. As you may, or may not know, in May'44, W approached OSS with a plan, which *inter-alia*, called for the elimination of Hitler and an immediate end-to-the-war. This plan, the old-plan, was ignored. I have no evidence that it was ever seen by PM and the President. A few weeks after D-Day, I got a frantic call from an SOE agent in Holland, that a German general, representing W was bearing a new plan. They believed that the new-plan deleted the objectionable elements from the old-plan, and urgently desired a meeting with British Intelligence. I dispatched B here, one of my most trusted subordinates, to meet with GG. Largely on the basis of his report, and after a tumultuous session, I concluded that it is SOE's duty to recommend that we support the W proposal for a joint Anglo-W operation.

"To truncate a long story, SOE has carried this matter as far as it can go.

To proceed further, we need the PM to modify or relax Un Su."

Grimly, Monty listened to Dir's rendition. Silently, he vowed that nothing was going to interfere with his own plans. He really didn't want to know more. He knew too much already. Neither WO nor PM had ever even hinted that such a plan existed, but he could see why the Dir, and Dulles before him, were so excited about its prospects. Sorry to say, it was not his cup-of-tea.

Monty stroked his chin, "Everybody has plans on what to do next. The Americans have theirs, and we have ours. From what you say, even the Germans have one! (Monty thought that comical,) I can see no need for another one—especially one as 'iffy' as W's. I cannot see anything to gain from it.

"Have you shown this to the PM?"

"No, that's where you come in, sir."

"I understand that time is at a premium, but this W plan has to be thoroughly studied by my staff before I can comment on it intelligently"."

"I'd rather not discuss the plan with others; the matter is really for your eyes only."

"Is the material that 'hot'? It is highly irregular for me to make up my mind without prior consultation."

"I understand, but right now I am soliciting your support in bringing this 'enterprise' to the PM's attention."

"I'm sorry, but if your enterprise—as you call it—cannot withstand scrutiny then I cannot be of any use to you.

"Look, old friend, just stamp your papers top secret/urgent and leave them with me. You will hear from one of my most trusted and discreet staff officers shortly."

Dir didn't care for this answer, but what could he do? He didn't want to offend the FM. Disappointed, Dir returns to London, wondering how long Monty was going to sit on his report. To his pleasant surprise, Monty's staff Intelligence officer pays an early call to London. Dir invites B to sit in on their conversation.

In strictest confidence, Dir explains the elements of the new-plan and its consequences. "What is this?—Some sort of a joke? They expect the British contingent to ward off the German Army, while these GGs carry out their 'Revolution'?" (The Dir suppressed a grin. MSO's reaction was similar to his own, when the plan was first broached to him by B. (See Section 7.6)).

"I wish it were. But, it is the most serious and far-reaching proposition to cross my desk in all my years in His Majesty's service. At the risk of sounding melodramatic, it has the potential to bring about an abrupt end to the war, and all that entails."

"Boy, that sounds ominous."

"Let me see if I've got this straight.

A very small number of anti-Nazi generals have concocted a plot to kill Hitler, and bring about a quick termination to the war. For politico-military reasons, they plan a joint operation, with a token British Airlanding force. They argue that the mere presence of the British triggers *Op Valkyrie*, that mobilizes the Home, or Replacement, Army which is under W control. We have been assured that there will not be any Regular German Army units in Berlin, but if a firefight does develop, it will be handled by the 'Home Army'.

MSO interrupts his summation, "You know, Berlin isn't exactly around the corner. It's a long haul, requiring dozens of gliders, tractor-aircraft (e.g., converted Halifaxes, Wellingtons, and other obsolete bombers) and a huge flotilla of long-range fighters to protect this air armada. Have you given any thought to the logistics of such a fantastic enterprise?"

"I haven't, but I hope that the GGs have. We are relying on them to direct the combined operation."

"Oh, oh, Monty will love that. He will never agree to a German-led operation."

MSO continues his observations: "Joint operations are inherently quite tricky. We've had enough trouble working with our close friends— the Americans—but an Anglo-W venture? Wow!" Philosophically, he continues with a barrage of rhetorical questions:

"How do you coordinate your movements with theirs? How can you execute a joint-venture with a clandestine organization about which we know very little? How do you link-up, and fight side-by-side, with a phantom army over which W has only tenuous control?"

B who had been quietly listening, entered the conversation. "You don't have to persuade me. We know that the 'enterprise', though simple in concept, may be very difficult in practice. However. it is not as convoluted as you seem to imply.

We realize that it would be preferable to deal directly with Rommel and von Kluge (he replaced von Rundstedt on 07/02/44.) but they both have shown no inclination to seek an Armistice. Only W is pressing forward. The whole point of the British detachment is to unmistakably show a relaxation of Un Su, and de-facto recognition of W. Hopefully it will generate an upsurge of support from the German Army and the People for the Provisional Government.

"Sure having the British along presents, as you say, 'logistical complications', but they are essential, if only as a 'stiffener', to assure the success of the 'Revolt'."

"Bravo! You've almost had me convinced. But, don't tell that to Monty."

Section 8.5.2 Response from FO

Admittedly, Dir wasn't relying too heavily on help from FO Despite being given the full 'top-secret/ urgent' treatment, the wait for the response from FO seemed interminable. He suspects that the delay was probably due to an internecine struggle between the Foreign Secretary and the PM.

Actually the response, terse, and to the point, was restrained but firm. FO feigned surprise that Dir was taking GG's plan so seriously.

"It's just a patched-up retread of the old-plan that has already been rejected."

"Un Su has served us very well, We have no intention of pressing PM to modify it in any meaningful way, While we are as concerned as anyone about the fate of hostage-Europe, we cannot deviate from our War Aims. This war is being fought to crush Germany, so that she will never again be able to threaten the 'Peace of Europe'; and to destroy the Wehrmacht, not to turn it over to W. GGs are not to be trusted. They are all militarists, cut from the same cloth. What they actually want is to regain control of the Army, in order to extort concessions at the 'peace table'. An anti-Nazi GG? that's an oxymoron. That you have managed to dredge up a few decent and honorable German generals doesn't change a thing.

"We haven't been asleep. We are continuously monitoring the situation. FO and PM are of the same mind on this matter. Nothing will be gained by an interview with the PM Should he and/or the President. soften their position—not very likely—we will act accordingly. But as of now, Un Su is non-negotiable. There will be no '14 points' to hobble us this time.

"SOE should keep its distance. It is concerning itself with matters beyond the scope of its mandate.

Stick to 'Sabotage and Subversion' and leave the future course of the war to us.

"You are straining the limits of Abs Sil. Future contact with the 'enemy' should be cleared by us. Be warned, you are perilously close to being in violation of the Official Secrets Act."

Section 8.5.3 Response from MHQ

The eagerly awaited response from Monty's HQ arrived shortly thereafter. It contained references to many of the points raised by MSO. It was clear that Monty was not going to jeopardize his grand-offensive to knock Germany out of the war, to be launched after the breakout from Normandy.

He had visions of WWI, where the German Army withdrawal quickly turned into a rout, resulting in the Armistice of November 11,1918.

"Monty has enough to worry about in Normandy, without taking on any new ventures. Superficially, it may look like the easy-way-to-go but upon closer examination, it is seen to be mired in problems. When we delve into details, its simplicity loses its luster.

"Putting it bluntly, he doesn't like the odds. It goes against the grain, to commit British forces to support a German-led coalition, well intentioned as they might be. Though anti-Nazi, W is still a German organization.

"Monty—the super-cautious—is a firm believer in the principle of overwhelming force—which he used to such spectacular effect at El Alemein. In this way, victory is assured and Allied casualties are kept to a minimum. The situation here is just the reverse—British forces are weak and are in danger of total annihilation. In good conscience, he cannot risk a single battalion, under these conditions.

Monty disputes the assertion that this is a 'minor operation' and if it fails, it will only be a minor setback to the Allied war effort. Superficially it may look like small-potatoes to us, but what if there aren't enough men to do the job? These operations have a way of escalating. How do we respond to an urgent distress call for reinforcements? Airlanding troops, which are in woefully short supply, play a pivotal role in his plans. He can easily see, if things go awry, how this 'enterprise' may impact adversely on his carefully crafted offensive, to 'end the war in '44'.

"I can see why you, and Dulles, are so excited about the prospects of a joint Anglo-W operation, but why trade-in a sound, well-thought-out plan, for one so fraught with risk?

"I'm sorry, old-boy, but from a purely military point of view, if asked, I would have to tell the PM that it has disaster, spelled out all over it.".

Section 8.5.4 Status of the Enterprise

Dir hadn't expected anything from the FO, and that's precisely what he got: nothing. He thought that he would have a better chance with the WO, but that proved to be illusory. With neither the 'diplomats', nor the 'soldiers' expressing any interest in the 'enterprise' he was at a loss on how to proceed from here. Yes, the situation could hardly be worse.

Rebuffed from all sides, it seemed as though they weren't making any progress. He was temporarily overcome by a strange sinking feeling of despair. He had a similar feeling during the 'Battle of Britain' when the Germans had to be stopped in their tracks—or a*lles Kapu*t. Perhaps he was looking back at those dark days for inspiration, but now it wasn't the safety of England that was at stake, but the rescue of 'hostage Europe'.

"We can talk of them in the abstract, but these are real people in occupied Europe, the POW compounds, and the CCs who daily face the horrors of Nazi tyranny."

Dir calls B into his office and invites him to bring along GP. He reviews the responses from FO and WO. Recovering from his temporary letdown, he angrily pounds his fist on the desk. "Those bloody fools at FO still cling to that bankrupt policy of Un Su. They made it clear, under a veiled threat of dire consequence, that we were to refrain from contacting W without prior clearance."

Monty is in no hurry to release the glider troops. He fears and detests any operation that might detract from his grand-offensive-plans. Ha! Even project ANVIL, the invasion of southern France, being pushed by Ike, draws his ire.

"We have yet to get around to requesting the RAF to supply the tug-aircraft and the 'long-range fighter protection'. With a sardonic laugh, he wonders how 'Bomber Command' will react when asked to suspend 'blockbusting', and bomb with leaflets, not explosives.

"Only PM could make order out of this mess, but so far, he hasn't' displayed any inclination to do so."

B and GP listened glumly to his diatribe.

B remarked that with his mention of 'leaflets', Dir introduced a new set of problems.

Strange to say, the purveyors-of-propaganda played an insignificant role in the war-of-words.

Since the Allied insistence of Un Su equated, intentionally or not, all Germans with the Nazis, there really wasn't anything for them to do.

"Now however they will have to lubricate their rusty propaganda apparatus, to spread the word all over Germany that a new day is dawning".

Propaganda is a touchy subject, It has to be employed with care. "I scarcely know where to begin. I suppose that W will have to supply its own propaganda message."

Hitherto, for its own safety, W had to be secretive, but to mobilize the support of the Deutsche Volk; they have to spread the message (without mentioning W by name).

"They can't just say, "If you encounter any Allied troops, don't panic. They are here at W's invitation, to help us jettison Hitler and the Nazis."

"W must undergo rapid transformation from anonymity, to ubiquity, but they must do so without attracting the attention of the Gestapo. Already it was breathing down their necks. Some of the leading civilian members of the conspiracy had been arrested, and others have gone into hiding. If the 'Revolt' is indeed imminent, then we are already running behind schedule, By now, our bombers should be pummeling the Third Reich with leaflets. Messengers from W should have been dispatched to those army commanders in the West, sympathetic to the conspiracy, alerting them to the impending uprising.

Section 8.5.5 The Plot Moves Forward

After his meeting with B, and the departure of the Lysander, GG heads for Berlin, to report back to the Colonel General. It was not a pleasant trip. The infra-structure of Germany, its trains, roads, bridges, etc., were under continuous attack by Allied aircraft. It was gut-wrenching for him to view the devastation brought upon the German people by Hitler. GG fervently hopes that Britain will join W, in applying the one hard shove, from the inside, on the pillars of Nazism, causing the whole rotten edifice to come tumbling down.

After many delays and detours, he reached his destination, WHQ on the Bendlerstrasse. The Colonel General was gratified that he had acquitted himself so well, but cautioned him to restrain his jubilation. Although he placed great stock in English participation, he was realistic enough to face the strong possibility that it might never materialize.

"Even if it does, it may be too late."

GG returns to his home in the Cleves-Julich area, near the Dutch border, awaiting the call from London. The month of June passes into history, but still no word from Baker Street. It was taking too long. At first he views this favorably, attributing the delay to the inevitable wrangling at the highest level, presaging a change-in-official-policy. However, when it stretched further into July, he began to worry. With the rapid deterioration of conditions on the WF, much of the reason for the 'plot' evaporated. Some of his co-conspirators, dismayed by the apparent lack of interest by the British, and viewing the joint-enterprise as a study in futility agitated to put Op *Valkyrie* on hold. People who thought like that didn't really understand the mind-of-the-GGs.

Although the motives of individual Resistance members differed, the glue that bonded them together was an all-consuming hatred for Hitler and his gang—consequently this position was dismissed.

The leadership of W, after reviewing all options, chose to go-at-it-alone, if necessary, as originally planned. This wasn't merely a gesture; it would show posterity the true face of Germany, not the ugly, revolting, contorted grimace inflicted on Europe by the Nazis. Clinging desperately to the hope of British support, GG pleaded in vain with W to wait a little longer, before writing them off. But some of the more cynical declared: "Why wait? We know what their answer will be. The Allies ignored the Dulles-Gisevious contact in May, and the English are showing their disdain for W, by ignoring us now."

Even Colonel General Beck who valued British help so highly conceded: The plot must go ahead as planned.

"W is as ready as it will ever be."

(Besides, Colonel Stauffenberg has his own timetable . . .)

Section 8.5.6 Time Marches On!

The biggest foe of the enterprise is Time. Despite its 'top-secret/ urgent' classification, the red-tape in working its way through the FO and WO took time—a commodity in tight supply—that they could ill-afford to expend.

"A day here, a day there, and before you know it, you are late."

Outwardly, Dir exuded confidence, but the 'time pressure' building up, was getting him down. Dir calls B, (and GP) into his office. He reviews the responses. FO and Monty's HQ didn't buy their arguments.

FO has them tied up in knots. They cannot even apprise W of the current state-of-affairs.

"To people clutching at straws, any news, no matter how negative will be interpreted as 'encouragement'"

Regrettably, Dir concurred. He thought that by simply ignoring them they will get-the-hint that they will either have to get rid of Hitler by themselves, or pack-in-the-plot altogether.

B felt the same way: "Let them think that we have abandoned them. Maybe our crude, uncivil behavior will have the desired effect, and they will heed our advice to sit-out-the-rest-of-the-war!"

But who are we to tell them what to do? They are 'big boys'. I'm sure that they will do, what they have to do,"

Dir notes that since the last meeting with GG, the German position has rapidly deteriorated. It was now in the middle of July, and the war on the WF and the EF had reached 'fever pitch'. The war was about to enter a new phase.

A break-out by the Allies from Normandy on the WF.

A break-through by the Russians into Poland on the EF, threatening a break—into Germany proper.

The Red Army drove the broken Wehrmacht out of Russia.

On the WF, with the GA on the verge of collapse, things weren't much better.

Caen fell to the British-Canadian forces, as the Americans advanced on St, Lo and cleared the Cotentin Peninsula, but still the German Army held on tenaciously. A knock-out blow, from which the Wehrmacht supposedly would never recover, OP Goodwood was launched. Realistically, how much longer can they stave off the inevitable?

Intently, GP listens to the conversation. He was appalled to learn that things weren't progressing as smoothly as he had hoped. He is shocked by the state-of-affairs. Failure to get British support hit them all hard, but him the hardest. He never dreamt that it would come to this. To think that he once thought that Dir was the big-hurdle, but getting him aboard was child's play compared to the problems facing them now: FO and WO (and presumably PM) didn't buy SOE's story.

He wasn't happy with their decision not to inform W (it's too-raw). He couldn't bear the thought of GG, waiting in vain, for the British support—that will never come. Although not as pessimistic as Dir and B, he did agree that with no likelihood of British Air-landing troops the risks might prove unacceptably high, but he was not ready to call-it-quits.

B interjects, "I think that GP may have a point there. We've played it by the book. We've gone through channels and have nothing to show for it. If we hesitate now, all of our arduous work will come to naught. Our carefully nurtured, logical, unassailable arguments have been adroitly side-stepped. Let's face it, we've been out-maneuvered. Resumption of our contact with W seems to be the only course left open to us.

"Desperate situations require desperate measures."

"You know, at the close of our meeting, it did occur to me to invite GG to return with us, even though I didn't have specific authority to do so. There was no way that I could guarantee what would happen to him, when we landed in England."

"It's a good thing that you didn't, It's not that he might be interned as a 'defector'; incarcerated as a POW or even, heaven forbid, be detained as a war-criminal (Wouldn't that be a scream?—But that's the way they think over at the FO), but we would be openly flouting the 'twin doctrines'."

If the FO wanted to be real nasty they could accuse Dir of trafficking with the enemy. It's one thing to be reprimanded for bending-the-rules and quite another to be charged with violating the Official Secrets Act.

Dir wonders. *Were B's instincts right, after all? He half-wanted to send B back to Holland to fetch GG. Ha! What an uproar that would make! But, in retrospect, with the benefit of hindsight, maybe that was just the 'tonic' needed to jar them out of their smugness and complacency.*

GP bewails that they seem to be losing sight of the objectives of the Anglo-W enterprise. "Recall, sir, it's not just a case of Allies and

Germans, but there is a 'third party', bearing the brunt of Nazi brutality in occupied Europe, the POW camps, and those cooped up in the CCs, as well."

Dir placates GP, but replies irritably, "My boy, we know what has to be done, but unfortunately we cannot do it by ourselves. We cannot, and I certainly will not subvert Official Policy, but as long as there is a glimmer of hope, there is no risk that I would not take for the sake of the enterprise."

But, was is it worth it, just to hand-deliver the bad news? No! He was convinced that W had already divined the truth: FO clung to Un Su; Monty refused to release the Airlanding units, and the PM made speeches. However, as they speak, B and Dir's earlier comments penetrate. Suddenly, they crystallize, and an idea pops into GP's head. He couldn't believe it, but he who had striven so valiantly to promote the 'enterprise' was considering volunteering to deliver SOE's message that it-was-all-over. and carrying Dir's remarks a step further, possibly bring GG back with him. Perhaps this should have been tried before but it wasn't. Things can't be any worse than they are now.

With a self-conscious grin, directed at B, GP blurts out," I'll deliver your message."

Dir wouldn't touch it.

"We have been skating on thin ice; for the time being the government has chosen to look away, but if we persist, all this can change abruptly." Sternly, he adds, "My boy, what you are suggesting is treasonous."

GP could understand his hesitation. As a loyal servant to the crown, Dir was duty-bound to uphold official government policy. But, these rules didn't apply to him. Who was he anyway? Just an ersatz pilot.

"I can understand your predicament, sir, but don't worry., No one is going to suspect me. Anyway, it's a small enough price for me to pay, compared to what hostage-Europe is going through. All I need are the necessary clearances and a satisfactory excuse, and I'm on my way." (And besides, he yearned to see the girl again.)

Was Dir secretly relieved that the flow-of-events had taken him off the hook? If so, he didn't show it. He sympathized with GP, but SOE was not in the business of rescuing anti-Nazi Germans, nor (with a wink) of furthering cross-channel romances of its operatives.

Dir appreciated his offer, but he didn't want to rush into anything that might exacerbate an already perilous situation. "Calm down. It isn't simply a matter of flying off into the wild-blue-yonder; there are others besides you and the GG, involved, and we must all pull together if the mission is to succeed.

"Tell me, are you absolutely sure that you want to go through with this?" Slowly, with conviction, GP answers, "I will deliver your message, sir."

Dir smiled, "I really think that you will, young man. We, in good conscience have done all we can. If GG wants to come, bring him back to England, on the return flight."

GP thinks: *If the British leaders will meet face-to-face with GG, then he can plead his case for the Anglo-W enterprise better than any of us. Hopefully he will have better luck than we have.*

Dir reasons: *If there really is a crime, in all of this, it would be not to make one-last-ditch-effort to bring official policy over to our way of thinking.*

"Let us take heart from the incessant skirmishing taking place in the 'House of Commons', which seems to indicate that political support for Un Su is eroding."

B muses: *Miracles do happen. Who knows? Although it has never happened before in this war, maybe something will break-right for W.*

Dir has his work cut out for him. He has some heavy thinking to do. He ushers them out of his office, cautioning them that preliminary arrangements may take a while.

"Why don't we sleep on the matter, and meet tomorrow for lunch?"

Section 8.6 A Surprise Visit

Section 8.6.1 The Dream of GP

That night GP had trouble falling asleep. This was rare for him. Time was (not too long ago) when he slipped into the arms of Morpheus the moment his head hit the pillow. The events of the day left him drained. The transition from happy-go-lucky to Atlas supporting the weight of the Anglo-W enterprise on his shoulders was catching up with him.

Although he got what he wanted, it was with trepidation that he approached the upcoming trip. He twisted and turned but these qualms would not go away. His dream was so real, so shocking, that he awoke In a frenzy. Shaken by this nightmare, he reassured himself that it was only a dream!

GP accosts B on the way to Dir's office. Before entering, he tells B of his dream. "I could have sworn that they were the GG and his interpreter. I started walking towards them, when the two men whipped around pointing their Walther 9mm pistols at me. "Halt**!"** I hobbled back to the airplane as fast as I could, but they easily overtook me. "Aha! We've got a live one here. Let's see what interesting stories he's got to tell us." They dragged me towards a waiting automobile; in the shadows, I caught a glimpse of the GG and the girl, struggling with a man in the backseat, but Incredibly, the only thing I **could** think of was**,** "My God, this is a replay of the Venlo Affair—when abruptly, with a start, I woke up. What if anything, am I to make of this?"

B shrugs his shoulders. "You've come to the wrong man. **I'm not an 'interpreter of dreams', nor** am I a soothsayer. These dreams have no predictive powers; they are merely a reflection of your agitated state-of-mind. Your subconscious seems to be telling you that you are too-late. Britain has dallied too long. She will not participate in the great enterprise. We've come full circle. It's W's party, and we are just bystanders. You, my lad, might just as well have stayed in bed."

"But, come, let's see what Dir has come up with."

"You are in luck, my boy. Your cover is a routine drop scheduled in the vicinity of your earlier rendezvous with W. For a 3-day pass, the pilot was glad to switch to a different flight. The SOE agent will be dropped off. The GG, with his Dutch Resistance escort, will be waiting for you. B will draft a message which will be committed to memory expressing SOE's regrets, and emphatically reiterating our warning against unilateral action.

"If he wants to come, you will bring him (and F, who never seems to leave his side) back with you on the return flight. Finalizing the arrangements may be a problem, but if all goes well you may be on your way as early as tonight."

However, hitches cannot be ruled out. Dir cautions that the military situation has changed drastically since GP's last trip. Cross-border activity has increased sharply and the GG himself, may have trouble, and even be in great danger, trying to enter into (and return from) Holland.

"Do not stay any longer than absolutely necessary. Keep your wits about you and if anything doesn't look kosher, abort the mission and depart at once."

"Don't worry so much about me. sir."

"But, we do worry. Should you fall into the hands of the SS or Dutch collaborators, our whole SOE operation, in NW Europe will be in jeopardy."

We braced ourselves as Dir gave GP his famous 'quickie course' on 'how to be an Intelligence Officer:

"Unless you absolutely must, in order to carry out your mission, do not tell anyone, anything, and that goes for GG and DR, as well, Remember, If you don't tell them, they can only guess."

Section 8.6.2 Second meeting

The tiny Lysander hove into view. GP saw the familiar L-shaped pattern of the landing lights. He was all agog over the prospect of meeting GG and the girl again, but the thought of delivering Dir's message, dimmed the joy of the reunion.

He dropped off his passenger, and waited. The DR guide left with the agent, who was more than a little surprised to see the airplane 'loitering' there. Usually the plane departs immediately after discharging its passengers. (But, true to the 'code of the intelligence officer', he asked no questions.)

"Getting into, and out of, the cockpit is a pain, so I remained on board in case I had to make a quick get-away". He had stricken the lingering effects of his nightmare from his mind—but he checked to see that his weapon was at the ready. It was eerie sitting there alone, when two figures appeared. Recognizing them in the dim light as the DR guide and the girl (masquerading as a boy) he dismounted from the plane and hastened towards them. With a bemused expression, the DRG watched as they happily greeted each other. She was attired much the same way as before, but was carrying a heavily loaded field pack, as if going on a trip.

Looking around, he inquired sharply, "Where is the General?"

"He left in a rush to take up his duties . . ."

"Does that mean that the Revolt is about to begin—or has it already begun? I have an urgent message from SOE to W."

"I'm sorry. I don't really know, but if you will give me the message, I will relay it to him."

GP hesitates." I am supposed to deliver it to the General in person."

Rationalizing, that since she was present at the earlier rendezvous, and well aware of the mission, GP recites the message.

It was the letter that Dir didn't want to dictate.

It was the missive that B didn't want to compose,

and it certainly wasn't the message that GP wanted to deliver. (But, he had volunteered.)

Although not unexpected, it was the news that she dreaded to hear.

Stripped of all persiflage, the gist of the message was simply:

"British help? Forget it. SOE advice? Disband. Any hope? Not much. Get rid of Hitler first, then 'call us'."

Bound together by the dream of a joint Anglo-W enterprise her hopes, like those of GP's, were dashed, All color drained from her face, but, on the whole she took the bad news rather stoically. Exclaiming that it may be too late, she thanked him profusely for SOE's concern. As Dir had surmised, W had guessed Britain's intentions—but he is sure that they will make their plans accordingly.

GP quickly comes to the point. "My orders are to bring the General and you to England at once, assuming, of course, that you want to join me on the return-flight. I'm sure that if the General were here, he would insist that you go. Should W prevail, you can return in a hurry, but if things go wrong, you certainly don't want to be caught hanging around here, in Germany.

"He pleads with her to return with him,

He uses all his powers of persuasion, but to no avail.

"I'm not going to let you escape this time."

She laughs, "You are not going to kidnap me, are you?"

Harking back to the Venlo Incident, she thought it was comical, that there must be something in the air around here that is 'conducive to abduction'. Impulsively he reaches out, clumsily wrapping her in his arms. Very strong, he inadvertently puts the 'crusher' on her, hugging here so tightly that she could scarcely breathe, planting a long, deep, ardent kiss on her lips.

Quickly releasing his grip, he steps back, sheepishly mumbling, "I'm sorry. Please forgive me. I just couldn't control my feelings." But, he held on to her hand.

"Whew! I thought that you English had a reputation for being cold, distant, and reserved. Do you always greet your female friends like this?"

"Only those whom I really want."

"Desire me? In this get-up-baggy-pants, jack-boots and all? I must look a mess, and you must be desperate. Is there a shortage of girls in England?"

It struck her very amusing: Even GP, who was getting grumpier by the minute at her intransigence, smiled, but he thought her mood light-hearted for one about to embark on so dangerous an assignment. This 'playful repartee' (which might have led to greater things), heavily weighted down by the gravity of the situation, was cut-short by reality. Sensing his displeasure, but touched by his concern, she said,

"Why are you making it so difficult for me? For years, all of our thoughts, all of our efforts, have been directed towards the planning and preparation for this momentous occasion."

Trying, not too successfully, to suppress her tears, she looked up at the ex-glider pilot, and said, "At any other time, under any other circumstances, there is nothing I would rather do than fly back with you to London, but now I cannot leave the General nor desert the *Vaterland.*

"You see, I will be needed, as interpreter, for discussions with the Allies."

GP thought cynically, *"Needs you? Ha! What they need is Luck. Discussions with whom? Perhaps the Americans. But from the British you'll draw a blank. Doesn't she realize that they have washed their hands of W?"*

The thought of her traipsing around war-torn Europe made him shudder.

"Does the General approve of you running around alone?"

"Please don't pull that 'big brother' act on me. If I were a man you wouldn't be so solicitous.

I can take care of myself."

"I know you can. You are one of the bravest people I have ever met, but war is a 'young man's game' and don't let anyone tell you otherwise."

His imagination ran wild. All that has to happen is for someone to figure out that 'she is not a boy' and she becomes prey for 'foe and friend' alike. He particularly dreaded the thought of her falling into the hands of the Gestapo. He admired her courage, but blasted her folly. Disconsolately, he dropped her hand,

"You're a good soldier. But there is such a thing as being overzealous."

Silently (to himself*), he salutes her filial devotion, her patriotic zeal for the 'new German democracy' that is to spring from W full blown, as Minerva from the head of Jupiter.* With a quizzical smile, he whispers to himself, *"Now how do I know that? It's in the manifesto.* There was a 'certain ring 'to that phrase that really got to him.

"I dislike long, mawkish, sentimental, good-byes, so I made mine short".

Resting his hands on her shoulders, he braced himself and (out loud) delivered a 'cliché ridden' farewell address. "The 'enterprise' is bigger than all of us. The fate of millions hangs in the balance. With— or without—British help, it must succeed." Sounding more like a sloganeer, than a soldier, he repeated SOE's motto:

"*VE Day, Liberation Day, Revolt Day—the same day!*"

I released my grip, and continued with my parting perfunctory, (but sincere) remarks. "Whatever course W ultimately chooses to take, I, (and, the downtrodden people in hostage-Europe), fervently wish you, the General and W, utmost success in your endeavors." He limped over to the Lysander, and with the assistance of DR Guide, he climbed into the cockpit. Securely buckled in, the old-music-hall-refrain, made famous by Gracie Fields, crossed his mind, and he 'wished her good-luck, as he waved her goodbye'.

With a wan smile, over the propeller noise, she shouted simply:

"*Auf Wiedersehen.*"

The landing lights, extinguished, F left with DRG, who escorted her to the frontier. He watched, as (like Bulldog Drummond) into the night they walked, rapidly fading from view. An eerie 'sense of foreboding' descended on the airplane, as he took off for the *return* flight to England.

Section 8.6.3 Second Return Flight

The magic was gone. He was in a foul mood. His Majesty's government had let him down! Suddenly, a long suppressed animosity welled-up in him. He was resentful that he hadn't been recruited by the RAF. It was funny that he should think of this now. He had purged all thoughts of that from his mind, a long time ago. He was a glider pilot, and proud of it. Chugging along at 160 knots, he enjoyed flying the Westland Lysander, but, just the same, he was angry that it wasn't a Hawker Typhoon.

In contrast to his earlier return flight (with B), where he was enthusiastic, full-of-hope, and confident that the Anglo-W enterprise would succeed, he was morose and feeling sorry for himself. B was right—he shouldn't have come. Disgustedly, he muses, *"Like everything else that brushes up against the enterprise, this trip is one-big-bust"*

GP rambles on, (for the second time) that HM government has let him down. With Britain out of the picture, all that SOE can do is give advice. "It's all up to W now. If W packs-it-all-in, the conspirators survive, but the goals of the enterprise are forsaken. Who is going to get rid of Hitler, bring a quick end to the war, liberate occupied Europe, free the POW's, and empty the CCs?"

"Who is going to make good our motto now? Realistically, without British help the odds of success have skidded precipitously, from reasonably high, to unreasonably low."

Fully cognizant of the stakes involved, which way will W jump? Like Schroedinger's cat, we won't know until after they do it.

GP muses: *"Yes, the 'enterprise' is bigger than all of us; but Britain has shirked its responsibilities, so W will do, what it will do."*

Section 8.6.4 Empty-handed

Flying had an exhilarating effect on him. His anger subsided, as the plane approached the English coast. He thought of the last-minute instructions given to him by Dir and B. If he is bringing passengers back with him, he was to use a secret cypher to contact SOE. He was to touch down at a little used corner of the airport at Tangier, before going on to Tempford. He will be greeted by B who will drive his passengers back to London with him. If not, he should proceed as if it were a routine flight.

The morning after his return, empty-handed, he reports to 64 Baker St. He observes that business—is-booming at SOE HQ, but it was 'silent as a tomb' at the GR Desk. He couldn't contain himself. It was bizarre. Here we are at the threshold of what may well turn out to be the most significant operation of the war, but no one seems to be particularly concerned. Here he was bringing the astounding news that the Revolt is 'closer' than imminent, (but further away than 'right now')!

He reports to his superiors, "I was shocked when the General didn't show, although the girl did. She wouldn't—or couldn't—tell me where he was, only that he left to take up 'his duties'. It was evident that W had given up on us, and the plot was on a day-to-day basis. I gathered that the final Putsch commences with the assassination attempt."

B recalls, that at their meeting, the General had informed him, that W is well organized in the West. "He is probably trying to make his way to Paris to line up the support of OBWest for W and arrange an Armistice with the Western Allies."

Dir thought it ironic: Here he was, in possession of this 'vital intelligence'—but what could he do with it? He had curtailed his appointments, and instructed SOE agents in the field to be on the lookout for any unusual activity or 'something big' taking place, 'Inside the Third Reich'. If so, SOE HQ must be notified immediately.

"For all we know, they may be making their Revolution right now."

"Just as it is hard for W to know what is going on over here in Baker St., it is equally difficult for us to be sure of what they are up to over there, on the *Bendlerstrasse*."

Dir informed us that there are persistent rumors that a few days ago, FM Rommel was severely wounded during an RAF strafing attack. While undoubtedly this was a 'great plus' for the Allied side, it must be viewed as a setback for W. FM von Kluge, who replaced von Rundstedt on July 2nd will be in sole command of OBWest.

"Some say that he is associated with the conspiracy, in which case it may, on balance, redound to W's advantage, after all."

B cautions, "Let's not go overboard. There were many prior attempts but they all fizzled out. They were really not part of a well-thought-out, meticulously planned operation. Who should know that better than the titular head of W, the erstwhile Chief of the Great German General Staff, Col Gen L. Beck.?"

Section 8.6.5 PM Pays a Call

There is a knock on the door.

"Who can that be? I'm not expecting any visitors."

GP jumps up, quickly opens the door, and two men—one a soldier, with his Sten-gun at the ready—rush into the room, looking about wildly. The other man, demands their weapons; B and GP were unarmed, but Dir placed his side-arm on the desk, saying, "Hold on there. What do you mean by breaking into my office like this?"

Suddenly, the secret service agent roared, "Attention, the Prime Minister!"

Dir was stunned, B flabbergasted, and GP didn't know where to hide. They all snapped to 'rigid attention'. Dir tried to interrupt; the agent glowered, as the PM silenced him by simply raising his hand, indicating that this was not to be a 'Questions and Answer' session, but a 'speech'.

"At ease, gentlemen."

"I am well aware of SOE's strong advocacy on behalf of the latest W plan, and I am not pleased. Official Policy prohibits all cooperation with the enemy—and that includes German Resistance movements."

Perturbed, he suppresses his annoyance, and continues in a more conciliatory tone.

"I know exactly how you feel. Like you, I have a penchant for a daring operation and few are more dangerous and momentous than this one. Remember, SOE is my baby. It is ironic: now that events have finally given SOE a mission worthy of its existence, circumstances dictate that Britain must pass."

With the invasion a success and the end of the war in sight, some feel that the reason for the continued insistence on Un Su seems to have vanished. This issue has been hotly debated, behind closed doors, and on the floor of the House of Commons. The leadership of both parties agreed that as a show-of-good-faith, the anti-Nazi elements should act to eliminate Hitler, before the British will consider active intervention.

"There is no way that these deliberations could be conceived as signaling any change in our official position. On the contrary, Un Su never looked better.

"W is addicted to wishful thinking."

PM complains that he scarcely knows the identities of the more prominent members of the conspiracy, and that he doesn't even know how to get in touch with them.

PM pauses for a few moments, before continuing his monologue.

Dir scoffs silently: *How can he say that? Does he expect anyone to believe it? Admittedly, in line with his famous Abs Sil edict of (January 1941) we had little contact with W, but with the continent a-flood with our agents, all that he had to do was ask!*

"It isn't cricket to bring up casualties. I needn't remind you that despite the huge losses suffered in the last war, we were left with 'unfinished business'. It isn't that the FMs took a ghoulish delight, from the length of the casualty lists, but it is in the Nature-of-War itself. It is easy to condemn war, but sometimes there is no other way. The appeasement policy of the thirties ended in a shambles, when the war we tried so hard to avoid, broke out in September.1939 with the brutal invasion of Poland.

No doubt, a quick termination to this conflict will save innumerable lives, but we cannot turn from our duty, without achieving our war aims. We owe it to the men who fought the menace of German militarism in WWI and WWII, that there will not be a third! Their sacrifices will not have been in vain.

"Few people are more ardently anti-Nazi than the President and myself. Few people are more concerned about the fate of 'hostage Europe'. Few people are more appalled by the 'Extermination Camps'. But, the primary objective of this war is not only to crush Hitlerism, but Germany itself, so that she will never again threaten the 'Peace of Europe'—and that means Un Su. Predicting the status of post-war Europe is hazardous at best, but one thing is certain: Our 'War Aims' must be achieved.

Post-war Germany will not be governed by Germans. There will not be a German head of state. What's left of Germany will be administered by an Allied Control Council. There will be no deals. No negotiations. No 'unfinished business'. No fourteen points. Just Unconditional Surrender.

"If W elects to move forward with their plan, they do so on their own. They must take sole responsibility, for any disastrous repercussions that will surely ensue, if they do not succeed. I do not wish them ill in their 'enterprise', but cruel—and heartless—as it sounds, it might be best, for post-war Europe, that they fail."

With that, he turned on his heel and left the room. Before exiting, the secret service agent turned towards us and said, "You understand, of course, this interview never took place." In a flash, it was all over, Left speechless, it took a few moments to recover.

Defiantly, Dir calls out after the retreating PM and his entourage. "You can have my resignation, but SOE will not retreat from its stand."

It struck him (with the impact of a small asteroid colliding with the Earth) that it is 'Now or Never'. Reducing the sound volume a few decibels, he continued in a more conversational tone. "Sir, with all due respect, I have some urgent, vital news to convey. Please hear me out."

Unused to being addressed in so brazen a manner, PM stopped, turned his head and glared at him. Others might have trembled under his withering glance, but the recipient of the 'Victoria Cross' in the first World War, answered unfazed, "Sir, you must listen . . ."

Dir hesitated momentarily (GP knew why. The last thing that he wanted to do was to bring attention to, and have to explain, the unorthodox means used to gather this information.)

"My sources tell me that an insurrection in Germany may be underway right now. My instincts tell me that this is not speculation, but the real thing."

PM really couldn't stay mad at them. The fact is that despite his outward show of indignation, he had a soft-spot in his heart for SOE. Not wishing to make light of this 'intelligence alert', he menacingly replied, "I thought that I made the government's position on this matter, quite clear. If your information is correct, we will know soon enough, won't we? Our opinion is that it is all bombast; they will not proceed on their own. But, if they do, and succeed, then as the Americans say, 'it is a new ball-game'. But, if they do not, well we warned them. Didn't we ?"

The SIS agents grinned, as they followed PM down the corridor. With a rueful smile, B says, "And we thought that the stars were on our side. So much for 'Truth and Justice'. For once in this wretched war, things were finally breaking-right, and a torrent of fresh air was about to sweep across the continent."

More to the point, GP queries innocently, "What was that all about, sir?"

"We just witnessed a tug-of-war between the PM's private and public views. On the one hand, he is the dashing, 'Soldier of Fortune' of the 'Boer War' fame, but as HM's first minister, he is the stodgy bureaucrat defending the 'Official Position'."

"But, *best that they fail*? Why he's no better than the Nazis."

"Steady, I wouldn't be so harsh on him; a failed Revolution spares the President and PM the ordeal of sitting across from Colonel General L. Beck at the Peace Table. Can you imagine negotiating with the Col Gen as the provisional 'Head of the German State'? The moral force of Beck would have engulfed them. Of course, FDR and PM were arch-foes of Hitler and the Nazis from way back, but Beck and his co-conspirators, put their lives on the line, risking everything to get rid of them.

"Well Gentlemen, you heard the man. He concurs with the others. In the same vein, the FO and the WO made it clear that they were not about to share their 'diplomatic triumphs' and 'military glory', respectively, with W. Barring a miracle, the Allies will not rescind Un Su, nor lend any support to the latest W plan, nor participate in the proposed Anglo-W enterprise. Yet, it must be recalled, that despite all this, they did leave the door slightly ajar:

"Consideration of British intervention was tied to a 'show of good faith'".

Scarcely had the visit terminated, when fragmentary reports started filtering in concerning '*Action in the 3rd Reich*'. Coupled with GP's news, this reinforced their supposition that the 'Revolt of the Generals' was at hand. But, why no speeches by Beck over the Rundfunk, as 'Head of the Provisional Government', exhorting the German Army and the Deutsche Volk, to rise up and follow W? Of course, it was still very early; hard news was sparse, but, still it doesn't bode well.

Section 8.7 The 20th of July1944

"A little encouragement to those Germans ready to risk their lives to free Germany, could have brought Peace before the Russians crossed the Vistula, and before the Western Allies had advanced beyond Normandy."

W. S. Casey, 'Secret War against Hitler' (1988), p.120.

Section 8.7.1 Der Tag

Meanwhile, W was rushing headlong towards its 'date with Destiny'. They had the man, the means, the access, and the opportunity. The man? Colonel Klaus von Stauffenberg. A much decorated officer, severely wounded in Tunisia, during the North African campaign (04/43), he was appointed Chief of Staff to Col Gen F. Fromm, Head of the 'Home Army', shortly before D-Day. Col Stauffenberg, a man of highest ideals, unusual courage, and nerves of steel, was the perfect choice for the job. The means? An attaché case carrying two 2 kilogram bombs. The access? As chief of staff he is frequently deputized to meet with Hitler and his advisors to discuss the Home Army's capacity to raise new units to replace the huge losses incurred by the Wehrmacht at the Front.

The opportunity? All that remained was to wait for the most propitious time to strike. Already an inordinate amount of time had elapsed since his appointment. The war was now in the crucial middle of July period. The Allies were pounding their way out of Normandy, and if W was to have any impact on the war they had to hurry.

Unbeknownst to SOE, there were several recent abortive attempts on Hitler's life. Incredulously, to compound Col S's problems, the conspirators thought that it was of paramount importance to decapitate the leadership of the 3rd Reich in the same explosion. To expect Hitler, Himmler and Goering to be clustered together—why, that's almost Astrologic!

On 07/11, at *Berchtesgaden*, the attempt was postponed ostensibly because Himmler and Goering were not present. On 07/15, they were all there, but Hitler was called from the room. These delays didn't make sense. This was deadly business, not the time to be playing musical-chairs. The German Generals 'Oath' was to Hitler—not to Himmler, or Goering, or anyone else. With Hitler eliminated—there was no-more-oath; a major obstacle to joining W was removed (making a 'civil war' unlikely).

Hitler's concrete bunker, in the Wolfs-lair, was under reconstruction; the meetings took place in a wooden hut. Thursday, the 20th of July, was a hot, sultry day, and the windows were wide open. This move had the undesirable side-effect (for the assassin) in that it muted the force from the explosion.

Col S placed the attaché case, containing a single bomb, in position to kill Hitler. An eye-witness to the explosion, he heard the blast, saw the devastation wrought, but it was impossible for him to know for certain what happened inside the hutment. A confederate, Col Gen E. Fellgiebel, Chief of Signals, was inside the compound. What exactly he was supposed to do, or actually did, is unclear. All that we know, is that for an operation where the key word is surprise, there was roughly a 3 hour hiatus between the explosion, at 12:42, and the activation of Op Valkyrie!!

Col S believed that Hitler was killed in the blast. He congratulated himself on a job well done. He had every reason to be satisfied—but fate was 'not through with W just yet'.

The insurrection froze, until Col S returned to Berlin. W finally swung into action. Op Valkyrie was activated, the Home Army mobilized, but the essential reliable, hard fighting, highly motivated core (e.g., British Glider troops) was missing. The seizure of the Communication Center ended as a fiasco, and there was 'nobody home' to defend the Bendlerbloc.

The revolt that started out with such high hopes collapsed when the word spread that Hitler had survived the blast. For all practical purposes it was over in single day. Col Gen Beck committed suicide; Col Stauffenberg was summarily shot in the courtyard of the Bendlerbloc; the other conspirators were rounded up, tortured, tried, and ultimately executed.

Section 8.7.2 The missing contingent

The mood at 64 Baker St. was glum, and getting uglier all the time. GP wondered: *What was it like at the Foreign Office, Whitehall, and 10 Downing St.? Jubilant?* The revolt in Berlin had run its course. The leadership of W was liquidated, on-the-run, or under arrest. What caused this 'implosion'? Hitler's survival left a vacuum. Without the release of the British Airlanding unit by Monty; without the propaganda blitz by Bomber Command; without the scrapping of Un Su by FO and without de facto recognition by the Allies, what could W offer the Germans to 'stoke the fires' of rebellion?

The Manifesto? "Ha! They couldn't even give them that, having botched-up the capture of the Radio Broadcasting Station!"

B's worst fears were realized, As B had predicted, W went ahead on its own. B always held that the W plan was flawed. But, SOE was convinced that the 'joint Anglo-W' enterprise had a high probability of success. Without the 'stiffener' supplied by the vital hard-fighting, reliable core, it was foredoomed. None of the glaring defects catalogued by B, brought to the attention of GG, during their meeting had been corrected. SOE had repeatedly stressed that failure to kill Hitler didn't necessarily signal the end of the rebellion. From its inception, the 'Revolt' began to feel the effect of the missing British detachment. According to the plan for the 'Defense of the Reich' to repel a foreign Invader, the mere presence of the British triggers Operation Valkyrie, which activates the Home Army, facilitating the issuance of orders for its mobilization and deployment. The 'Home Army' units would follow directions without asking potentially embarrassing questions (As occurred during the 07/15/44 attempt where Valkyrie was prematurely set-in motion. Fortunately, they managed to pass it off as an 'excercise'.)

W had struck! But a concatenation of unfortunate events, some fundamental, others accidental, conspired to throw the Revolution into disarray. Considering that Col Gen L. Beck, a former Chief of the Great German General Staff, and Col Gen E. Hoepner, who as Commander of the 4th Panzer Army Group, that led the final tank assault on Moscow (12/41), were active in the planning stage, one might have expected W to have launched a 'model campaign'. It strains credulity, but the plan that emerged was slip-shod, and their response to the alarming news of Hitler's survival was listless, uninspired, inept, fatalistic, and too late: a recipe, just ripe for defeat! Much has been written criticizing W's plan. Yet, despite all of this, they came within a cat's whisker of pulling it off.

Section 8.7.3 Foci of Rebellion

The foci of the Revolt was in the two capitals; Berlin was a lost cause, but Paris was a different matter. There, adherents of W occupied key positions. Colonel General Stuelpnagel, the Commandant of Paris, acted swiftly; the SS and SD agents in Paris were rounded-up and incarcerated. The way was now open for W to take control of Paris and try to initiate immediately talks with the Allied Army on the Western Front. FM von Kluge's cooperation was essential—but was he up to it? The Field Marshal hesitated. As CIC OB West what did he have to fear? There was no way that Hitler could get at him. He was the 'man on horseback'—but could he find a horse?

Section 8.7.4 To Salvage a Revolution

But, that was before.

Could Britain have done anything after the failed attempt on Hitler's life to help W salvage its 'Revolution'? There was a ray-of-hope, but could W rely on a vague promise of their intervention? Was it sham or substance?

It was a matter of interpretation. Will this futile attempt qualify as the 'show of good faith' they were supposedly on the lookout for? True, the 'Revolt' in Berlin was over in record time, but all was not lost. At this stage, the apparent success of the uprising in Paris bought some time for what was left of W's leadership. While the revolt was still alive, there was time for Britain to make its move. But, how do you reconcile 'good show' with 'best that they fail'?

Even the PM couldn't do that. Maybe he was right. Maybe he didn't know how to get in touch with them after all, but it does seem as though PM would rather treat W as a faceless monolith. He really didn't want to know who they were, or how to get in contact with them.

A Britain prepared for such an eventuality, might have been able to take full advantage of the 'turmoil and confusion' rampant in OBWest, but they had to move like-lightning before the impact of the revolt wore off, if it was to do W any good.

Realistically, though, without prior establishment of 'lines of communication', it would have been difficult to synchronize operations between the Allied Army in Normandy and von Kluge's HQ. But, there is little evidence that the English ever had any intention of even 'lifting a finger' to assist W, regardless of what transpired.

The British never understood that by helping W they were helping themselves. The 'enterprise' was never an 'Anglo-W' operation, but an Anglo-'hostage Europe' affair. W was only the 'tool' for accomplishing Allied objectives: Eliminating Hitler; bringing a quick end to the war; liberating occupied Europe; freeing the POWs, emptying the CCs, and minimizing Allied casualties—civilian, as well as military.

In a way, the 'collapse' took everyone off the hook, but it left hostage-Europe dangling, to fend for itself. The people in 'occupied Europe'; the soldiers penned up in POW cages, the hapless denizens of the CCs were now compelled to wait for the inevitable Allied victory before their harrowing ordeal would finally be over.

Section 8.7.5 The Reaction of the Senior German Generals

The Field Marshalls and Senior Generals were strangely silent. No Sr. General, in command of a Field Army stepped forward in support of the Provisional Government. Unfortunately, the Generals in W were the main problem. Their errors in judgment proved catastrophic.

Apart from Col Stauffenberg, the most critical jobs fell to Col Gen E. Fellgiebel, the Chief of Signals, and Col Gen P. von Hase, the Military Commandant of Berlin. Col Gen Fellgiebel was in the Wolfs-Lair when Col S struck; his task was to telephone Berlin immediately the results of the explosion and then seal off FHQ from the rest of Germany.

Some say that no word came from *Rastenberg* to WHQ in Berlin, but others assert that W was informed on 1330 hour that Hitler was alive. Bewildered as to what to do next, they waited for the return flight of Col S.

But, Col S actually knew less than they did. Likening the explosion to a direct hit from a 155mm shell, he insisted that Hitler was killed. It was unnerving to learn that he had survived the blast. Whatever, nearly 3 crucial hours elapsed, between the explosion and the activation of Op Valkyrie.

Col Gen Beck had to get on the 'air' before Hitler did. W had been lax in not using the pretext of Valkyrie, to set-up a transmitter in the *Bendlerbloc*. His famous, "Tyranny is dead . . ." speech to the *Deutsche Volk*, had to wait for the takeover of the Communication Center in Berlin.

The 'Home Army' was the military arm of the Revolt in Berlin. Ostensibly, it was under W's firm control. Col Gen von Hase was responsible for the seizure of the Communication Center and the protection of WHQ in the Bendlerstrasse. He dispatched the crack Guards Battalion, with a known Nazi sympathizer at the helm, to the Rundfunk. Its seizure ended in a disaster, and as for leaving the Bendlerbloc undefended, what can one say?

B had had his doubts about the Home Army; Would the zeal of the Deputy cancel the lack of enthusiasm of the Chief? Col Gen Fromm, at first non-committal, turned on W with a vengeance when things went sour. Betraying his trust, he arrested the leaders and summarily had some of them executed.

Knocked out of action, during a strafing attack on 17 July, the loss of FM Rommel was a bad break for W. But, quixotically, FM von Kluge, who had relieved von Rundstedt on 2 July, took sole command of OBWest. Although not a member, W had reason to believe that he was favorably disposed to their plans. He had been in-and-out of the conspiracy for years. Which way will he jump now?

(It is ironic, that neither of these FMs, would join W, but they might just as well have, since they both were 'dead men' anyway. Ultimately, they suffered the same fate as the conspirators.)

Section 8.8 Aftermath

Section 8.8.1 Window of July

It will be the last time that they will meet together officially to talk about the 20th of July and its aftermath. B and GP enter Dir's office. His orderly, who had prepared a nice little spread, took their requests, and 'set up a round'.

GP felt so low, that (as Fred Allen, the radio and early TV comedian, might have put it) he could 'walk under a snake, with a high-hat on'. "Leave the bottle on the table. If there was ever a time to get drunk, it was now."

Dir had been busy perusing the latest communiqués from the front.

"The 'Battle of Normandy' is over. We and the Americans are following up their respective breakouts from Caen and St. Lo". He walked over to a wall map of Northern France. Sweeping his hand over the map, he traced their movements. "It appears that Monty is taking the high-road, while Patton, fanning out from Avranches, takes the low-road, swinging eastwards to the Seine valley. I presume that von Kluge will pull back as fast as he can to avoid encirclement." Smiling, he whistles an 'air', "The Allies are breaking out all over."

The month of July—what a memorable month that was! At the beginning of the month the Germans were fighting like tigers, making us pay dearly for every step, but, at the end of the month, they were fleeing like scared rabbits. Surrendering in droves, they were straining the capacity of the Allied POW camps. What happened in the interim to break the morale of the German Army?

Section 8.8.2 Side-effects

The 'Revolt' had come and gone, but its impact on the future conduct and course of the war lingered. Teams of SS and SD operatives scoured the land in search of anyone associated with the conspiracy. The destruction of the German High Command, begun in earnest in 1937, was completed in the weeks following 20 July 1944. This was accompanied by a purge of non-Nazi officers further weakening an already debilitated German Army. The Wehrmacht was virtually denuded of non-Nazi Generals. (And there still are some Allied chauvinists—particularly American—who blithely tell us that the 'Revolt' had no palpable effect on the war!)

FM Rommel was out of course, but how long would von Kluge hang in there?

Section 8.8.3 A Toast

Of course, they were overjoyed by the spectacular progress of the Allied forces. Dir raises his glass. "To the Allies." "Hear, hear."

"But, specifically, what do we have to celebrate?"

GP had perfunctorily drained his glass, but his heart wasn't in it.

Sensing his discomfiture, B reminds GP, "We feel as you do, but a basic rule of Intelligence is: Never allow yourself to become personally involved."

"We could drink a toast to the joint Anglo-W enterprise—potentially the most exciting and decisive single operation in the war—that never 'got off the ground'."

Dir sighed:

"We have little to be ashamed of, but of much to be proud. We struggled mightily against time, and an overwhelming opposition to the 'enterprise'. Finishing his drink, Dir stopped for a moment before resuming his little speech:

"It all made perfect sense to us, but, regrettably, not to them. SOE's powerful, irrefutable arguments, painstakingly developed, all came to naught. They failed the 'big test'!"

B noted, "It's almost surreal". He had the impression that they were talking to themselves, going around in circles, unable to draw the British Government into the loop. "It was as if we were in separate 'universes', and there was no way to cross-over."

"Yes, my friend, simply put, FO wasn't interested in W's diplomacy; Monty wasn't interested in their military strategy; and the PM wasn't interested in W's political agenda. In fact, they weren't interested in anything we had to say. Already the enterprise has been relegated to being—or so they would have the world believe—just another 'minor episode'—a footnote to WWII.

"Is it my imagination, or is nobody talking about it anymore? There is little, if any, mention of it in the popular press." (And so it remained, until well after the war ended in May 1945, when documents pertinent to the 'Revolt of the Generals' became readily available to scholars, and a very, very different picture emerged.).

Section 8.8.4 Post-mortem

Dir stopped. The orderly (who must have been a mind reader) quickly came in with refills. "If it wasn't so deadly serious, we could settle back, and have a good laugh."

"For a minute, we thought that what we said and did meant something in 'the scheme of things'. For a while it looked as if we and W might leave our mark in history."

GP retorted," Who cares about history? It is the fate of hostage-Europe that worries me. It isn't often that one gets the chance to save millions. We had ours, but the 'enterprise' ended in unmitigated disaster, much worse than any of us ever imagined."

Adding to Dir's previous remarks, B points out that SOE and Official Policy diverged on the advisability of W pursuing the revolt on its own. But, if W elected to take that route, it was stressed that they follow SOE's dictum

"Once started, there is no turning back."

Despite assurances that W was ready for all emergencies, when the chips were down, it was unable to cope with adverse situations as they developed. Part of the problem was fundamental and part accidental. Unfortunately, W was the victim of both.

Colonel Stauffenberg was aware that the meeting at the Fuhrer's HQ in Rastenberg, was to take place in a large wooden-hut on a hot July day, with the windows wide open, and with only a single bomb in his briefcase, (the second one was jettisoned, as he left the compound) all of which would militate to mute the effect of the blast. But that was the plan, and there was nothing that could be done about it.

B rose from his chair and after a short peripatetic excursion, turned, and addressed us in his inimitable way, as if he were lecturing back at the University.

GP smiled. At one time, this posturing annoyed him but he had learned to appreciate his idiosyncrasies.

As his won't, B pontificated: "Assassination does not a Revolution make. (. . . nor iron bars a cage." Our thanks to the Elizabethan poet, Mr. R. Lovelace.) W focussed too much on Hitler's demise and too little on the nuts-and-bolts of the revolution. As an assassin's tool, an 'explosion is basically unsound' (excuse me, Mr. Thomas Hood). "Explosive systems generally require too many steps. Any miss-step, whether due to a miss-calculation or purely by chance, can botch-up the whole operation."

In Nov1939, the explosion scheme devised by Georg *Elser* failed because Hitler left the Munich *Brauhaus* early.

A Focke-Wulfe Condor flying Der Fuhrer back from a meeting with FM von Kluge, CIC Army Group Center, in Russia, March1943, to Berlin, carrying explosives packed in a 'liqueur box', timed to detonate in mid-air, misfired.

B mistrusted explosives. It's one thing to throw-a-bomb, so that it acts like an aimed-missile but quite another to plant-a-bomb and hope that the intended victim (in the explosion area) will be killed by the blast."

Yet, on the 20th of July, 1944, immortalized as the 47th attempt on Hitler's life, everything, apparently, went off like clockwork. Yet, Hitler survived the blast, but Colonel Stauffenberg did not know it!

Col S had every reason to think that he had succeeded.

However, a basic flaw (in the plan)—

There was no way that he could know for sure the effect of the explosion in the hutment.-

Combined with the following unpredictable act—

The briefcase was inadvertently moved from the position where the Colonel had left it, to a place where Hitler was partially shielded from the full force of the explosion.-

Conspired to 'dash W's hopes!.

(Who ever heard of a bomber without a radio?) Well, the He111 carrying Colonel S back to Berlin didn't have one. This meant that for the crucial first three hours at the start of the rebellion, he was out-of-contact with WHQ.

Why procrastinate, while waiting anxiously for his return? He knew less than they did. All that he could do was repeat: "It was as if the hut was struck by a 155 mm shell." He insisted that Hitler was killed, but upon his arrival in Berlin, to his dismay, he learned otherwise.

GP listened to the exchange between Dir and B. He had no patience for their cool post-mortem. While they seemed to have no problem stamping—finis—to the episode, he had a tough time coming to terms with the events.

"Yes, we did all we could but that does not remove the stigma from our-side."

GP quipped: *"I'll tell you one thing. With the British contingent present, W wouldn't have been so quick to throw-in-the-towel!"*

Section 8.8.5 Tyranny is dead!

As it was, the Revolt had no staying power. The German People weren't given any time to absorb what was happening, nor to choose sides. It was all over. Inside, GP was devastated. Keenly aware of having left hostage-Europe in the lurch, he just couldn't let go. He had a vision and it was trashed by events. Although unfit for combat duty, he imagined himself accompanying the British detachment on its mission.

"I wanted to see the expression on the 'little Doctor's face' as he opened the door to the Propaganda Ministry and stared down the muzzle of a Sten-gun (which insolently, stared right back at him).

After securing the Central Communications Center they scurried to take up their position on the *Bendlerstrasse*.

"In my vision, I bounded up the stairs to Col Gen L. Beck's office in the Bendlerbloc. I heartily saluted him, and congratulated the others in W. "Escorted by us to the Rundfunk, he delivers his famous speech outlining the 'Rights of the German people' in the new post-war Germany, as per the Manifesto".

Everybody in Germany knows of that savage, unprincipled, demagogue, Adolf Hitler, but who is this General Beck who has the audacity to challenge the 'Leadership of the Third Reich'? In July 1944, a relative unknown, even within the German Army, and certainly to the populace-at-large, he had to identify himself. He had to gain their confidence and support for the 'Revolt of the Generals'.

"My friends, the German people. Let me introduce myself. I am Colonel General L. Beck, erstwhile Chief of the Great German General Staff. Today, I am interim Head of the Provisional Government of a 'new, and more glorious Germany' that we can all be proud of. "As some of you may recall, after vigorously protesting Hitler's Rearmament plans and Foreign Policy—while still at peace with our neighbors—I resigned my position as Chief of the General Staff on 18 August 1938. I invited the other generals to join me, but they elected—or were coerced—to 'follow Der Fuhrer'.

Now after five years of relentless and debilitating warfare, we can step back and leisurely gaze on Hitler's achievements: inexorably, his policies brought the entire world down on us, causing the destruction of the once invincible Wehrmacht, and utter devastation to our beloved *Vaterland*. The amount of pain, suffering, and death, which the Nazis unleashed on Europe, is beyond comprehension. That the German Army could have, unwittingly or otherwise, been accomplices to such cruel, ignominious, despicable crimes defies imagination."

Yes, I desperately wanted to hear Beck's oration. I wanted to hear him announce triumphantly—"The 'Allies are on our side! They have thrown their unqualified support behind W's efforts to overthrow the Nazis, and restore sanity to the world. If you meet Allied soldiers in the street—greet them. They are our comrades . . . They have joined us in the great struggle to free Germany and hostage-Europe from Nazi oppression . . . We have waited too long. We should have stopped this fiend many years ago. and spared Europe senseless carnage and slaughter . . . Only we can liberate Europe; only we can partially atone for the monstrous crimes of the Nazis. Only we can end the war today and rid Germany and Europe of this chimera forever!"

The news spreads rapidly—like a 'firestorm' ignited by a 'thousand Lancaster bombers'—over Germany, creating an unstoppable upsurge in support for the Provisional Government.

"I saw all this clearly in my vision, but in the real world, dreams don't count."

It was not to be!

"I don't know what went through von Hase's mind when he entrusted the Guards Battalion, commanded by a Major E. Remer (not a member of the conspiracy) with the vitally important assignment of cordoning off the government quarter of Berlin. (Count Heldorf, the prefect of police, a co-conspirator, had repeatedly warned that he was 'unreliable'. Why take chances? There was no dearth of officers, loyal to W, who would have been eager to lead the Battalion.) Be that as it may, he would probably have carried out his assignment, without question, (The German Army was great for 'following orders'—the 'Der Hauptmann von Koepernik' syndrome.) if not for an alert fanatically pro-Nazi junior officer on his staff. Noticing, what seemed to him to be an upsurge of 'military activity' in Berlin and ever mindful of a possible Putsch, he persuaded Remer to visit Goebbels, who connected him directly with the slightly injured Fuhrer in Rastenberg; Promoted on the spot to Colonel, Remer's men captured the WHQ in the Bendlerbloc.

Unbelievable! W mobilized the 'Home Army' to take possession of the Communication Center. and to protect WHQ, but Hitler turned the tables on the conspirators and used the Guards Battalion to deny W access to the Radio Broadcasting Station and seize the Bendlerbloc. Far from being the 'military arm' of W, in its only significant action, the Home Army deserted W and brought about the precipitate downfall of the Conspiracy. Incredulous? But—sad to say—true. The `Revolt' in Berlin had collapsed!

Berlin was a disaster for W, but everything was in place to succeed in Paris. The war, of course, was marching-on; with Operations Greenwood (7/18/44) and Cobra (7/25/44), the Allies positioned themselves to sweep the Germans out of Northern France. But, Hitler had his own ideas. Not acting immediately after 20 July 1944, boomeranged on FM G. von Kluge, He had his hands full. Overburdened, he had to cope with the Allies and, simultaneously, execute Hitler's orders to retake Avranches, and split the British and American forces (e.g., the First Battle of the Bulge.).

It's a fact! For a couple of days in the middle of August,1944, von Kluge was 'missing' from his headquarters, at *Le Roche Guyon*. Earlier, on several occasions, Col Gen *Stuelpnagel*, and others, before 20 July, had demonstrated that it was possible to make contact with the Allies in the field. Some say that von Kluge had disappeared in order to attend a pre-arranged meeting with British operatives to discuss a cease-fire and a general withdrawal of the German Army—*ala* 1918—from the Western Front, but the British did not show.

On 8/16, F.M. von Kluge was relieved of his command of OBWest, and replaced by FM W. Model. He was recalled to Berlin; however, en route, he took poison. (Did these events actually occur as recounted here? Conflicting evidence, and interpretation, surrounds this affair. What really transpired will forever remain as one of the many 'unsolved mysteries' of WWII.)

In summing up, GP said to B, "You were right from the start, Sir. You sized up the situation, and immediately put your finger on the problem. Before W could hope to succeed, they had to shed their 'sense of despair' that permeated all their actions, and to discard this fatalism that dogged all their ventures. This is where we came in. They really couldn't do it without us. It was not merely a case of manpower, but more of morale and reliability."

B mused: *They couldn't make so many mistakes, and fail so many times purely by accident—but—as the ancient Greeks knew—something beyond our comprehension must have been at work.*

Section 8.9 A secret meeting

Section 8.9.1 A crisis

Three men met privately in a secluded, little used, dimly lit room in Downing St. Barely visible to each other, they were ensconced in large roomy chairs, so comfortable that the mere act of closing one's eyes could bring on a deep sleep.

"I've invited you gentlemen here to discuss a delicate matter which unless handled speedily, and with care, might lead to grave political consequences. The matter concerns W; its ill-starred venture; SOE and the Official Policy of the British Government."

The heavy-set man took a few puffs on his cigar, and continued, "As you know, SOE has far exceeded its mandate. Some might say that it has been guilty of meddling in the 'Affairs of State'. We could hit them with violating the Official Secrets Act but that might precipitate a messy scandal.

"Fortunately, there are relatively few people who are acquainted with these events, and fewer still who could link them with the Revolt of the German generals."

"Very few? How many are we talking about?" asked the distinguished looking gentleman.

"Although there is widespread opposition to Un Su, the principals engaged in vigorously pushing the Anglo-W enterprise are the Director, the Head of the German Resistance Desk, B, and their Pilot, GP.

"B seems to have been the prime mover, but he was constantly being prodded by GP—who couldn't possibly believe that we would hold back from seizing this opportunity afforded us by W."

The 'host' flicked the cigar ash into a tray, and proceeded darkly, "The question is what is to be done with them? All rumblings must be nipped in the bud. No one is to know the extent of SOE's involvement with W. Aside from information already cleared for public consumption, all reference must be expunged from the Official Record."

"I see what you mean. These events never happened." said the Foreign Secretary.

"Reports filtering through, tell us that a fearful vengeance has befallen W."

Angrily, PM continues, "Certain prominent members of your Department have been extremely vituperative in denouncing the GGs in W. Tone down the rhetoric. These courageous men deserve admiration, not condemnation, from us."

Wincing, the Foreign Secretary replied, "I'm sorry, but you must realize that we are ardent supporters of Un Su, and it would have been catastrophic for our post-war European policy, if W had succeeded. As much as I disapprove of SOE's actions, and despite their violation of our security laws, OSA, we can afford to be magnanimous."

The heavy-set man thought for a few moments, then turned to the other man, "You are the thaumaturgist here, what do you propose we do to make the problem disappear?"

"My vigorous opposition to SOE is well-known. I've certainly had my differences with Dir.

While it is true that he has transgressed, and as such should be held responsible, I can't help being impressed by his persistence and zeal."

The third man briefly reminded them of the clandestine meeting between the heads of MI6, OSS, and the Abwehr, in late 1943. He recalled how Un Su forced them to terminate their talks with Adm. Canaris.

For the same reason, the Dulles-Gisevious contact made no headway with the U.S. State Department in May 1944.

"I'm no fan of Un Su, but so long as it is Official Policy, we are duty-bound to support it. But, sometimes I wish that I had had the courage to challenge the establishment on that issue. Yes, I can 'play the magician', but there must be a less onerous way."

P.M. thanked the Foreign Secretary and 'C', for sharing their thoughts with him, but noted that the responsibility was his alone.

"As for us, this meeting will be our own 'little secret'. Remember our discussion must be held in strictest confidence. We will refrain from all mention of this episode. If pressed—improvise. Stick to the 'best that they failed' routine."

Section 8.9.2 Solution

They took their leave. He relaxed; it was rare that he had such an opportunity for self-reflection. He leaned back; closed his eyes, blew a few smoke rings, as he digested the comments tendered by his guests. He was gratified that they didn't expect him to hold SOE 'strictly accountable', to the letter-of-the-law. He rose and walked slowly about the room for a few minutes. Suddenly, he stopped; he had reached a decision. His peripatetics over, he sat down at a desk and quickly scribbled a terse characterization of each culprit.

Dir has submitted his resignation. A loyal subject to the crown, he takes his duties as seriously as we do. Despite his braggadocio, he is petrified at being brought up on charges. For his 'peace of mind', it is supposed that he would be delighted if the episode were forgotten.

B is a different matter. How is he to be kept quiet ? He yearns to return to the University. It is the business of a professor to write articles and books. Can he be trusted to suppress the urge 'to tell all'?

GP is a typical tough, gritty Tommy. He wants to return to his 'old outfit'. Right now he's fed up, but he is the sort of chap we want to keep in the post-war Army.

After disposing of the matter, the old-man stretched out in his chair, taking a few nervous chomps on his cigar. He wanted to savor the moment, but couldn't. Why was he so agitated?

"Bizarre, bizarre! I should be ecstatic. The news from the front couldn't be better. Monty has taken Caen, and smashed out of Normandy. COBRA has struck; Bradley has entered St. Lo and broken out of the Cotentin Peninsula. From Avranches, Patton's 3rd Army has fanned out, with its main thrust directed east-ward to the Seine. The enemy is in full retreat, as the Allies prepare to sweep the Germans out of France."

But, he couldn't get the thought of W and the '20th of July' out of his mind. Brooding, he muttered to himself, what he wouldn't say to anyone else (not even Clementine).

"The 'Battle of Britain' may have been England's finest hour, but our dastardly treatment of W must be our most shameful."

It grieved him greatly to think that his name would forever be linked with both!

The old corsair hesitated, and as if as an afterthought he ingenuously enquired:

"Would it really have been so terrible, if we had employed W as a 'tool' for achieving our war-aims?"

"True, W is German, but then again aren't we all?

Fantastic! Our Teutonic heritage stretches back over fifteen centuries and during that extremely long time interval we have had many occasions to work with them in the past".

A strong sense of family pride—difficult to contain—welled up within him at the thought of his great ancestor the First Duke of Marlborough teaming up with the Austrian Prince Eugene of Savgrowthoy to defeat the French in a series of spectacular victories as they battled Louis XIV of France for the hegemony of Europe, in the War of the Spanish Succession, during the reign of the 'good Queen Anne' (1702-12).[xv]

For the next 300 years, or so, the Churchill's have been actively engaged in British politics. In a way it is truly astonishing that the two most illustrious members of the Churchill clan were present in positions of leadership, power and influence at the crucial growth and decline stages, associated with the 'rise and fall' of the British Empire, respectively.

Whatever, as if to 'break the spell' his rotund face lit up and smiled: "It will be the next millennium before the remaining documents pertaining to the Anglo-W enterprise will be open to public scrutiny. By then the World will have other things on its mind, than this *Minor Incident in a Major War*' to worry about." He switched off the light and exited the room.

CHAPTER 9

60 plus Years Later

Section 9.1 Reprise

I looked around the club. The crowd had thinned out. It was late, and I was getting tired.

"That was an astounding story. I've heard many stories about aspects of WWII, but this was the most disconcerting.

"You were right. I agree that you were neither a *schicke* nor *mushugenah*."

"How's that?"

"My little joke—*Yiddishisms* for 'drunk nor mad'—but I think that you are being too harsh on your compatriots."

"I don't think so. If anything, I am too soft. There may have been a time during the war, when Abs Sil (01/41) and Un Su (01/43) made sense, but by the late stages of the struggle, they had long out-lived their usefulness. The only thing that 'slavish adherence' to the twin doctrines accomplished was to extend the duration of the war, and prolong the pain and suffering of those in hostage-Europe. The end of the war, though near, was still too far off for many of them to wait.

"Realistically, so long as the Germans were winning there was little hope of mounting an effective German Resistance movement."

I could see where he was heading. "That's not strictly true. Even in those years Hitler wasn't really winning. It was only an illusion. He had been stopped at Moscow (a fluke?) in '41, wiped out at Stalingrad, (a blunder?) in '42, and routed at Kursk, (a bad judgment call?) in '43. I helped him along by reminding him that the German Army was destroyed in three mammoth battles in Russia: code-named Operations Typhon, Blau, and Zitadele, perhaps more commonly known as the Battles of Moscow, Stalingrad, and Kursk, respectively.

GP brushed aside my remarks, and continued, "GG contended that Stalingrad (12/42-02/43) was the most propitious time to overthrow Hitler, but instead of vigorous Allied support, what did W get? Un Su! To the everlasting credit of the Heads of Allied Intelligence they did meet with Adm. Canaris in late 1943 to try to make something happen. But, how much negotiating can you do with Un Su hanging over your head? The Dulles-*Gisevious* contact followed, before D-Day, in May1944. These efforts were greeted by 'stony silence' in Washington and London.

I got up, stretched, and mulled over what he had just said. Obviously, he knew what he was talking about. Here I thought that I was something of an authority on the '20th of July', but on Anglo-W relations, I was no more than a tyro. Anticipating his line of thought, I said, "Let's look at the record. Chronology tells all: Succinctly put,

before 18 December'40, Hitler couldn't lose.

After 18 December'41, he couldn't win.

After18 July1943, the initiative passed over to the Grand Alliance. Once lost, it could never be regained."

GP acknowledged my comments and resumed his diatribe, "Despite the fact that the Wehrmacht was still an extremely formidable fighting force, from that time on, it was all downhill. The German Army never again launched a major offensive. By D-Day (6 June '44}, however, the Western Allies were facing a simulacrum of the once mighty Wehrmacht. Its effectiveness had dropped faster than an 'internet stock' during the collapse of the hi-tech bubble on the NASDAQ at the end of the twentieth century.

"The Allies no longer had anything to fear from the Nazis; with their overwhelming superiority in men, machines, and material, they were free to pursue their 'War Aims' with gusto: eliminate Hitler; bring a quick end to the war; liberate occupied Europe; free the POWs; empty the concentration camps, and minimize Allied losses (civilian, as well as military)."

Section 9.2 Thunderclap

The Allies were fond of saying that casualties were the 'price of victory'. But, the fact is that the Allied High Command was acutely concerned with Allied losses. Monty repeatedly said that to shorten-the-war by a single day is worth everyone's utmost effort. The war was dragging on—the casualties were mounting, the public, restless, and the military, uneasy—as the Allies desperately groped for an abrupt end to the war. Hence Project Thunderclap. In a last ditch effort to demonstrate the validity of the 'Douhet Doctrine' (*'Command of the Air'* (1921) by the Italian Air General, *Giulio Douhet*), British Air Marshal 'Bomber' Harris (the architect of night-time saturation-bombing of densely populated civilian areas)

sold the RAF and the USAAF on the 'Fire-bombing of Dresden' (02/45) as the means of delivering the one-punch-knockout blow to the Third Reich, but it fell short in achieving its objective.

Convinced that the invasion of Japan would be very costly in American lives, Pres. H. Truman came to the same conclusion. However in the time-interval from (2/45) to (8/45) warfare had been changed forever. With the advent of the Atomic Bomb, a new chapter 'on War' was about to be written. He hastened the coming of 'Victory in Japan Day' by dropping the A-bomb, not just once on Hiroshima (08/45), but twice, on Nagasaki as well (a few days later).

In perspective, it is estimated that Dresden suffered from ten to thirty times the casualties incurred in NYC on 09/11/01 (some 3,000). As for the A-bombings there is no way to put their carnage in perspective. (These events occurred after those chronicled in this book.

However, in this regard, they undeniably show that the Allied leadership, obsessed by saving Allied lives, was thinking along the same lines as W. Yet the Allies did not support the W plan!)

It is evident that other more nefarious considerations were in play. The crux of the matter is that the Allies would do anything to shorten-the-war (no matter how heinous) rather than work with W.

Section 9.3 A Tale of Two Cities

Whew! That was quite an indictment.

"I never looked at it quite that way. I'm beginning to see what you mean. There are atrocities by commission, like the Nazis (e.g., overt oppression, persecution, and genocide) and there are atrocities by omission, like the British (e.g., indifference, neglect and duplicity).

"By leaving hostage Europe—especially those in the CCs—in the lurch, the British have a lot to account for. But, in their defense, they didn't engage, as a matter of policy, in war-crimes, and besides, they had a 'War to Win'."

GP listened to my comments, and fired back: "True, but the concatenation of events, created circumstances, where the Allies were caught in the middle. Like it or not they had to become involved.

This was not a spectator sport. The GGs in W committed themselves; they plunked a feasible plan down on the table, but it was hostage-Europe's so-called friends who balked."

Mesmerized by his saga, I had been loathe to interrupt. But, I had an irresistible urge, to put my two cents in, and give vent to my pent-up feelings. Supporting my head in my hands, I cried out, "What a colossal mess. What a convoluted story."

By itself, it would have made for an interesting tale. Who would have dreamt that the 'twin doctrines' could wreak so much havoc?

To avoid a general European war, the 'Appeasers' wanted the Allies to cave-in to Hitler's demands.

To avoid a general European war, the German Resistance to the Nazis wanted to oust Hitler. Intentionally, Absolute Silence (01/41), during the 'Battle of Britain', wanted to clamp down on the so-called 'Defeatists', who sought to make peace with Hitler.

Incredibly, and inexplicably, Unconditional Surrender (01/43) was used against W whose goal was the same as the Allies: to eliminate Hitler and bring a quick end to WWII.

The 'twin doctrines', elevated to dogma, severed all communication between Britain and W. This was interpreted to mean that Britain could play-the-ostrich, and abandon her obligations to hostage—Europe with impunity. Amazing! Ah! Why wouldn't W just go away?

Dropping my hands, I raised myself up and continued: "Let's see if I've got this straight. After Venlo, the British resolved, 'Beware of German generals bearing gifts.' At Casablanca, the two greatest Hitler fighters of the age, (in a startling reversal from prior statements) loudly proclaimed, for all the world to hear, that '*all* Germans are our enemies'. UnSu sounded great, but unwittingly, it was also a 'death warrant' for millions. Having been subjected to inconceivably inhumane treatment, the *worst atrocity was the refusal of the British to support the proposed Anglo-W efforts to bring an abrupt end to their ordeal.*" Furthermore, the British had no plans to exploit the ensuing chaos and breakdown of morale of German soldiers on the Western Front that must follow the 'Revolt of the Generals'.

"Moreover," I continued ominously, "It sounds duplicitous to me."

Why be surprised? To the amazement of all, W acted in good faith, but the British didn't even consider intervention.

"Simply stated, they didn't live up to their end of the bargain, causing one to conclude that they had no intention of 'raising a finger to help them' regardless of what happened."

I really hadn't intended to lambaste the English, but the facts speak for themselves. After all, the plight of the inmates in the CCs, on the 16th of August was little changed from what it was on the 20th of July, and despite the smashing victory at the Falaise Gap, they had to wait—what to them must have seemed to be an eternity—before their torment and persecution would finally be over, and they could regain control of their lives.

This short declamation, left me exhausted, but it was GP's turn to be astonished, "That's about the size of it."

Smiling, he said, "B couldn't have put it better himself. I can see him rambling on in his unique pedantic style, "Harrumph! If *'Our Mutual Friend'* hadn't absconded with the name, the title, *"A Tale of Two Cities'* could be just as easily ascribed to the 'Revolution of the 20th of July' as it was to the 'French Revolution'."

The epic tale of 'how, what was supposed to have been, the most decisive action of the war, ended up as a footnote (to WWII) was finished. I have heard, and read. many stories about the war, but this was the most fantastic. Positively! GP was right; it was the 'last great story' to come out of WWII.

"All of these happened eons ago, but it hurts every time I think of it." Looking back in anger, he had stricken the entire episode from his mind. However, over the years GP had mellowed somewhat and was now able to view those events dispassionately.

"I have even taken to reading some of the more recent definitive histories written on the subject."

Conversationally, I (e.g., the author) recalled how this episode first piqued my interest. "I remember reading a brief article on it in the *'Stars*

232

and Stripes'. It didn't make any impact on me at all. Many years later, while browsing in one of the many second-hand bookstores located on 4th Ave in NYC, I ran across a paperback on the plot to assassinate Hitler.

"The store had a collection of these cheap paperbacks; hurriedly and poorly written, half-truths, that flooded the market, of the 'How I almost won the war single-handedly' variety. There I first read about the exploits of a Colonel Stauffenberg. It was an interesting tale, but a failed plot by some GGs to 'shut down the war' seemed hardly credible. I thought no more about it, until, quite by accident, I came across J. Wheeler-Bennett's *Nemesis of Power* '(1961 ed.) This excellent book presented a thorough 'History of the German Army, and its place in German Society' from the 'Treaty of Versailles' to the end of WWII'.

It rekindled my interest, in 'my war', and in particular in the 'Revolt of the Generals'. There have been enough books written on WWII, to fill a small library and shelves of them have been devoted to the ill-starred 'enterprise'. I must have perused (or at least thumbed through) a fair percentage of them, but references to combined Anglo-W operations were generally from sparse to non-existent."

To cover up their abominable treatment of W, the Allies tried to suppress their failure to act by belittling the 20th of July and characterizing it as a non-event.

Ike's memoir, *'Crusade in Europe'*, makes short shrift of the plot, but, significantly, a biographer (M. Miller, *Ike the Soldier*) was careful to point out that it had just about `zero impact' on the war'. In a British contribution N. Hamilton's biography of the FM—Monty and the

PM engage in some tom-foolery—but one is hard-put to see what the hilarity is all about.

Although military historians had long pondered on the devastating effect of the 'Plot' on the German 'will to resist', it waited for the bio, *'Monty, the Lonely Leader'* (1994) by A. Horne and D. Montgomery (Monty's son), to set the record straight, give credit, where credit is due, and proper recognition to W's contribution—a half-century after the event! (During the war, JWB and other staunch proponents of Un Su, endorsed the FO official policy, as expressed by the FS's private secretary, to the effect that 'Britain's enemies are both the Nazis and the Generals'; that we should make peace with neither, and that it is to our interest that the 'coup fail'. (see N. Annan, *'Changing Enemies'*).

As if in atonement, he wrote the above-mentioned book, extolling W, but he couldn't resist trying to justify his wartime position with the old refrain—it was *'best that they failed'.*)

To this very day, the story, inexplicably, still holds a magnetic-grip on the reader's imagination. Upon finishing a book on the '20th of July' you, my dear reader, closes the volume but cannot put it down. You are left unsatisfied. You shut your eyes, lean back and think. There seems to be something missing. It didn't have to end this way. Nothing ever broke right for W—and if it seemed to—it was really a 'trap' in disguise.

But, alas, no matter how many different books on the subject, you read; how desperately you want them to succeed; how you try to point out ways to avoid the pitfalls and blunders, the ending is always the same: Colonel General L. Beck a suicide and Colonel K. Stauffenberg gunned down by a firing-squad in the courtyard of the *Bendlerblock*).

Section 9.4 Arch-Cynic

July1944 had been a rough time for all of them. At times the stress was almost unbearable, and they had 'weathered' markedly, during the interval surrounding the incident. Dir had staked his reputation, B his intellectual integrity, and GP all his hopes on the Anglo-W coalition.

"I admired Dir, but I really liked B Dir, the arch-cynic—whose favorite aphorism was that the Cynic is right 90% of the time.—got caught up in the idealism of the 'Great Enterprise'. He was supremely confident in his ability to navigate the' treacherous waters of intrigue' on the way to its adoption.

"B, the philosopher, unabashedly followed wherever logic led him. He strove to remain aloof, but was trapped by the irrefutable logic of his own powerful arguments."

"But what about you? How did you survive the ordeal?" He was reluctant to talk about himself, but I prodded him. "You were a naive, starry-eyed optimist, certain that everything, despite the plethora of difficulties surrounding the 'enterprise', would eventually fall into place. How could you keep your hopes up-so-high as the 'flow of events' unfolded."

He shrugged his shoulders. "Because it was the right-thing-to-do and the right-way-to-go."

"Yeah, I know. As King Richard II tells us, "Heaven still guards the Right."—and we all know what happened to him.

I noted that he and Dir had switched sides; in the end, Dir was the idealist, while he was the cynic." GP laughed (It was good to hear him laugh; there hadn't been much humor in his 'doleful yarn'). "You've got it—except for one little thing: after this wretched business, the cynic's odds jump to 95%."

Section 9.5 Protagonists

GP glanced at his watch. Sensing that he might be getting ready to leave, I quickly enquired, "What happened to the protagonists in your saga?"

"Well, Dir submitted his resignation, but it wasn't accepted. To avoid the appearance of dissension, in the Tory leadership, he was asked to stay on until SOE was disbanded in 01/46. With a profound sense of relief, he accepted the PM's offer. He was subsequently knighted for his long record of outstanding service. B never did return to the University, and resume work on his 'magnum opus', "A Comparative Discourse on the Generalship of Gustavus Adolphus, King of Sweden, Leader of the Protestant Cause; Albrecht Wallenstein, (Duke of Mecklenberg, Sagan, and Friedland, Prince of the Holy Roman Empire), Generalissimo of the Imperial Army; and Johann Tserclais, Count Tilly, the 'Brabanter', Lieutenant. General of the Catholic League, during the Thirty Years War (1618-1648)."

"But, he was recruited for a Senior Administrative position with the British Control Commission. While carrying out his duties in the British Zone, his jeep ran over an anti-vehicle *Teller*-Mine buried in the road and was killed.

(I was saddened by the news.

From GP's description he must have been quite a man. I appreciated his wit and his epigrammatic style—modeled after the writings of the famous Roman author Marcus Martial (40-104 AD). In particular, as a retired professor, I—like him—enjoyed spicing-up my lectures with references from the classics and the contemporary popular media.)

"As for myself, I only wanted to rejoin my 'old outfit'. Of course, my wounds at that time, precluded my return as a glider pilot, but with a few good words from B and Dir, I was assigned to Sect G-2 (Intelligence) of the 1st Division, just in time for the disasters at Arnheim (09/44), and to a much lesser extent, at Wesel (03/45), after rejoining the 6th Div.

"You know, for over 50 years, I've wondered: Did those fiascos mark paid to Monty's refusal to risk a brigade on behalf of the proposed joint Anglo-W enterprise? All I can say is that they lost a heck of a lot more men in those aforementioned Airborne operations, which, at the time, were advertised as vital, but were really unnecessary.

"After six-years of warfare, with the 'new found egalitarianism' of C. Attlee and the Labor party, combined with my wartime-experiences, and a recommendation from the ex-PM (or so I was told), I was belatedly admitted to Sandhurst, to become an Intelligence Officer—and a Gentleman! Imagine me a 'gentleman'. Struck by the humor of the situation, we both laughed: "I guess that you had finally overcome your fear of 'high-ranking Officers'."

"Actually, I had outgrown that phobia, during the dark days of our struggle for the 'Great Enterprise' back in 1944, when I saw that many of them knew less than I did, about the war."

"Ain't it the truth. It is one of Hiram's maxims that the 'Understanding and Knowledge of Warfare' varies inversely with military rank."

Section 9.6 London by Night

.He had finished his narrative, but he still hadn't told me what I wanted to know. Off-handedly, I quickly asked, "What about GG and the girl?"

He hesitated. I feared the worst, but he simply shrugged, and gesticulating with his hands, replied, "Ah, that's a long story."

"Can't you give me an abridged version?"

"Hang on a little longer. The strangest part is yet to come."

"I don't doubt it—but frankly, I've had enough for one evening. What could possibly be more amazing than what I 've just heard? Why should I listen to this?"

"Because it is True."

Smiling inwardly, I thought, sardonically, *"A double-feature! This is my lucky day, If the sequel, is as fascinating as the original, I don't want to miss a word of it, But, right now, I couldn't take another session."*

My meeting was scheduled for the next day, and I craved my beauty sleep. I was tired: the drinks made me drowsy. 'I'm not so young, as I used to be', as the Scottish music-hall entertainer Harry Lauder, used to say, and I was struggling to keep awake.

More and more frequently, I find myself taking an unintended nap at the movies, or while watching TV, or even at the concert-hall—not from boredom, since I am a classical music enthusiast, particularly of the great Baroque composers—hooray for Handel!—so I girded myself against dozing off, as he regained his second wind.

Over my protestations, he launched into part two of his story. Disgruntled, with an empty glass in hand, I slumped into my chair as he droned on, "It was 'Springtime in Bavaria'. Awestruck, one could only marvel at the rugged beauty of the terrain. It was a mystery why the Germans felt compelled to covet the land of their neighbors, not nearly as well endowed by nature. The Third Army had been driving relentlessly through France, from the breakout at St. Lo (07/25/'44) to the Rhine River, which was crossed by Patton's forces about eight months later. (Patton won the bet. He pissed into the Rhine before Montgomery.) Once across the Rhine, it was full-speed-ahead into Bavaria. After this wild-ride, the 3rd Army took a well-earned rest, as they readied for the final push of the war, crossing Czechoslovakia into the Danube Valley.

"Two Germans, a man and a woman, approached along a country—lane leading up to the field HQ.of one of Patton's toughest infantry divisions. The man, although bent over somewhat, was rather tall, but looked as though he had seen better days. The young woman's step was light and springy as she strove to keep up with him . . .

Startled, I was shaken awake by one of the 'cleaning women', "Excuse me Sir, but the gentleman you were with left you this letter". I thanked her, opened the envelope, and read his brief message.

"I was half-through my with my rendition when I realized that I was talking to myself. "Sorry to have put you to sleep, old chap, but I wasn't aware of the extraordinary soporific power of my tale. You looked so comfortable that I hadn't the heart to interrupt your slumbers. It's a shame that you are in no condition to hear the rest of it, but take it from me, it's a terrific story. We will have to continue this tete-a-tete some other time.

The complete 'Adventures of GG and the Girl' will have to wait until we meet again. It will give us something to talk about."

I was disappointed, "Oh well. Until then." I raised my empty-glass. "I'll drink to that."

I went into the men's room, refreshed myself, and exited the club. The streets were largely deserted, and I decided to walk back to my hotel. Invigorated by the cool late-night (early-morning?) air, the brisk stroll did me a world of good. I took the elevator to my room on the 24th floor. Staring out the window, I was greeted by the magnificent spectacle of 'London by Night'.

Hypnotized by the view, I searched 'through-out the panorama—not for a 'sign of Royal Gamma' (Princess Ida's father)—but to amuse myself by identifying some of the more prominent landmarks that I recognized: The Thames, the bridges, Big Ben and the Houses of Parliament, and other tourist sites that were readily made out.

I don't know why, but, with a smile, I warmly recalled a trip, many years ago to the now defunct Soviet Union, where as a guest of the Siberian Academy of Sciences, I presented a technical paper at the XI International Symposium on Non-Linear Acoustics, in Novosibirsk, Siberia (sound's impressive, if you say it fast).

The meeting over, my wife and I took a side-trip to Moscow, where we stayed at the 'Cosmos', an immense tourist complex. Anxious to get settled down in our room, and then to visit downtown Moscow, we seemed to be waiting an inordinate length of time in the lobby. It turned out that our taxi-cab driver (from the airport) assumed that we wanted an upper floor. The girl at the desk told him (in Russian, of course) that everybody wants one, and that we will have to wait. So here we were waiting for a an upper floor, that we couldn't use anyway.

The reason? My wife shuns elevators—She wouldn't take one in New York City—let alone Moscow. To make a long story short, without further ado, we were immediately given a room on the 4th floor, with a beautiful view of the yard, complete with clanking garbage cans, and an occasional 'blood-curdling scream' from a Moscow stray, outside the kitchen service entrance. But, I wasn't to be denied my birds-eye view of 'Moscow by Night'; that evening I simply took the elevator to the roof while Erika waited below.

I mused, "*Look at what I'd be missing, if I had dragged her along with me!*" I still had some lingering effects from the 'imbibing at the club'. The excursion to the hotel had cleansed the cobwebs from my mind, although subconsciously it was still digesting the evening's proceedings. The room had a small balcony. I went outside for a better view, and with a firm grip I clutched the guard-rail. Uncontrollably, I shouted out, so that not only London, but the entire world could hear—

"Just think! A thousand Schindler's lists!"

I went inside and fell across the bed, into a deep sleep.

But,

'A sadder, and a wiser man, I rose the morrow morn'.

Chapter 10

Springtime in Bavaria

Section 10.1 US 3rd Army Encampment, Bavaria, April 1945

Two Germans, a man and a woman approached along a country-lane leading up to the field HQ of one of General G. Patton's hard-fighting Infantry Divisions. A rather tall man, he was bent over somewhat, and, upon closer examination, looked as though he had seen (much) better days. The young woman's step was 'light and springy' as she strove to keep up with him.

There was a fair amount of activity going on. The war was rapidly grinding to a halt. What was left of the German Army was weak, disorganized, demoralized, and in total disarray. German soldiers were surrendering in droves—giving themselves-up to anyone who would take them prisoner.

The GIs were in good spirits. Although fraternization was banned, there were more than a few German civilians, mostly women, milling around. Some undoubtedly wanted to get an early start in doing 'business' and making useful contacts with the Americans.

Working their way towards the makeshift orderly room of C-company, they were stopped by First Sergeant D. "Where do you think you're going? This area is off-limits—you know—'Verboten'!."

The 1stSgt wasn't pleased at this mixing with Germans. He had given his men a pep-talk cautioning them against complacency. "Keep your wits about you, and don't forget to have your rifle handy at all times. Be extra-careful 'we don't want any more casualties'."

"Take me to your company-commander, I must see him, it's urgent."

"What about? You can tell me. I'll pass it along."

"Please, if you don't mind this is for him alone."

His first impulse was to kick them back into the road, but after thoroughly checking them out (especially the girl) for concealed weapons, he knocked on CO's door.

Relaxed, CO was lounging around, with his feet on his desk, aimlessly, throwing darts, at a dartboard hanging on the wall. This diversion, a staple in the English pubs, was enthusiastically adopted by the American troops. Dart contests were frequently held before the invasion. If they had stayed in England a little longer. they probably would have formed a 'Dart-throwing-league'. Who should enter, but his 1st Sgt.

"Don't you know better than to barge into my office, without waiting for an invitation?"

"Sorry about that, Sir", the Sgt laughed, "Haven't you heard? Such formalities went out of style when we hit-the-Continent." He and the Captain had been together for such a long time, they might just as well have been brothers.

"You've got a couple of visitors; a tough looking cookie, and a Fraulein who speaks pretty good English." (Pretty good? She spoke the King's English better than 90 percent of the guys in the outfit!)

"Yeah, what do they want?"

Lately, every time they stop and pitch camp, they get a delegation of Krauts with stories—every one of vital importance—but in the end they all turn out to be veiled requests for special treatment.

"She wouldn't say. Just said that it is urgent, confidential, and she needs your help right now."

He was curious: What variation of the *'me nichts Nazi'* routine would she use? Ha! In all of Germany, he never once ran into a Nazi ! "Show them in."

Literally, he` exploded' out of his chair'. He hadn't jumped so high, so fast, since Gen Patton paid a call—unannounced. He conceded: Germany has loads of good-looking Fraulein's. but not many as attractive—and she talks English, to boot.

"Just my luck, a girl like this stumbles into my tent, and we have to pull-up-stakes in a few days."

Quickly, he rearranges the papers on his desk. Picking up a few sheets, he glances over them. Feigning interest in their contents he takes out his pen, and initials the documents, (to lend some credence to an otherwise bald subterfuge). She watches his antics with amusement.

"Can't you see that I have a lot of work to do? What do you want from me? If you have some information to peddle, take it over to Battalion Intelligence; they get paid to listen to this stuff. Don't forget to tell them I sent you." Giving the girl the once-over, he adds with a lascivious leer, "I'm sure they can use another interpreter."

"You don't understand, I haven't the time to go through channels.

There is a saying in the German army that if you want something done in a hurry, go to the smallest unit that can do the job—and that's you."

Sarcastically, he replies, "Is that so? I never heard of it. Is that what they are teaching at the German General Staff School nowadays?"

She bit her lip. "Are you making fun of me?"

"What? Me an officer in the U.S. Army taking advantage of a gorgeous Fraulein? Never!"

"This is not a laughing matter." Quietly (aside) he adds, "*War never is.*"

"This is not the time for 'playful banter', the lives of many brave men are at stake."

Taken aback by the ominous tone in her voice, he says, "Slow down. The war will be over in a matter of weeks."

"Yes, but these men may not be around for more than a few days."

Grumbling that he is very busy, he signals for her to continue. But before she could say anything, he suddenly interrupted, "I'm reasonably certain that you are not a Nazi, but don't tell me that he isn't one either."

CO walked over, and closely inspected him. "He looks like a soldier to me. What happened to his uniform? Where did he get those civvies? Where are his papers? How come he isn't up-front giving his 'Alles fur Adolf'?"

"You Americas have all the answers. You talk too fast for me. You are right: '*me nichts Nazi*' and neither is he." CO suppressed a grin, as she went on, "Let me start the story at the beginning, and please don't interrupt."

Annoyed at her abrupt change in attitude, he motions her to sit down. Answering brusquely, he retorts, "Get to the point, and make it short." Chastened by his rebuke, she replies contritely, "Okay. I'm ready." "Get on with it, I'm listening."

Section 10.2 Special Prisoners

There is a Concentration Camp nearby at Flossenberg on the German-Czech border. As the Allies have been over-running the CCs, the Nazis have been transferring the inmates to more secure camps. Many of these inmates did not survive the brutal marches. Recently, however, a number of Special Prisoners have been trucked into Flossenberg and Dachau. Amongst them are some who were connected with the German Resistance to Hitler.

"Did you ever hear of the 20th of July, 1944 'Plot to kill Hitler'?"

"July 1944? That's ancient history."

She gave a brief review of the aims and aspirations of the of the conspirators, and the disastrous end to the 'Plot'.

"But, now that you mention it, I did see a couple of paragraphs in the *'Stars and Stripes'* about a power struggle amongst the Generals that ended badly for some of them. Whatever did happen to those guys?"

"It would make things a lot easier, if you had heard of the *'Widerstand'* as the anti-Nazi Resistance movement in Germany came to be called.

The Captain shrugged.

"A-lot of those guys, as you contemptuously put it, whom the Gestapo could get in their clutches, were rounded-up, tortured, tried and executed.

"But, there were a few of them, caught-up in the dragnet, who for lack of hard evidence, were nevertheless, kept in custody, in certain Concentration Camps. These camps, had a block of individual cells, usually bordering the perimeter of the main camp, reserved for the so-called 'privileged', or Special Prisoners. A 'Special Prosecutor' from Berlin has arrived. That's strictly bad news."

"What's the big hurry. If he just came, it will take a-while for the accused to prepare their defense . . ."

"Defense? Are you naive! SS Standartfuhrer Huppenkothen is coming with warrants for their execution in his pocket."

"So why bother with this charade?"

"Everything must be done legally, according to the 'Laws of the Third Reich'; the Nazis are sticklers for that."

Section 10.3 Ci-devant Panzer Commander

"How come that you are so familiar with all this?" She dreaded that question. This was the crucial point in the interview. Will it turn him off, or will he be sufficiently intrigued to let her continue? How to put this in a favorable light? She had to trust someone. Without further hesitation she decided—tell the Truth!

"M here is a security guard at *Flossenberg.*"

"A CC guard!" Instinctively he reaches for his '45. "These CC guards are on the Allies 'most wanted list'. You've got your nerve, bringing this thug onto a US Army compound. I should turn you both in."

"Don't be so melodramatic. He plays the key role in this mission. I had to bring him along. He knows full well that a CC guard is anathema to the Allies, but he insisted on accompanying me, and suffer the consequences (if need be). Listen to my story, then call for the MPs if you like."

CO mutters, "You may be right, but your tale better be a good one."

He places his weapon on the desk with the pistol-grip in easy reach of his right hand.

"How come that you, an implacable foe of the Nazis, are on such good terms with this cut-throat. He looks like a pretty tough customer to me."

"If you spent 3 years on the Russian Front you wouldn't look much better."

"Touché."

M a former tank commander was wounded twice—once during the retreat from Moscow, and again at the failed attempt to pinch-off the

Russian salient at Kursk. He was given a choice: return a third time, or relieve a CC guard for active duty at the Eastern Front. Reluctantly, he had himself posted at Flossenberg—not an extermination camp, but a place for the disposition of 'unwanted political prisoners '.

"So you were with the Panzers in Russia. What type of tank did you command?"

"That depends. At Kursk, I had one of a new breed of tanks, a PzKw V (Panther), designed to wrest control of the battlefield from the Soviet T-34s."

"It's little I know about the details of that great tank battle—some say the greatest and unlikely to be repeated ever again—but I understand that you guys took quite a trouncing there."

"In the summer of 1943, I was with von *Hoth's* 4th Panzer Army, driving into the Kursk salient from the South. He was a first-rate Panzer general, but I really didn't like him—too 'National Socialist' for me."

"Our problem was that there were too few Panthers, and what was worse they suffered from operational and mechanical difficulties."[xvi]

"I take it that there were several outstanding Panzer Generals, but who was the best? Tank-General! You know, that designation Is seldom used in the American Army. I suppose that the closest to it is my big-boss, 3-Star General George Patton."

"In my opinion Col Gen E. *Hoepner* was unsurpassed, and apparently the High Command in Berlin thought so too: They put him in charge of the 4th Panzer Army Group (comprising the 2nd, 3rd, and 4th Panzer Armies respectively), for the investment of Moscow, way back in 1941."

Somberly—with a break in his voice—M continued, "A fine gentleman, but, unfortunately, a leading member of the conspiracy; he was due to become CIC of the Army of the Provisional Government, but was executed after the plot to kill Hitler failed."

CO was genuinely sorry to hear that; he would have liked to continue the conversation, but they had other things to worry about. They had given F quite a workout. Having to flip back-and-forth, from English to German, and from German to English wasn't easy. CO quipped (to himself), "*Either M was there, or he spent a-lot of time researching that campaign.*"

Section 10.4 An Escape Plan

M learns from a fellow guard that there are half-dozen formerly high-ranking military officers and civilians, headed by ex-*Abwehr* chief Adm Canaris, associated with the German Resistance on a 'short-list'. He surmises that this must be a group of VIP prisoners. M tries to contact W.

"Why you?" She shrugs her shoulders, wistfully replying,

"There are so few of us left. The others are either dead or incarcerated."

"Why are you so concerned with the fate of these men? I must assume that you have more than a casual interest."

"Never mind. M has a plan. He needs transportation, and a few men to support the rescue operation."

Vexed, CO is dissatisfied. "Either full disclosure, or it is—as you Krauts say—Auf *wiedersehen*." CO regrets his stern admonition. "Look, I believe you. I think your story is true. But thinking is not knowing. I can't risk my men on a hunch. Isn't there someone who can verify your story?"

"There were two Englishmen at the meeting between British Intelligence and the *Widerstand*. (She never did get the subtle distinction between SOE and MI6.) One, a Brigadier did all the talking. The other, a young man, was the pilot. He moved about, painfully, with a pronounced limp. Ha! He called it a present from my countrymen on D-Day."

"What did they talk about?" She hesitated, but he gently added:

"At this late date, you can tell me. You wouldn't be violating any trust, but it will help me track down your tale. If it will make you feel any better, just skip the details."

She briefly recounts the meeting between B, GG, GP, and herself, as interpreter, in Holland. "Who is the General to you? Is he one of the men you want to rescue?"

"Well, as they say, much water has flowed under the bridge since then. There are no secrets now. He is my father, and M's former General in France and Russia." As an afterthought, she mentioned that she did meet with GP again, just prior to the 'Revolt'. She left him, to catch-up with GG in Brussels, but he was picked-up by the SS and sent to a CC in NW Germany.

With the war rapidly winding down, the Special Prisoners thought that they had managed to escape the reign-of-terror and survived. But now, belatedly a cache of hitherto concealed documents supposedly linking their names to years of involvement with the German Resistance activity had been uncovered.[xvii]These men were condemned. SS *Standartfuhrer Heppenkothen* was sent down from Berlin, a few days ago, to make it all legal. "It seems to me, that your obvious course of action is to head straight for the British Zone and seek help from them."

"I would, but they are up-there, and we are down-here" (aside). *Besides, the English play by the book; irregular operations are more to the American's style".*

"Let's see if I've got this straight. M works here as a security guard. A Special Prosecutor from Berlin arrives with a 'short-list'. M surmises that he has uncovered incriminating evidence. Aware of your connection with W, he alerts you. Both of you think that one of the high-ranking military officers is your father. M has an escape plan, but needs transportation and some firepower (if necessary).

"I suppose that's where I come in. Using stealth, without creating a ruckus, M and his confederate smuggle them out of the cell-bloc undetected. It's all over in a flash, and we whisk them away.

What about the other SPs?"

"They aren't in any imminent danger."

Tension was building up inside him. CO got up from his chair and exuded a deep sigh of relief: Of all the units in the 3rd Army why did she have to pick mine? CO had already made up his mind. It was the least he could do for those who had risked everything to get rid of Hitler. Too bad they failed—but those are the 'fortunes-of-war'. He wasn't going to let their names be added to the toll of Hitler's victims. No! Not if he can do anything about it.

The seriousness of the situation gradually dawned on him. Realistically, what if anything could he do? CO thinks that she is 'on the level'. No one could concoct such a convoluted tale if it wasn't true. His thoughts were racing ahead.

It seems that there was a recent incident, where a rather large task force, consisting of tanks and motorized infantry, had raided an Allied Officers POW camp (Offlag XIII at *Hammelburg*) deeply behind the German lines. Unfortunately, it ran into 'strong anti-tank defensive forces' and was 'cut-to-pieces'. All he knew was that Gen Omar Bradley was furious. As a consequence, all units were under strict orders not to stray too far ahead of the front lines.

.He had a Reconnaissance-in-Force scheduled. What he could do was stretch the range of the mission to encompass Flossenberg. Instead of a Lieutenant he would lead the patrol himself. He would take a jeep, a half-track with a half-squad of good men (tossing in a light 30 caliber MG, and a couple of bazookas, just in case) and try to reach the CC undetected.

There are no guarantees. He had no doubt that his men could overpower the cell-bloc guards, but 'if we get hung-up in a 'firefight' it will rouse the entire garrison; the ensuing commotion may well cause the mission to be aborted; in that case, we quit the area and head for home, 'as soon as possible'. He had no desire, to stick around, so deeply in enemy territory.

CO laughs (to himself), *"Some patrol this one is. We are supposed to be on the lookout for enemy military activity, not avoiding it. Oh well, We can do that on the way back."*

He wonders if he might be walking into an elaborate trap. With all this talk of 'Werewolves' and an 'Alpine redoubt' being bruited about, who knows? You can never be too careful. (This was reality, as far as U.S. Army was concerned. General Eisenhower deployed the 3rd Army to sever the 'National Redoubt' from Germany.) But he was getting ahead of himself. Before proceeding further, he still had to verify her story, to his satisfaction. He wasn't going anywhere until he got confirmation; it would be folly to do otherwise.

Section 10.5 Too Late!

CO has an idea. Occasionally, he had seen British agents around at Division HQ. With the help of a friend in G-2 he gets in touch with a British Agent, who gets through to London. London replies that B is no longer with SOE, but is now a Senior Administrator with the Allied Control Commission, in the British Zone.

"Yes, he recalls the meeting between SOE and 'W'."

"Yes, GG was accompanied by a girl, disguised as a boy, as interpreter, but he didn't really get a good look at her.

"My pilot conversed with her on two separate occasions. He is in a better position to give you the proof that you need. He is back with the 6th, in G-2, and took part in 'bouncing the Rhine' at Wesel."

GP backs up the gir'ls story, but the only way, "That I can give you the 'positive ID' that you seek is if I talk to her face-to-face."

"I only saw her briefly, a couple of times, yet I have often thought about her. Imagine how relieved I was upon learning that she was alive and well with the Americans.

"Would I be willing to take a quick trip to South Germany to Interview this young woman, if it could be arranged? 'Try and stop me!'"

B exerts his influence. Pulling strings, he obtains a 'special duty, safe-conduct pass' and GP hitches a flight to 3rd Army area in Bavaria, where he is picked-up by CO. Overjoyed, GP and F spontaneously embrace, but their elation is tempered by the grim task ahead. Everything seemed to be in place, but CO was skeptical. It looked like a precise, delicate scheme but M assured him that it could be done. They planned to arrive late at night, during the overnight lull in Camp activities.

It was a strange sight, that Bavarian night, as a British ex-Glider Pilot, an ex-Panzer Commander, a Jewish Infantry Captain from Brooklyn, and a German General's daughter left for the Czech border. With M as guide, they travelled over deserted back-roads, through desolate areas where the likelihood of encountering German Army units (and civilians who might recognize US Army vehicles) were minimized. His accomplice had arranged matters so that they would be the guards on duty in the corridor holding the cells.

They were lucky. The trip was uneventful. They reached the vicinity of the CC. CO couldn't help noticing that there seemed to be 'a lot of noise for what he had expected to be a quiet night'. M entered the cell-bloc where he was met by his friend. Nervously, the Capt. deployed his men, and waited. A few minutes later, M emerged in a state-of-shock.

"We are too late. The short-list is no more! The rest of the SPs are being transported to Dachau."

Then he threw a bombshell.

Rumors of American forces hovering nearby worried the Camp Commandant. Anxious to abandon Flossenberg, he urged the Special Prosecutor to speed up the 'trials' and quickly finish his 'business'. Compressed into less than 2 days, the assembled court, came down with its verdict and sentence at an unheard of rate of speed, even by Gestapo standards. The last batch of prominent members of the German Resistance were executed on (04/09/45).

Overcome by the news, F burst into tears. Quickly regaining her composure, (aside, *she exclaimed that 'there will be plenty of time to mourn her loss, privately.)* and steeling herself, she resumes her role as interpreter.

Section 10.6 Conversation with the Enemy

CO has to get back. His outfit is all set to pull-out. He tries to contact his unit, but the signalman has trouble getting through. Communication is disrupted by local German transmissions. M recognizes the call letters of Army Group C, the German Army in Northern Italy, Col Gen Vietinghoff commanding. CO reasons that the SPs, will be better off in the hands of the German Army. CO gambles. He instructs M to alert Bolzano to be on the look-out for a convoy of SPs heading for Dachau from Flossenberg, with ultimate destination, perhaps, the Italian Tyrol.

Astonished, the German radio operator, replies "Americans here? The GA has nothing to do with this. We don't have the time to look for SS convoys."

"Well, you better make time. The SS commander has orders to kill the SPs, rather than turn them over to the Allies. If these SPs. are liberated unharmed, I will put in a good word for you. If not, I personally will see to it that the entire headquarters staff is held responsible. Take your pick: a de-Nazification hearing' or a 'War-crimes tribunal'. Sign off: HQ Gen Patton, 3rd Army."

CO laughs: "That will light a fire under them, If nothing else, it will make them think about 'life in post-war Germany'."

Proud of his `coup', CO smiles and addresses M, "Why don't you and your friend come back with us? Since both of you were in GA combat units, I might be able to palm you off as P.O.W.s."

"That's a tempting offer. I'd like to, but we think that we should stay. The SS commander isn't such a bad guy, but as you know, they have orders to kill the SPs, if need be. Several of the SS guards are former soldiers, and have had their fill of this infernal 'business'. But, the heavily armed SD might be a problem. We might be of more use to the SPs if we went along."

"I can appreciate that. Good Luck. Now, let's head back.

CO muses: *It almost restores one's faith in human nature.*"

Section 10.7 'Short List' revisited

Upon their return, CO dropped-off GP and F at the C-company Field HQ. 1st Sgt. D made their stay comfortable as they awaited his return from Bn HQ.

CO reports to Battalion on his observations. "Things were pretty quiet, we didn't run into any 'stray Tigers' or anything like that. There was some commotion in the vicinity of Flossenberg, though. We learned that the CC is being evacuated. Some SPs are being trucked to Dachau. It is probably too late to intercept the truck convoy, but how are the other inmates supposed to make the long trek—on foot?"

The Bn Commander sympathized. "I'd like to help but this is way over my head. I'm sure that 'Army' is prepared for these eventualities. Even if we could do something, we'd have to stop and wait for the medics, and the other auxiliary units needed to tend to the welfare of the survivors. I'll pass your report along but as of now, our orders are explicit; we head down the Danube Valley and cut-off the National Redoubt. Get your men ready Captain, we may be leaving as early as tomorrow."

Meanwhile, hungry, thirsty, and tired, GP and F were grateful for a light repast prepared for them. The 1st Sgt. topped it all off by filling their glasses with wine from CO's 'private reserve'. Magnificent! Superb! GP's eyes lit up; aches and pains from the cramped ride 'on patrol' vanished. Not that he was a connoisseur, (A 'pint of beer or ale' at the Minden Arms, was more his speed.), but he had no doubt that this was the finest wine to be found anywhere.

(In passing through Oppenheim the company was billeted in the home of a local Nazi bureaucrat. In the cellar, the casks were full with newly vinted wine. The men drank so much of this stuff that (like the 'King of Barataria' who had nothing but Rhenish wine to drink,) they yearned for simple water. CO had a few bottles left over that were doled out on special occasions.

Savoring his drink, GP loosened up a bit. Relaxed, he complained to F : "Why is it that we never seem to have time to talk. Maybe, with the war just about over, we will meet again under more pleasant circumstances and make up for lost time."

"I'd like that. There will be nothing to stop me from accepting an invitation to visit England now."

More voluble than usual, but still at a loss for words, he extended his regrets; (Although GP (and B) had met him only once, they were very impressed with GG; in their view, he was 'representative' of Germany's 'finest'). It is ironic, that except for the most notorious 'War Criminals', a preponderance of the other, lesser, Nazis, after perfunctory de-Naziification, would land on their feet, while those associated with W will have long since departed from the scene.)

"I'm very sorry that we were unable to help those men but I*'ve* been thinking. It's all your fault, you know. Ha! I never thought about anything until I met you."

She laughed, "Thinking isn't so bad, is it."

"For a soldier, it usually means trouble, but anyway, I've asked myself a few questions. "Why were those on the 'short list' singled out? The presumption is that the incriminating evidence pertained to them in particular, and not to the conspirators in general.

"You recall that in our meeting with B, GG remarked that he couldn't talk for Adm. Canaris or certain other Senior Generals who had anti-Nazi, anti-War leanings, because they might have had been 'hatching their own plots' independently of W. If the intent was merely to get rid of a few prisoners why the need for the ace-SS Special Prosecutor?

"My conclusion? GG could not have been on the short list. Those men on it were (long-time) resisters, while GG was a relative newcomer. These men were somehow the objects of Hitler's personal vengeance— and GG was highly unlikely to have been one of them."

"I hope that you are right, but when it comes to 'good news', the record of W isn't very encouraging."[xviii]

CO rejoined them. "I'm sorry for the delay but the de-briefing took longer than I expected."

CO grinned broadly. GP looked the picture of a man 'who had the feeling that he wanted to stay/ when he knew that he gotta go' (as the one-and-only Jimmy Durante, might have put it). Yes, he was certainly reluctant to leave, but he had a 'plane to catch'.

Good naturedly, CO said, "I'm not trying to get rid of you, pal, but, your transportation to shuttle you back to the 'Westphalian Plain' is waiting. I hear that Monty can use every man he can get. If you hurry, you can catch up with your outfit, and resume that long—delayed trip on the Autobahn, to the Elbe River, Berlin and beyond."

CO just couldn't resist getting in that last little dig, but it didn't go unnoticed. No sooner had he uttered that fatuous remark, than he regretted it. (aside), "*I should have realized that he would take umbrage at any patronizing reference to Market-Garden.*"

GP liked CO a lot and didn't want any arguments. He decided to let it pass.

Blandly, as if nothing untoward had transpired, CO quickly continued: "Give the girl a good 'squeeze and a kiss' for the rest of us, and get a move on." After 'following the Captain's order' and the usual farewells, GP left.

"What a 'great guy'. You can go through an entire war, and never cross paths with one of his caliber."

Section 10.8 Anglo-American friction

Newspaper coverage of the war was an important source of irritation.

"The British and the Canadians do the fighting, the Yanks do the advancing and the press gives them the headlines."

A. McKee "The Race for the Rhine Bridges" (1971), Chapter 23, pp. 327-329

(Note: McKee was a British Military Historian during WWII.)

The return flight to the British zone, was on a C-47 (Dakota) delivering some military cargo to the US 9 Army. There were a few GIs, who, surprised to see a Limey, welcomed him aboard. But he wasn't in the mood for small talk. Listlessly he sauntered over to the side-door. Staring out of a porthole, he looked down at the rapidly receding countryside:

"Glad I'm not a paratrooper."

CO's innuendo stuck in his mind. Unexpectedly, it triggered a chain-of-thought that extended back to pre-invasion times. With conscious effort he had managed to tune-out the events of the past year. But CO's ingenuous remark—uttered in jest no doubt—reopened old sores. It all began with the early-May, 1944 *Gisevious*—Dulles contact (see Section. 4.2).

A few weeks before D-Day (6/6/'44), W submitted a plan for a combined Western Allied-W venture to eliminate Hitler and keep the

Soviet Union out of Central Europe. This attempt to split the Grand Alliance was ignored.

A few weeks after D-Day, W submitted a new-plan, with the anti-Soviet provisions deleted. But, the initial success of the invasion mitigated the urgent need for a joint-enterprise. One smashing victory followed another, but still the war rolled on.

GP recalled GG 'pounding the table':

"Externally? No way! "Internally? The only way!"

He couldn't have been more prescient. Forced to act alone, the collapse of the 'Revolution of 20 July 1944' meant that the liberation of hostage-Europe would be piecemeal; their ordeal would not be officially over until VE Day (5 May 1945).

GP groaned, "The Anglo—W enterprise!

Such a short patch of Sunlight, in Such a long, dark, brutal war."

The first 'Battle of the Bulge', Normandy 8/7-14/'44. nearly wrecked OB West (see Map 1).

Opportunity knocked—loud and clear.

The Allies proceeded without significant opposition. The ratio of Allied/German in men and material had escalated dramatically. Literally, there was nothing in the way to deter the relentless pursuit by the Allies towards Germany. Logistic problems, however, seemingly retarded the advance, giving the foe, time to stabilize the frontline from Arnheim, in the North, to the Swiss border, in the South.

(Up to about mid-1944, the undivided attention of the Allies was single-mindedly directed towards the complete and thorough Military defeat of the Axis. However, the last year of the war was really 'All about Casualties'. Each passing day inflated the losses. The last 7 months cost the Western Allies a staggering one-half million men, but for 'hostage Europe' they were incalculable (see M. Cooper "The German Army 1933-45", p.515). Monty had always held that to 'shorten the war' by a single day is worth everyone's utmost effort. Yet, ironically, he himself didn't follow his own dictum when he had the chance. (See Section 6.5).)

The Field Marshal had a plan to 'end the war in'44' (8/23/'44). Uninterested in playing second fiddle, US 12Army Group pressured SHAEF to reject his proposed '40 Division—single thrust' offensive, but to the amazement of all, Monty the super-cautious substituted a daring, but ill-thought-out, much watered down version, codenamed Market-Garden.

(In the Spring of 1945, the Allied Armies approached the Rhine almost simultaneously. It may be hard to believe, but Combat Engineers, Sappers, and even sailors, by the tens of thousands, were assembled to erect Bailey Bridges, clear minefields, deactivate booby-traps, etc. The German Army was in such a sorry state, that every Allied venture worked. In sharp contrast, early planning had anticipated that 'bouncing the Rhine' would be a very tough proposition.)

Lt Gen. C. Hodges, US 1 Army was lucky. On 7 March 1945, they surprised the Germans at *Remagen*. They captured the bridge intact, but it was a railway bridge that didn't lead anywhere—it had problems as a bridgehead and wasn't fully exploited.

Besides—more to the point—it didn't fit in with the Allied plans which scheduled the British 21stAGp's crossing for 23 March 1945. In a classic set-piece exercise—complete with aerial bombing, artillery barrage, and British and American Airborne Units—Monty overwhelmed a stiff, determined German Defense, concentrated at Wesel.

All though clearly later than Hodges, Patton was determined to beat out Monty. To regain some of his lost prestige, Lt Gen George Patton hit the Rhine 'on-the-run', crossing on 22 March (before Monty), but what he forgot to tell us was that Oppenheim was virtually undefended.

US 3A had a good laugh at Monty's antics, deriding his massive preparations, but the Brits, who had suffered heavily at Wesel and had still not fully recovered from the debacle at Arnheim (9/17-24/ '44), were not amused. They thought their reaction 'mean-spirited' and unworthy (of the Great U.S. Army). There was little love lost between the British 21AGp and the US. 3 Army, and some held the U.S.12AGp accountable for its (behind-the-scenes) interference and machinations.

This was more than just a case of intra-Allied rivalry. Apparently the excitement emanated from an attempt by a 3-star American General bent on up-staging a British Field Marshal! GP knitted his brow in disgust:

"*Nasty business, but what did the Tommies and GIs have to do with the 'squabbles' of the Generals?*"

Section 10.9 An Excursion Above and Along the Rhine

"Hi, Tommy. You've been pretty quiet. Haven't heard much out of you. Anything wrong?"

Snapping out of his reverie, GP quickly replied, "No! No! I'm sorry. You must think me a perfect boor, but I was trying to sort out some things on my mind, and I was loathe to interrupt my thought-processes."

"Okay, fair enough. I don't mean to pry", the co-pilot said, "but there has been a slight change in flight-plan. We have to put down at a makeshift airstrip, West of the Rhine, near Wesel. As you know, Simpson's US 9A is back with the Brit 21st, so we had no difficulty in arranging ground transport. I hear that Monty is heading for the Jutland peninsula to reach Denmark before the Soviets. He's moving at a rapid clip and you may have a ways to go before you catch-up."

"Want to see a fantastic view? Come on over to the cockpit."

While they were talking, the pilot had been steadily reducing altitude as they flew lengthwise above the Rhine. GP stared out the windshield, stunned speechless by the panoramic vista. He did not know if 'awesome' was the proper word to describe the carnage-strewn landscape, but that's what it was. (Incessant aerial bombing is bad enough, but when a modern city becomes a battleground all that remains is a hollow, eerie, uninhabited shell).

Hitler's orders for the Rhine bridges were simple enough:
Anyone who failed to blow-up a bridge in time—*wird erschossen.*
Anyone who blows-up a bridge too early—*wird erschossen.*

Not much room for error! (Were these orders ever carried out? See A. McKee.)

Following the curvature of the Earth, in quick succession, and in pairs, the original Deutsche *Brucke*, and its Allied replacement popped-up into view. (Die *Brucken* had historic or picturesque names (e.g., the *Ludendorf* Railway bridge at *Remagen*). A picture of the demolished 'Hohenzollern' bridge at Cologne (1945) is given on p.288, McKee.)

"You've got to hand it to those Combat Engineers. The last time I flew over Wesel die Brucke was a heap of rubble—take a look at what's spanning the Rhine now. Isn't she a beaut?"

"These guys can throw-up a Bailey Bridge faster than it takes *der Ober-Niederreisen Offizier's bericht* (report) to reach the bunker-in-Berlin.

'*Mein Fuhrer!*.

Die Rhenischer Brueke sind alle zustort.

Der Verfluechener Englander und Americaner soldaten muss jetzt uber-schwimmen.

Haw! Haw!! *Heil* Hitler!"

Not so quick, Adolf—the men barely got their feet wet.

The Army—built bridge seemed to be open for business, with its 2-way traffic controlled by the MPs. Somewhat surprisingly, German civilians, mostly women (by far) mingled with the allied military personnel and vehicles streaming across the Rhine.

"You guys have all the fun. You get to see these spectacular views, while as an erstwhile glider pilot, all I ever got to see was the rear-end of an 'Albermarle' (or Halifax), farting, and polluting the pristine atmosphere all the way to the 'Landing Zone'. "Laughing at his own joke, he joined in the hilarity with the Americans . . ." and what's more let me tell you—those exhaust gases really stink."

The co-pilot invited the others into the cockpit. "*Trinken ist streng* Verboten (while on duty), but for this occasion, and for one tiny shot-glass of *schnappe*s we can make an exception.

"To the British—the greatest, most dependable Ally one can ever hope to have. Yanks and Limeys, may they always stand together in the never-ending battle for "'Freedom and Justice': Comrades-in-arms—Forever."

"Hear! Hear! I'll drink to that. Down the hatch."

Beaming (aside) GP exclaimed, cryptically, *"I don't care who knows it; I Don't care what anybody thinks or says; Damn it all—I like the Americans!*

Section 10.10 All's Well that Ends Well

CO consoles F, "I'm sorry that we arrived too late. I know how bad you must feel with all of this taking place so close to the end of the war. But, we can at least hope that the other SPs might survive. Maybe there is some mistake. Maybe he is with the other group. After all, they were listed under code names, and M didn't have a chance to get a close-up look at the prisoners. You, yourself, remarked that people may 'suffer severe transformation under duress' and being confined by the Gestapo was no picnic."

F interrupted him. "I thank you and GP for your concern."

She repeated the essence of her conversation with GP.

"Well, he certainly has a point. I forgot that he knew your father from the meeting with British Intelligence, but his reference to Canaris came as a surprise. I'm convinced that his argument is compelling. In that case all you have to do is find him."

"As soon as Munich is taken and Dachau is liberated, I will begin my search."

"Sounds great, but in a few weeks Europe will be one-big-morass. Upon Liberation, Europe will be inundated with displaced persons: Foreign workers, Concentration Camp refugees, returning German POWs, and don't forget the 'black-marketeers'.

To cheer her up a bit, he goes through his 'little-Caesar' act' "I'm a tough guy, see. If you ever have need for a 'hard-fighting', 'hard-drinking', 'hard-loving', wise-cracking, son-of-a-bitch officer in the U.S. Army, then give me a 'ring' (Call it coincidence, but the codename for the 'little Admiral' at Flossenberg was Cesar.). Perplexed, despite her fluency in English, she didn't quite get the drift of what he was saying, but from the way he said it she burst into laughter.

"What you don't believe me?"

"You men are all alike. The General worried about me all the time. GP feared for my safety: "A girl traveling alone faces some pretty scary prospects." M wouldn't hear of it. He insisted on accompanying me as we eluded the sentries. And now you. What do I have to do to show that women are not as fragile as you men seem to think?"

"Fragile? Far from it. The 'bard of Avon 'wrote, "Frailty, thy name is woman." But, he didn't know you. "I shudder to think of the hardships that you endured this past year, but the fact is that you are quite vulnerable, and I can get around much easier than you can."

Her blue eyes glistened through her tears. "Even though unsuccessful, I shall be forever grateful to you and your men, GP, and of course, M, but, nothing ever broke right for W. From its inception, everything about the 'Revolt' was 'star-crossed'. It enfolded like a Greek Tragedy. This is the way it had to be. How can I even hope that the GG somehow escaped?"

CO responds emphatically, "No. That's the way it has been. That's all in the Past. Things have a way of changing, maybe, now for the better. That people like those men in W existed bodes well for the future. Despite tremendous devastation, Germany will now have the chance to start afresh, as a Democracy, we hope, and live peacefully with her neighbors.

"I have to move out now. Maybe I'll see you on the way back."

She looked up at him, smiling, "I can't take a chance. I'll tag along behind."

"I'd like that, but the U.S. Army frowns on 'camp followers', especially when they are in violation of the 'No Fraternization' policy. *Auf wiedersehen!*"

Epilogue

CO heads East for the Danube. GP returns to his unit in NW Germany, just in time to liberate the infamous concentration camp at Bergen-Belsen. M is back on duty guarding the SPs. The trucks move on to Dachau, joining up with other SPs. Gen. Patch's 7th Army takes Nuremberg (04/19/45), and advances on Munich. It gets 'too hot' for the SS. A convoy evacuates SPs from Dachau, and heads South to the Italian Tyrol, where German Army Group C, Col Gen H. Vietinghoff commanding, has its HQ at Bolzano. The convoy stops at Niederdorf (in German, Dobbiacco in Italian).

(Meanwhile, unbeknownst to the others, A. Dulles, the Allies, and SS Gen K. Wolfe, were engaged in secret talks about the surrender of AGpC. These negotiations had been moving forward for quite some time and Gen. Vietinghoff didn't want any complications. The net result was the unofficial capitulation on (04/29/45). The official date (05/02/45) was only a few days earlier than VE Day (05/08/45). It may not seem like much, but when the casualties are totaled, even at this late date, every day is crucial. (see M. Gilbert, *The Day the War Ended*)).

The SPs dismounted from the trucks, and loitered around. While waiting, one of them, a Colonel, slips away and telephones an old friend in Bolzano, explaining their predicament. (Slips away? Makes a telephone call? Where were the guards? Was this done with their connivance?)

Now, we don't know if CO's bluff, had any effect, one way or another, on what transpired, but Jerry couldn't afford to take any chances. All that we do know is that Bolzano responded quickly. Gen. R, acting jointly with SS Gen. Wolfe, dispatched Capt. A with a squad. This was followed shortly thereafter by a company of German soldiers.

There were 136 SPs, 30 SS guards, and 20 heavily armed SD escort troops. The SS commandant had the orders to kill the SPs in his pocket. Why didn't he carry them out? We can only speculate. Maybe he thought that he could barter himself out of War Criminal status, or then again, it could be that after years of suppression, a glimmer of humanity surfaced in him. All that we know is that he didn't.

The Italian partisans were swarming around, and he certainly didn't want to be captured by them. So, when the unit dispatched from Vietinghoff's HQ arrived, he was only too happy to turn his charges over to them. Some of the men stayed behind, (including M and most of the 'old soldiers') and 'gave themselves up', while he and the others melted away, hoping to make their way back to Germany.

With the rescue from the SS, the long ordeal of the SPs was over. It was a regular 'League of Nations' that was liberated (05/05/45), a few days later, by the 50th Division of the U.S.7th Army. Besides Germans and Austrians there were French, Russians, and many others from the occupied territories, surprisingly, some of whom were Jews. Also, strange to say, quite a few from England.

Two of them had an amazing story to tell. For them,

'World War II began with the kidnapping of the British Agents Captain S. Payne-Best and Major R. Stevens at Venlo, Netherlands on 11/09/39.

It ended, after 5 ½ years' incarceration mainly in Sachsenhausen, as Special Prisoners, with their liberation by the U.S. Army at Niederdorf, Italian Tyrol on 05/04/45.

Thus, the 'War in Europe' concluded on a 'happy note'. As CO had prophesized, a 'new and better day' was dawning. How the World will actually respond to this opportunity (as G. Heater, the WWII commentator, might have put it),

'Time and time alone will tell.'

GLOSSARY

List of principal characters, organizations, and abbreviations.

Allies:

G(lider) P(ilot). British 6th Airlanding Division.

B(rigadier, acting) Head, G(erman) R(esistance)Desk, SOE

Dir(ector) S(pecial) O(perations) E(xecutive)

C(ommanding) O(fficer), Company Cmdr. of Infantry Division, US3A

German:

G(erman)G(eneral) A leading member of W.

F(raulein) Interpreter

M(anfred) Tank Commander.(later, C(oncentration) C(amp) guard).

W(iderstand) Name given to 'GGs against Hitler'.

Organizations:

M(ilitary) I(ntelligence)6,

O(ffice) of S(trategic)S(ervices), WWII predecessor of Central Intelligence Agency.

Ausland/Abwehr, are the S(ecret)I(ntelligence)S(ervices) of Britain, US, and Germany whose Chiefs were 'C', William Donavan, and Admiral Canaris, respectively.

S(chutz)S(taffel) State Protection

S(icher))Dienst) Central State Security

Others:

Abs(olute) Sil(ence)

Un(conditional)Su(rrender)

h(ostage)E(urope)

S(upreme)H(eadquarters) A(llied E(xpeditionary)F(orces)

S(pecial)P(risoner)

Bibliography

This book is a 'historical novel'. Readers interested in delving deeper into the history of the events chronicled herein may consult any of the vast number of tomes written on World War II, and the 'Revolution of the 20ᵗʰ of July, 1944'. Each of them usually has an extensive bibliography. However, some perhaps lesser known, less widely distributed, works, of particular interest to us, are appended in the very limited bibliography below.

General: World War II in Europe:

Cooper,.M. 'The German Army, 1933-45'. 'McDonald & James, London 1978.

Seaton, A. 'Russo-German War', 1941-45, Holmes & Meir, New York, 1981.

'The Fall of Fortress Europe,—!943-1945'

General: Thirty-Years War,1618-48.

Mann, Golo, 'Wallenstein: His Life Narrated', Holt, Rinehart, Winston.1971.

Wedgewood, C.V.,'30-years War', London, NYRB Classics,1938.

Limited bibliography:

Bender, R. J. and W. W. Odergard, "Panzertruppe", R.J. Bender Publ. 1980

Bradley, Omar 'A Soldier's Story', Henry Holt and Co. N.Y. 1951.

Brown, Anthony Cave. 'C', McMillan, N.Y.,1987.

Crookenden, N."'Drop-Zone, Normandy: Story of the American & British Airborne Assault on D-Day, 1944", Ian Allam, 1976

Dulles, A. "German Underground: The Anti-Nazi Resistance". DeCapo Press, 2000

Gill A. "An honorable defeat", Henry Holt, 1994

Goerlitz, W., "History of the German General Staff, 1657-1945, NY", Praeger, N.Y., 1957.

Hoffman, P. "History of the 20th of July", MacDonald and James, 1977."

""Stauffenberg"

Hohne, H. "Canaris", Bertelman, Munich, Cooper Square Press, NY,1976.

McKee, A. "Race for the Rhine Bridges", Stein and Day, Souvenir Press Ltd.,1971.

Payne-Best, S. "Venlo Incident", Sky Horse Publishing, 2010

Turney, A. "Disaster at Moscow", University New Mexico Press.1970.

Wheeler-Bennett, J. "Nemesis of Power"

West, N. "MI6", Random House, 1983

ENDNOTES

i   It wasn't too long ago when the problem of combatting the mighty Soviet Submarine Fleet, was a top NATO priority. True, since the breakup of the Soviet Union and a thaw in US-Russia relations, a more relaxed atmosphere currently prevails, but good relations, notwithstanding USW is here to stay.

ii   My, how warfare has changed over the years. The grizzled old warrior, Count Tilly (see Section 9,5), who never lost a battle in over 50 years, scoffed at Wallenstein's plan to raise an Army of 100,000 men, declaring that it is beyond the capacity of one man to control and direct an army even half that size.

We are amused at the Brabanter's naiveté', but account must be taken of the primitive state of battlefield communications and the logistics of supplying a large army in the field, during the 30-years War. At the pivotal Battle of Breitenfeld (1631), King Gustaphus Adolphus' (generally considered to be the 'Father of Modern Warfare') Army of 41,000 Swedes and Saxons, overwhelmed Tilly's vastly outnumbered 31,000 Imperialists.

After sacking the Protestant stronghold at Madgeburg, the Imperial Army was in poor condition. Awaiting the arrival of reinforcements (on the order of 10,000 men) from the conclusion of the 'Mantuan War', Tilly was unready for battle. But FM Pappenheim, the commander of the Imperial Horse, forced his hand, causing him to abandon his defensive positions and attack. Tilly is said to have exclaimed "He has robbed me of my reputation, and the Emperor of his lands!"

Too bad. The veterans from the Milan campaign might have 'leveled' the battlefield but would they have changed the outcome?

iii   The job of silencing MB fell to LtCol T Otway's 9th Parachute Battalion (750 men). A sizeable quantity of heavy weapons, signaling gear and other equipment deemed essential, was to be brought in by (5) supply gliders. In addition (3) assault gliders were scheduled to plunk-themselves-down in the midst of the gun emplacements ala the Fallschirmjaeger at Fort Eben Emael, Belgium (May 10, 1940).

The dispersion of the paratrooper drop was so high that only 20% of his men were assembled in the zone. Further, none of the supply gliders arrived nor did he get any direct help from the assault gliders. With great daring, consummate skill and grim determination, he and his men set out for the MB.

The battery was defended by the 716th static—low category division—with a large contingent of Ost-trupppen (e.g. recruited from East European POWs).

A couple of strange, but significant sidelights to this operation should be mentioned:

After a brief but sharp struggle, rather than engage in a fight-to-the-finish with the tough British paratroopers the remaining survivors of the (160 man) garrison were only too happy to surrender to them

Also, to their astonishment, they were startled to find that instead of the expected battery of 150 mm coastal defense guns, capable of hurling 96 pound shells, they were merely 75 mm field pieces!

iv True. The German attitude had its roots in the '30s diplomacy when the West was desperately seeking ways to halt the spread of Communism. There might have been a time when they would have welcomed German participation in such an enterprise, but with the takeover of Czechoslovakia, the Russo-German non-aggression pact, and the invasion of Poland the time for a policy of 'containment' had long since passed.

v WWI was the first major war that was Scientifically and Technologically driven, The war lasted so long, the advances in technology so rapid, that weapon systems in their infancy, or even unheard of, in 1914, were fully operational by the Armistice, with the Air Force ending up the war on a par with the Army and Navy. These systems (e.g., Airplanes, Submarines, Tanks etc.) emerged as the weapons-systems of the future, reaching a peak in development during WWII

vi Neville Chamberlain, the British P.M., was then and still is now, the subject of much controversy. He has been called everything from an 'abject appeaser' to a 'shrewd, hard-headed realist'. Whatever, the former Mayor of Birmingham, recognized that the British & French were woefully behind the Germans in modern weaponry, and that they needed time to catch-up. Fortunately, Britain took advantage of that one-year reprieve, to get the 'Hurricanes and Spitfires' into production, and it paid off handsomely in the 'Battle-of-Britain'. Unfortunately, however, it was paid for at the expense of Czechoslovakia.

vii   In exchange for supporting Hitler in his in his struggle with Capt. Ernst Roehm of the Sturm Abteilung (07/'34), the Army thought they had extracted from Hitler, a sort of 'Pledge of Autonomy' - ostensibly putting the Army on an equal footing with the Nazi Party in the Third Reich. The 'honeymoon' phase which began during the 'Night of the Long Knives' (07/'34) ended abruptly when he outlined his Foreign Policy offensive plans, and ordered the GGs to follow him without question (11/'37). Hitler outwitted the '3 Titans of the German Army'. 1938 began with the dismissal of the 'Minister of War', Col Gen W. von Blomberg; the forced resignation of Col Gen W. von Fritsch, Commander-in-Chief of the Army; and the voluntary resignation of the Chief of the Great German General Staff, Col Gen L. Beck on (08/19/'38). Beck vigorously opposed Hitler's rapid Rearmament plans and his truculent Foreign Policy which would put Germany on a collision course with the Major Powers and lead to the destruction, possibly the obliteration of Germany. This opened a rift between Hitler and his Generals which culminated in the dismantling of the German High Command, following the defeat at Moscow (12/'41). To the outside world it may have appeared that they were happily goose-stepping in lock-step, together, off into the 'sunset'. This inspiring picture, promulgated by Gen. Fredericki (1939) was a fiction.

viii   After the war, Liddell-Hart wrote the 'Other Side of the Hill', based on interrogations of some German Generals. I could visualize B gathering information for a monograph tentatively titled, "The Other Side, of the Other Side, of the Hill'. Lest one think of this as a feeble attempt at humor, and that it is a simply a play-on-words, B's account would be drawn from the anti-Nazi Generals in W, who, unlike Liddell-Hart's 'set of generals', didn't survive the war (and get to write their memoirs).

ix   Commissars (e.g., Communist Party officials attached to Red Army units) were subject to on-the-spot summary execution. But, in practice, this directive was applied indiscriminately to Partisans, the so-called 'Intelligentsia', and of course, the Jews.

x   We all agree with P. Knightly that in war, 'Truth is the First Casualty' but the 'Big Lie' is something else again. The great contribution to 20th Century Political Philosophy, attributed to the 'ace-Nazi-propagandist' Dr. J. Goebbels, may be succinctly written as: "A Lie, if Big enough and repeated often enough, becomes the Truth.'" This formula has been enthusiastically embraced, indiscriminately, by all regimes, Democratic and Totalitarian alike, to transform - in the manner of the Alchemists of old - 'Lies into Truth'. Although it may have had its origins in politics, big-lying has universal appeal. It is routinely practiced in all walks- of-life, with the important caveat that the higher-up on the social scale, the more elaborate and inventive the lie.

xi   Once considered to be Germany's ablest Field Marshal, von Bock's reputation has fallen steadily since the end of the war. In strong disagreement with this assessment, I always wanted to read his personal account of Operations BARBAROSSA and TYPHON, but he, apparently, never did get to write his memoirs. For some unknown reason (another mystery?) in May '45, he had his staff car driven into the British zone, where he was killed trying to circumvent Hamburg, in what must have been one of the last strafing attacks of the war (which officially ended on 8 May 1945.)

xii   One need look no further than Italy, where the GA under F.M. Kesselring fought the Allies to a standstill. Just imagine what a FM of that caliber, unencumbered by Hitler, could do on the Western Front.

xiii   Dulles would talk to anyone, even the infamous SS Gen, K. Wolff, if it meant shortening the war. As it happened, the lengthy Dulles-Wolff talks eventually led to the surrender of the German Army in Northern Italy, commanded by Col Gen Vietinghoff on 05 May '45 (3 days before VE-Day). Doesn't sound like much, but if one reads M. Gilbert's account in 'The Day the War Ended', one is struck by the difference a day made to those in 'hostage Europe', at that time.

xiv   Not long afterwards, the power base of Admiral Canaris evaporated as he lost his struggle with *Reichsführer* Himmler, over control of *Abwehr*, which was transferred to SD *Sturmbannführer* W. Schellenberg (our 'old friend', of 'Venlo Affair' fame).

xv   After the First Duke of Marlborough died (1722) England's military fortunes gradually declined until-- in coalition with some of the German States---she scored a decisive victory over the French at the famous battle of Minden (1759) during the Seven-Years-War (1756-63), known in America, as the French and Indian War.

But the last time was when the Duke of Wellington joined up with the Prussian FM Bluecher to put an end to the Napoleonic Era at the Battle of Waterloo (1815).

Now we must not lose sight of the fact that in those days German was a loose collection of Sovereign states of varying size and shapes, before the unification of Germany under Kaisier Wilhelm I following the Franco-Prussian War (1871)

Kaisar Wilhelm II, obsessed with Germany's great military strength was perceived as a direct threat by England, causing a reshuffling of alliances amongst the major players in Europe, pitting Great Britain, France and Russia against Germany, Austro-Hungry and the Ottoman Turks (more commonly known as the Allies v. the Central Powers).

xvi   *Col Gen H. Guderian, at that time Inspector General of Armored Troops, attributed these malfunctions* to insufficient testing; he didn't want them employed until properly de-bugged. Also he favored building up a strong strategic force of Panthers (and Tigers), rolling off the assembly lines, rather than commit them piecemeal. On these and other grounds, he strenuously opposed *ZITADELE*.

xvii   Admiral *Canaris* had been one of Hitler's earliest and trusted supporters. However this relationship had long since cooled. For a long time, Canaris had been suspect, while still Head of the Abwehr, on the grounds of Faulty Intelligence, Incompetence, and Defeatism. On the basis of this newly found trove of incriminating material these charges were upgraded to 'Treachery', a capital offense.

xviii   Hitler went berserk when informed of these hidden papers. To a man in his warped state-of-mind, this explained everything. True-to-type he flailed around seeking a scapegoat, and in the Admiral Canaris group he found one. For years, as far back as before the war they had been engaged in anti-Nazi-activity, undermining the German War effort, contributing to its ultimate downfall. What had the 'little Admiral' prophesized? *'Finis Germaniae'*! Not quite! It was the end of the Third Reich, but not of Germany!

Printed in the United States
By Bookmasters